THE EXCLUSIVE

MEL TAYLOR

BRIAN SHEA

SEVERN RIVER
PUBLISHING

Severn River Publishing
www.SevernRiverBooks.com

This is a work of fiction. Names, characters, businesses, places, events and incidents are either the products of the author's imagination or used in a fictitious manner. Any resemblance to actual persons, living or dead, or actual events is purely coincidental.

ISBN: 978-1-64875-600-9 (Paperback)

ALSO BY THE AUTHORS

Booker Johnson Thrillers

The Exclusive

The Arrangement

BY MEL TAYLOR

The Frank Tower Mystery Series

Investigation Con

Investigation Wrath

Investigation Greed

Investigation Envy

BY BRIAN SHEA

Boston Crime Thrillers

The Nick Lawrence Series

Sterling Gray FBI Profiler Series

Lexi Mills Thrillers

Shepherd and Fox Thrillers

Memory Bank Thrillers

To find out more, visit

severnriverbooks.com

1

Heat clung to him, wrapping his skin like a second layer, as beads of sweat traced down worry lines in his forehead. He made no move to wipe the sweat drops away, refusing to waste a precious second. He had to pack. Now. His hands worked in haste, tossing a flurry of clothing into the duffle bag with an urgency borne out of desperation.

Cotton shirts, underwear, and a pair of socks that hadn't seen their mates in months, all crammed hastily into the gaping maw of the bag. No time for sorting or neat folding. No time for anything but to pack and flee. His eyes darted across the tight space of the bedroom, scanning for every last necessity for the coming days until things cooled off, or at least until he could stop long enough to plan his next move.

He flicked his wrist, the dim glow from his watch reminding him he was out of time. A curse accompanied his breath, expelling worry into the heavy air. "Dammit. Get going!" He commanded himself, attempting to override the urgent pounding of his racing heart and gain some modicum of control.

His movements were frenzied as he zipped the bag shut and sprinted toward the door. In his haste, his right foot caught on a loose shoe, tripping him. He grabbed the back of the couch and stayed upright. He swiped at the car fob on the counter and dropped the fob to the floor. Twice. Upon reaching the front door, he did a quick mental checklist, ticking off the essentials. House keys, cell phone, a wad of cash, all jammed into the depths of his pockets. He left the custom-made door ajar in his wake and stepped into the encroaching dark of night.

The muggy air seemed cool to his overheated skin. All of his loud, quick movements contrasted the calm silence outside. His head swirled in paranoia, checking over his shoulder, staring down the road. He tossed the duffle bag inside the car. The ignition roared alive, the purring engine reminding him he was one step closer to putting all of this behind him.

The sleek two-seater Audi moved down the street, past his $850,000 ranch-style Florida home. Most of the lights were left on in the place, along with the just-installed laser lights encircling the pool. *Was the water left running in the kitchen? Screw it. Just go!*

A half mile away, he tapped his cell phone. He crammed the phone up close to his ear. When he spoke to the caller, his words were coming out like water gushing from a broken dam. "I'm outta here. You've got to leave now. Get away from these people. Go now!" On the other side, a voice tried to convince him to stay. "No way! You hear me? Just go. Never mind."

He hung up and kept driving.

Three more blocks and he would hit the interstate. The cityscape was a blur as he pounded the gas. Three measly blocks between him and the freedom promised by the state road. His eyes darted back to the clock on the dashboard.

2:37 a.m.

Just as he was about to increase his speed, he felt the vibration first. Then, a loud explosion. Gunshot? He felt the chilling sensation of his right front rim grinding on the road. Each jarring rotation of the wheel felt like a gut punch. His time gained by a quick departure was rapidly diminishing.

"Not now!" he yelled to himself. He gritted his teeth and thought about what he would do next. There was no time to fix a flat. And that explosion? What was that? He weighed his options. The tri-county train was within sprinting distance. He examined the tire. It was shredded. He swallowed hard, tasting the bitterness of desperation on his tongue. His well-laid plans were as useless as the car.

He hated to leave the Audi but there was no other choice. Not right now.

He reached for his duffle. And felt someone's hand press down on his left shoulder. The grip went from firm to painful. He looked back but could not see a face, only the black panel van. The hand on his shoulder moved to the back of his neck and forced him to look down. A second later a gun was pressed into his back. He dropped the duffle and was guided to the van. No words were spoken, yet he knew without seeing who had come for him. And why. Worse, he knew what was coming next.

The directions were given in tugs and pulls. Inside the van, the pressure of the muzzle against him was eased and a hood was placed over his head. His hands were tied and his ankles bound, then he was pushed down to the floor of the van. His only hope would be to plead with the man in charge.

There was no way to guess how long he was driven around and kept in darkness. No words were spoken. Time was an elusive thing when cut off from the world in the dark vacuum of confinement. All he knew was the ride turned from smooth pavement to bumpy, like driving on grass. The vibrations carried through the corrugated metal flooring, rattling his teeth.

He thought about all his moves made in the past seven days. Moves that could have been avoided. None of that mattered now. He was facing the tragic fallout of those decisions.

The van came to an abrupt stop. The engine cut off and so did the jostling. The reprieve came with an eerie calm.

He heard the driver's door open, followed by the approaching muted footsteps which meant the next phase had been reached. The door opened. Bindings were cut. The hood stayed on, for now. A hand pulled at his clothes. Unspoken directions had him removing all of his clothing.

He was now naked and vulnerable.

A zephyr of a wind moved around his bare skin.

The hood was removed and he saw what was in front of him. His eyes were transfixed on it. The machine was a contraption that started off as a woodchipper, only he could see many blades were added. There was no protective cowling. The thing was propped up with four jumbo tires.

Leading away from the chipper were several planks of plywood used to roll it into place. He knew what that meant. No tire tracks would be left behind. Nothing to investigate.

The time to speak up was now.

"I didn't tell anyone what we were doing. I promise." He got no response. "I didn't say a thing. I just wanted out. That's all. Just go on my way."

Still no response. The man behind him held his head firm, making him stare at the machine. It was built, he reasoned, to devour and cut.

He kept pleading. "I screwed up. I know that now. We can talk about this." Fear boiled up inside him until he felt his own bile forming at the back of his mouth. He started to jerk backward away from the machine. The strong hands kept him in place.

The machine started up. The sharp edges started swirling, starlight glinting off the turning blades. The motor sounded powerful. He again pushed back when he heard it start. The man behind him smashed him to the ground. Bits of grass and sand were embedded in his mouth. He was made to kneel in front of the beast. The turning blades were almost hypnotic, with a promise that anything going inside would never come back.

The prospect of certain death gave him, a man of limited physical strength, a surge. He pressed back against his captor, trying to wriggle free. He tried screaming but not much came out. The blades appeared to move even faster.

He jerked back again, pushing back only to be held down. Strength was waning throughout his naked body. His heart was exploding into a chest-pounding rhythm. He was finally able to vocalize screams. He yelled and hollered as loud as he could. All he could see was the whirling mass of blades in front of him and the guttural drone of cutting tools.

When he was done trying to yell, a voice whispered into his ear. "Once in, you can't leave the group."

Standing there, he knew what it meant to have his wallet and clothes taken away from him. *Almost nothing left for anyone to find.*

The blades, sharp as a surgeon's scalpel, seemed to beckon him. Each revolution etched a chilling melody in the air, the last symphony he would ever hear.

Suddenly, he was picked up, two hands holding his legs and upper body. He was being lifted into the air and held there. In the quick few moments left, he thought of the people in his life, a family he never contacted for months. The strong hands moved him closer to the blades.

He was thrust into the air. He was flying now. His arms swung wildly in a vain attempt to redirect his direction, yet his landing spot was not in his power. He felt the thrust but now he was just wrapped in the warm summer air. No manner of twisting or bending would change anything. He never saw the person who held him, only the large collection of turning blades turning so fast they were a blur, getting bigger and closer as he started his downward arc. Razor-sharp blades just waiting for him.

2

Booker Johnson held the hot wash towel to his face a full minute, then checked himself in the mirror to see if he looked ready enough to withstand the stares when he walked into the newsroom. He knew they would all anticipate how he would react, ready to whisper what he did when he arrived.

Nothing in the entire world moved faster than newsroom gossip.

Johnson did what he did on most days. He wore a shirt and tie and no sport coat. Summers in South Florida for TV reporters meant casual wear under the broiling sun. In case he needed to be on set in the studio, a dark gray jacket was hanging on the cubicle wall in the office. If he got there early enough, there would be time to sip on some Cuban coffee and get a jolt of adrenalin before he headed out the door. Cuban coffee was so strong only a small amount was enough to get the blood rushing. This morning maybe he needed a full cup.

On this day, heading out on assignment would be far different than any other since he first started at Channel 27. Johnson walked past the three Emmy Awards on his hallway bookshelf. Next to the Emmys was an arrangement of photographs showing him standing before a camera doing a live shot, one taken in the Florida Everglades, and another photo on vacation in Chicago with his then-girlfriend Misha Falone. His six-foot, two-inch frame towered nearly a foot over her, yet in their time together, he'd never felt as though he looked down on her. Misha was his equal, his partner, his soulmate. Or at least that's what he believed until the day it ended.

In the photograph, he wasn't smiling. He seldom did so during news stories, since they were all usually so serious. For Booker, this was a time of loss. The breakup with Misha also meant she took her dog Bruno with her. He missed them both.

He stopped at the door of the second bedroom. Two small piles of dirty clothes remained on the floor. A single red, rather expensive gym shoe was propped up by the doorjamb like it was the work of some rogue animal marking territory. No sounds coming from the room, just the silence of the morning. Booker started to knock, then stopped, and whispered to himself. "I'll talk to him later."

He looked around the room to make sure he wasn't leaving anything behind. The Emmys marked the highlight in what was a brilliant career.

And now this.

Demoted.

Booker was ready for the rumors. There was one rumor that he was headed to a rival news station. Another had him moving back to the Midwest. The strongest rumor pegged him for leaving the TV business altogether and becoming a Public Information Officer for the police department. They would all wait to see what he did when he walked in the door. And that moment was now.

During the ride to the station, he kept the radio turned off.

He entered the Channel 27 TV building and went down the hallway into the newsroom. Most of the time, a television newsroom noise level was the equivalent of a library. Quiet, except for scattered conversations on the phone or typing.

Not today.

Booker heard it within steps of entering the building. Breaking news. Assistant assignment editor Armond Conner had the loudest voice. He was barking out details to the gathering of producers and a few reporters.

"He just hijacked a car! We have a chase! Down Federal Highway!" Conner moved back to his setup of police scanners.

Booker stopped at the executive producer of the noon newscast. "What's going on?"

"Escaped prisoner," she said. "Broke free from an inmate bus, ran off, and just now hijacked a car."

Booker made a walk up to the desk. Conner was yelling more information. "I've got two crews headed a mile ahead of him. We have the helicopter in the air. We'll be over the scene in six minutes. I've got three crews headed to the original scene. And just in case, I have one crew going to the hospital. Trauma center."

Behind Conner, Claire Stanley stood, checking the monitor showing the camera view of the helicopter in flight to the chase. The camera is mounted on the front of the helicopter. She was chewing gum, hard. She had a notepad propped up on her arm and she was taking notes and listening to officers on the police scanner. Stanley was the chief assignment editor. A job that required her to send crews to their stories. She also ran the morning meeting where the stories were discussed. Stanley was the most admired person in the newsroom. In front of her, bolted to the ceiling, were six televisions. Each television had its own purpose. On three of them, Stanley and the assignment editors could see the other stations. One was dedicated to the helicopter, one to Channel 27's broadcast, and the last one to video feeds coming in from the network.

Stanley stopped chewing. "We need a crew following that car."

"On it." Conner picked up the phone and called a reporter in the field. More people were added to the story. With the phone jammed up to his ear, Conner shouted again, "The helicopter is on scene. Our helicopter is over the scene." On the monitor, the fleeing car darted in and out of traffic, nearly hitting other cars. The car was picking up speed.

In the studio, a news anchor was already in position behind a clear desk, microphone on, with paper for writing. In his ear, he heard the word from a producer and he started talking. Viewers would hear the anchor and see the live pictures of the car chase. "We are breaking into our regular programming to bring you this breaking news story. You can see this car moving in and out of traffic. We are told an escaped prisoner hijacked a car and is leading police on a chase north on Federal Highway. In a minute, the highway bends east and will be very close to the beach. We have several crews working this from many angles. We are told two schools near the chase scene are on lockdown. No one in or out of those schools right now. As you can see, Sky 27 is over that brown and white car. The car just missed hitting a truck and is moving faster. We do not have any information yet on the person who escaped and is in the car."

Booker quietly approached Claire Stanley, ready for directions on where he should be headed. "Where do you want me to go?"

Her eyes were fixed on the monitor with the view of the helicopter. "We're good, Booker."

"Good? I can help. You want me at the hospital? I know it's just me but I can do something."

"Booker. We don't need you right now. We're good."

Booker Johnson couldn't believe he was not in on a major breaking story. *So this is what it's like to be demoted.*

He stepped back. And for the first time since he arrived as a reporter, he was not asked to be a part of the action. The assignment desk was the greatest source of noise in the building. The sales offices were upstairs. On the main floor, producers were always busy writing stories for an upcoming newscast. In another section, they were writing for the website. At the assignment desk, noise had a home.

"He crashed the car!" Connor yelled to all assembled. On the screen, you could see the car crash into another car. The prisoner, wearing a bright orange jumpsuit, emerged and started running. Within seconds, eight cars converged on the smashed car, officers out and running toward the escapee.

Booker stood off to the side, looking like someone in need. Stanley continued to ignore him. A few seconds later, the prisoner was down on the ground. Officers were handcuffing him. Other officers arrived. The breaking news element of the story was ending. There would be plenty of work to do before the noon newscast.

Booker tried one more time and again approached Stanley. "I know I'm working alone. But send me anywhere."

Stanley had almost thirty years of experience. And like most newsrooms, she did the job of eight people. They were enveloped in a cacophony of police scanner conversations. Only a trained ear could decipher and understand the chatter. A seasoned assignment editor could pick a true news story out of that mass of talking and get a crew going. Booker looked into Stanley's eyes and waited for an answer. She pulled him from the desk and found a quieter spot a few yards away. "You shouldn't have been put into a one-man band. It's not right and I argued against it. You're way too good a reporter for this."

"But you lost the argument." Booker held tight to his reporter pad.

"I do have to send you somewhere." The hard gum chewing started again.

"Where?"

Stanley paused like she was being forced to do something she didn't want to do. "It's out at the old park. There is a smell of something dead."

Booker's face looked confused. He tried to hide his disdain. "A smell? You want me to check out a smell?!"

"I'm not used to you asking me for a story." Claire stared into Booker's face. "Most of the time you come up with your own stories." Both of them conversed while keeping a close listen to the scanners. Finally, she asked the question. "You okay?"

Booker was still in mild shock. "Just let me get through this first day." He gave a quick glance at the room. No one was looking in his direction. Then again, most of the nine daytime reporters were already out the door, working the breaking news story.

She stared at her notepad as if looking for one more specific piece of information. "There's not much else."

"A smell? No body? No crime scene?"

Stanley checked her notes one more time. "No, just a few patrols there, I think. They're checking it out."

Booker fought back the urge to argue for another story. "Claire, it could be a dead animal."

"Could be," Stanley said. "They just don't know. And if it's something, call me."

Just as he was about to walk away, she pulled him back. "You're one of the best reporters in this shop. Since you'll be working by yourself, I'll give you all the support I can."

"Thanks." And Booker was headed into a new world as a one-man band. After sixteen years in South Florida, working with a photographer and at times a producer, Booker was now by himself, relegated to working alone, traveling in a news van and responsible for setting up his own live signals, editing, and getting the video back to the station. Some loved working this way.

Not Booker.

His new swipe entry card was updated to allow him into the photography room, where he would pick up a camera and keys to a news van. So far, no side comments from anyone about the new role. Johnson drove past the guard at the gate, who stared at him like he was seeing someone returning from the grave.

Booker kept driving.

3

Clifton Park was two miles off the busy I-95 Expressway. Most stayed away from here as there were no playgrounds for children. The entire place consisted of a hiking trail, a pond off to one side, and several benches near the water. Even the cyclists didn't use the park since the trip around was too short.

Booker got out and did something he didn't have to do for many years, since his days starting at a small station in the Midwest. He picked up the news camera. The thing weighed several pounds. Many photographers in the biz suffered shoulder problems later in life. Booker noticed it right away.

The smell of death.

A familiarity with the decaying odor had stayed with him since his first homicide scene years earlier. A putrid presence carried on the breeze.

He scanned the area. Two marked police units were near the water. There were also two TV news crews. When Booker approached, all attention was on him.

"I can't believe this! Booker, where's your crew? It's just you?" The questions came from Clendon Davis, veteran reporter and a challenger to get the story first. His photographer, Laura McDaniel, almost never spoke unless someone got in the way of her camera.

Booker rested the camera at his feet. "Life goes on." He turned to the two police officers. They looked confounded. Smell but no clear direction on where to look for a body.

Davis had his own idea. "This is a big waste of time. Gotta be dead fish. I'm giving it ten more minutes." Booker could feel the burn of the stare from Davis. "I still can't believe this. Booker Johnson, working alone like a cub reporter. What did you do?"

Booker ignored him, hoisted the camera to his shoulder, and walked off. He was trying to figure out where the odor was coming from and where did the smell dissipate. He got some forty yards away and smelled nothing. From this vantage point, he looked over the ground for a victim.

Nothing.

Human death stench had its own way of getting into a nose or the very pores of your body like nothing else.

Booker was convinced there had to be a victim.

He received four messages from the newsroom. They wanted Booker to leave the park and move on to another story. Just not the escapee story. He called and spoke to someone on the assignment desk. Booker kept things one-sided. His side. "No, I'm not leaving. I just have a feeling, that's all. I'm staying." He hung up, knowing a report would go up the channels from the assignment desk to the executive producer and possibly the news director. Defying a newsroom directive was tantamount to begging to be suspended.

For the moment, he was free to move about the park. Booker took advantage of the opportunity. While keeping a close watch on the officers, he walked the immediate perimeter. Every time he stopped, he recorded more video. All kinds of angles, different perspectives. Booker didn't know what angle recorded now might be really important later on. When he reached the farthest spot away from the search, he saw a man approaching. A hiker.

Curiosity was emblazoned on the face of the sixtyish man. He was wearing blue sweatpants, a faded University of Miami shirt, and running shoes. No hat.

"What happened?"

Booker put the camera down on the ground. "They're looking for something."

"Looking? For what?" His blue eyes moved from left to right, scanning the park.

"You come here often?"

"Twice a week. Get my steps in. I try to do ten thousand steps a day."

Booker sized him up. Every person he had ever interviewed had to measure up to Booker's bullshit meter. In a matter of seconds, he had to weigh whether a person was telling him the truth or some sort of evasion, planned on the spot. The man before him had clean hands, no cuts or bruises, meaning he didn't seem to have had a history of hard-driving labor. The polo shirt was clean, almost barstool-at-the-golf-clubhouse clean. The man obviously took time on his appearance. Booker's instinct said trust his words.

"Okay if I ask you about how quiet this place is?"

The man thought for a moment, rubbing wrinkled hands through salt and pepper hair. "You're Booker Johnson, right?"

"Yes."

"I've seen your work. You do a good job. I don't know anything about this but I can talk about the park."

Booker put the camera on his shoulder. With his left hand, he extended a microphone. This would be so much easier, Booker thought, if he was working with a photographer. "You come here a lot. Are you surprised to see police searching the park?"

"Yes. Usually, it's just me and the birds. Maybe an alligator. I hate to see the peace of this place interrupted. It's a nice part of the city."

Booker's arm was already getting tired holding the microphone. "You see or hear anything last night or this morning?"

"No, not really. My house is close by. I thought I heard some rumbling noise two days ago."

"Two days? You see anything?"

"No."

Booker thanked him. "That's all I need. Thank you."

He nodded and turned around. In the coming hours, detectives would be by his house, asking the same questions and probably more.

Booker walked back to the van and continued to watch. His phone hummed three more times. He ignored all of the calls. Then came the text messages. LEAVE NOW! CALL THE STATION. NOW!

Still, Booker ignored the demands. He was all in on what was unfolding before him. His day was already borderline terrible, and he was sure everything was about to get worse.

An unmarked car rolled up slowly and parked near the two police cars.

She got out of the car.

Detective Brielle Jensen looked at the collection of reporters. When she spotted Booker, her facial expression turned grim. She was quite easily the last detective he expected, and he really didn't know what would happen next.

Booker wanted to melt into the jagged-edged Florida sawgrass.

4

Booker, more than anything, was sorry he didn't leave as instructed. He hadn't seen Jensen in months, not since a very failed attempt at asking her out for a date. Reporters and detectives don't mix, he'd kept saying at the time. Plus, she held him responsible for getting a written reprimand.

Jensen approached the officers. She was tall, medium build with a confident walk and arms that showed plenty of time spent in the gym. When she approached them, the conversation was quiet and Booker was too far away to hear anything. Booker moved back to his original spot. She kept her hair pulled back. No polish on the nails and always the game face. Up until the incident with Booker, her arrest rate was pretty high. Booker kept track.

Jensen and the officers spread out. She put on a pair of white booties. They started a grid search, looking down at the ground, examining everything.

"That's it, we're outta here." Davis and his photographer packed up. He shouted to Booker. "This is like waiting for your hair to turn gray." The second crew also got ready to leave. The park got quiet once their vans moved on and out the front gate. It was just Booker as the lone reporter. His gut still told him to stay.

Davis approached Booker. "Sorry they're doing this to ya man. We're going, and I think it's a mistake to stay."

"I'll be fine." Booker never looked at him, keeping his gaze on the officers.

Davis kept at him like picking a scab. "You really staying?" He turned to his photographer. "You believe this guy? Milking a nothing story. Looks like this is your new life, Booker. Standing ground on wasted time. By yourself."

"Do what you need to do. Let me work."

Davis left, smiling all the way back to his van.

Booker's cell phone hummed and he ignored the calls another four times. He was disobeying a directive, multiple times. He imagined the conversations at the station. Booker knew this could be grounds for a suspension or even the thirty-day countdown to a dismissal. He sent back one text: NOT LEAVING YET.

Two minutes later, more police help arrived.

A sniffer.

An officer let his cadaver dog out of the back. They walked directly to Jensen. The officer and his dog worked the scene. Booker started to shoot video. The officers, the dog, Jensen, everything that moved.

The dog was a German shepherd. Playful, the dog looked eager to get going. The officer got a briefing from Jensen. With the dog working, everyone stopped what they were doing.

All those in the immediate search area put on Tyvek gear. Crime techs opened and stretched the white protective material. One person struggled to get the gear on. Seeing them in the white gear and head topping gave Booker's video an eerie look.

The dog moved quickly, going through the wide area of wild periwinkle and tufts of mondo grass.

Booker studied everything. Jensen worked one part of the search pattern, far away from the dog. She carefully checked in and around the trees. From memory, Booker recalled the city planted several trees of all kinds. The trees were placed strategically to hopefully stop a car from driving off the road and going into the pond.

There were no homes or businesses on the other side of the water.

Whoever was here used the same road Booker used to gain entry to the park.

For a moment, Booker thought about Jensen's arrival. She was sent to a possible nonevent just like him. And she was working by herself.

About twelve minutes into the dog's search, he sat down and barked and got his reward, a rubber ball and some strong hugs from his handler. Jensen approached the officer. Words were exchanged. Jensen cupped her hands and yelled. "Stop! The dog has found something."

One officer yelled back. "Where?"

Jensen spread out her arms in a waving motion. "Everywhere!" One officer approached Jensen. "What do we have?"

She looked at the now-growing search grid. "As of now, we don't know."

5

Booker could hear what Jensen told the officers. "I hope you brought more shoes because the ones you're wearing are going into property for a few days." She pulled out her phone and started a conversation with someone.

Booker tried to see what the dog could be alerting on. Using the camera, he zoomed in on the ground. What wasn't evident before was actually right in front of him.

Tiny bits of what looked like flesh. The stuff was everywhere near the bank of the pond. He zoomed in and also found three fifteen-to-twenty-inch pools on the ground, resembling red soup.

Booker looked down and around where he was standing and saw nothing. The scattered parts of flesh were all located close to the pond. Eleven minutes later, a crime scene van arrived. The crime tech checked in with Jensen.

The tech used utensils to pick up the bits. Moments later, the tech found what looked like bone shards. Booker had it all on camera. A field test was done. More minutes passed. And another conversation with Jensen. The officers were now out of their shoes, leaving them for the crime tech to photograph and examine. A stack of brown paper bags would be used to collect what was found on the ground.

The officers started putting up crime scene tape. Lots of tape.

And, of course, they made Booker move back. He looked around and could not find the one thing he could use right now.

Shade.

He estimated his time in the park had reached the fourth hour. Four hours standing in the grueling summer Florida sun with no trees nearby for comfort. Some reporters put up tents and set up camera positions for long stakeouts for waiting on someone to come to a microphone. No tent for Booker. He could easily move to a tree some twenty yards off, and then lose the best angle to get video of any action. He stayed put. If he stayed for the six p.m., he would log a full eight hours in the blare of the sun. No matter the skin color, every reporter and photographer Booker ever knew made regular checks with a dermatologist.

He watched Jensen work. Booker and Jensen had talked during dozens of crime scenes, leading eventually to a chance meeting at a coffee shop. More conversation. For just a moment, Booker thought something clicked between them. Maybe. Maybe not.

The moment was now. Time to wave his hands and see if Jensen would come over and talk to him. Maybe their last meeting was behind her. Would she forget the fact he once found some critical evidence that she missed and left behind at a crime scene? Evidence Booker pointed out in a live report to a large viewership of South Florida. Everyone watching saw it, along with Jensen's boss, the captain. She had to come back to the scene and collect the evidence. Not pretty. All thoughts of getting an answer to his attempts at dinner were gone.

That was months ago.

Booker waved for her to come over. Some detectives talked to the media at the scene. The usual step would be to refer reporters to the Public Information Officer. A PIO. A person, sometimes a fellow officer, who would speak and give updates on the investigation. Most times, a minimum of information.

Booker was shocked. She took off her protective outfit and started walking in his direction.

"Booker..." Jensen said his name like it was a swear word.

"Detective..." Booker snapped the camera into a tripod.

She looked him up and down. "Who'd you piss off? All by yourself now?"

"Long story."

She glanced back over her shoulder then back at Booker. "I'll be real brief 'cause the PIO is coming. We have human remains. The remains are all over this section of the park. We are very early in the investigation and don't have much more than that right now."

Booker grabbed for his microphone and got ready to fire up the camera. "Okay if I get this on camera?" He could see she was thinking about his request. Her temple muscles flexed.

"Sure, but it'll be short."

Booker recorded twenty seconds of an interview with Jensen. Interview over, Booker confessed. "I'm in a new position. They're calling me a pilot project. Working alone. A cheap way to save money in one of the biggest markets in the country. But I think they're sending me a message, trying to make me leave."

She took it all in and did not say anything right away. "Management gave you a slap?" She turned to walk away. "Now you know how it feels." Jensen returned to the crime scene, stopped, and turned back. "The last time I worked around you, I almost lost my position in homicide." She was gone.

Booker pulled out his phone and pressed it to his mouth. Claire Stanley answered. "Stanley..."

"It's Booker."

"Booker, we've been trying to reach you for more than an hour. The producers are pissed 'cause we want to move you to another..."

"Before you say anything else. We got human remains spread out all over the park. I can do a live hit for the noon show. Tell them there are no other reporters here. This is an exclusive."

6

Booker had to do several things at the same time. He first contacted the feedroom at the station and talked to the engineers so they could find the signal coming from his news van. The feedroom was the central location in the TV station where all video arrived from outside sources. And that included the signal coming from Booker's van. Once the signal was established, he started the process of editing his video. He cut a nice collection of video lasting just under one minute. He used a wide establishing shot first, then close-ups of the search, and finally bags of evidence. Booker fed the video back to the station and set up his camera and tripod for his live broadcast. He used phone earbuds to hear the producer's directions in his ear by dialing a number that also gave him on-air audio.

All the while, he kept a close watch on the crime scene. When the Channel 27 anchor read the introduction, Booker spoke and then moved out of the way to show what was going on. He detailed what he could, tastefully, about the tiny bits of body parts found on the ground, then back at the station, they showed the video clip of Detective Jensen. Booker then wrapped it up and tossed it back to the anchor.

Not more than fifteen minutes later, Clendon Davis and his photographer rolled up in their van, screeching to a burned rubber stop. He got out and slammed the door, walking straight to Booker. "Score one for you, you kicked my ass. The next chapter starts right now."

Booker ignored him. In all, he had enough video for a documentary, recording as much as he could. He did that because Booker knew the police's next move was about to happen.

An officer came to Booker, Davis, and a third crew and announced. "You guys need to pack up. We're moving you all back behind the gate. This entire area is now part of the crime scene."

Davis was losing his chance to get any close-up video and protested as much as he could. No doing. He got back into his van and drove out past the entry. Booker parked along with them in a new spot. He understood the need to move reporters. Detectives had to map out and determine what vehicles drove into the park. Maybe there were tire tracks. Too many people around could F up the scene. The answer was simple: move everyone out of the way and do your investigation.

With his camera full of video, Booker turned to other areas. Who was this person? Was it more than one victim? How did they do this? Was the murder done here in the park or somewhere else? Right about now, reporters jammed together would share theories on what happened. Not today. Booker could tell Davis was angry about leaving the scene and then being forced to come back.

For the five p.m. newscast, Booker put together a full two-minute video package. He included the earlier sound clip with Jensen, and a new sound interview with the PIO kept everything short and clean. No speculation.

Exactly one minute to Booker going on the air for the five p.m. newscast and telling a South Florida audience about the murder find, something happened. The something occurred every day somewhere in the television world. In Booker's case, the problem was immediately evident.

In his earpiece, Booker heard, "We lost your signal! We can't see you." The problem had to be attacked on two ends, the station and Booker. The loss in the feed was on Booker's end or theirs. While the station checked the incoming feed to see, Booker checked his gear. He wriggled the cable and he heard, "We got you back! You're good." He did the five p.m. cast and showed no worries about the problem with the feed. He was done. A great first day on his own. He got a few atta-boys from two reporters still in the station and a smile from Claire Stanley. The smile was all he needed. Next to come would be a drink.

7

Booker Johnson entered his apartment and heard music coming from the second bedroom. The clothes were picked up and the kitchen was actually clean. Even the red gym shoe was gone. Johnson opened his laptop and checked the websites of his competitors, the other stations, to see if they had more information than his own reports. Nothing special. He read the stories of three bloggers who centered their attention on city happenings. None of them had anything about Booker's story.

He typed a note to himself for a possible day-two follow-up on the chopped-up body parts.

A person emerged from the other bedroom. "What's up, Book?"

Johnson looked at his face and could easily see himself in the tall, angular body and brown skin tones of Demetrious Moreland.

His half brother.

"Had a bad one, huh? I saw the news." Demetrious opened the refrigerator and stood there looking at the shelves for food choices.

Booker thought about calling his ex-girlfriend, then gave up on the idea. "Bad is right." The sound of fingers moving items on the fridge shelves echoed from the kitchen.

Demetrious held up what looked like half of a store-bought turkey sandwich. "Ya know, Book, you should tell them why you were late for most of those assignments. It was my fault, not yours. I made you late."

Johnson rubbed tired eyes. "You don't have a car. Had to get you to those job interviews. I'll be okay."

"Okay? You said you're working by yourself? That's not okay. Tell them." He examined the sandwich then bit into the meal.

"Don't worry about it. I'll get through it." Booker turned on the television in the living room and used the guide to look for a sports game. Any game. A half glass of red wine was getting warm. He gave up on finding a game on TV and decided it was time to turn things down. Let sleep heal him.

Demetrious walked across the room, munching on the sandwich. "Thanks for giving me a place to stay." He was still wearing the bright red gym shoes.

Both of them shared their mother's large brown eyes, but Demetrious had those other features from a different father. He was broader in the chest and two inches taller than Booker's six-foot-two frame and two years younger. Demetrious would sometimes slap his hands against his leg when he was trying to make a point.

"Half bruh, I promise to get a job tomorrow. Like tomorrow."

Half bruh was his newest nickname for Booker, who always had the same response. "You're not my half anything, you're my brother." There was weariness in Booker's voice. All those hours outside, working the story. A Florida sun could sap your energy.

Meal over, Demetrious wiped his hands on his pants. "Tomorrow, you see. A job. I promise. I promise."

Booker did not hear him. He was asleep on the couch, still wearing the clothes he had on that day.

8

Booker Johnson arrived early to the newsroom, something he did on a regular basis. He had all kinds of follow-up ideas to pitch to anyone on the assignment desk. Before he could say anything, Claire Stanley shoved a piece of paper in his direction. "We've got a new mall opening. We need you on it. Give us the jobs angle, impact on traffic, you know the deal."

Booker held the paper like it was laced with poison ivy. "I thought we could do a day-two on the body parts. Try and connect a name with the crime. See if there are any witnesses."

Stanley was waving her hands as if swatting back his proposal. "All the producers want on that is twenty seconds. A mention. That's all. We can get an update with one phone call from here on the desk. What we need is the new mall story."

A dejected Booker headed to the photography room for his camera. There was one more directive from Stanley.

"Booker, I want you to meet Lacie Grandhouse. Your intern."

"My what?"

The five-foot-six skinny college student held out her hand. Booker shook her thin fingers. She smiled, "I've watched you for years."

Stanley moved back into her position on the assignment desk, back into the cacophony of noise. "You could use the extra help."

"I'll bring the van around. See you out front."

Universities across the state worked with newsrooms and provided college students who majored in Journalism. Future TV news reporters, anchors, and producers. They got college credit and the news stations got hungry, maybe brilliant students, willing to work hard. One of them might, just might be a great find.

Booker drove until he exited busy I-95 and headed for Clifton Park.

Grandhouse, the intern, turned to him. "I thought we were going to the mall. Isn't that the story?"

"We'll get to the mall. I want to check something out first."

A reporter's notebook stuck up out of her purse. No heels, she wore a good pair of running shoes. Her hair was pulled to the back, away from her face.

Booker asked her his standard question he asked every intern. "So, do you want to be in front of the camera or in back of the camera?"

"Reporter or producer? I want to be in front." The edges of her face turned up into a smile. "As a kid, I used to stand in front of the mirror and pretend I was on TV, doing the news. Yeah, I've been aiming for this for a long time. I want to learn everything from you."

In fourteen minutes, Booker drove through the entrance of the park. The yellow crime tape was down. He stopped in the lot and noticed other cars were there. Once he got out of the van, he saw why. Detective Jensen was back. She and another detective were still going over the scene. There was no one walking or riding through the park, as though the place was still shrouded in death.

Booker stood out from the van, prominent as he could, to catch Jensen's attention. There was a worried look on the intern's face. He could tell she was probably thinking, I'm assigned to a rogue reporter. He put the camera on the ground, for Booker a sign he just wanted to talk.

Jensen acknowledged Booker and made her way to him. She was wearing a fresh pair of gloves, shoes covered in booties. Jensen started talking before she reached him. "All information is coming through PIO."

Booker pressed on anyway. "You do an autopsy, as best you can?"

"You know I can't talk about that. I can tell you one is being done, blood work done, DNA, and we'll do a check with missing persons." She turned and walked away. "Bye, Booker."

He lifted up the camera and started to record some video. The intern Grandhouse was four feet away from him, her face twisted up as if confused and a bit shaken.

Booker stopped what he was doing to explain to her. "You smell death before?"

She shook her head.

There was still a strong lingering pungent aroma from flesh and bone still not recovered. "If you think you're gonna be sick . . ."

"I'm fine."

"You sure?"

"I'm fine. Is this your story from yesterday?"

"Yes. I came back for a quick check. I'll get some video and head off to the mall." When he was done recording a few minutes of video, he turned to the intern again. "This your first crime scene?"

"Yes."

"Take it all in. Check and remember how detectives do things. They took a ton of photographs yesterday. They might come back today and get some more. Sometimes they'll fly a helicopter overhead and get a wide shot." Booker packed up the gear and stowed away the camera in a locked metal box.

Booker studied her. She looked fine, not apparently affected by the smell. Grandhouse tucked the reporter pad back into her purse. She pointed to Jensen. "She's in charge?"

"Yes."

Grandhouse kept a glued watch on Jensen. "You know her? She seems like she knows you really well."

"Sort of . . ."

Over the years, Booker Johnson worked with and trained dozens of interns. They all came with a truckload of educational skills or the ability to work a computer. And what they lacked in life experience, they made up for it by asking a million questions. What Grandhouse asked next made Booker think.

"Why here?"

Booker started the van. "Here meaning why was there a murder here?"

"Yes. I looked up your report. They could have done this anywhere. Why pick a quiet deserted park?"

"I'm not sure. At least not yet. Good question."

The trip to the mall took about twenty minutes. He figured he was about fifteen minutes late for the start of the news conference. He saw all the other TV stations there. And something he did not expect.

"Shit," he said to himself.

A row of black SUVs and two state trooper cars left just as Booker was getting out of the van. He recognized the entourage.

"Wow," Grandhouse said. "Who was that?"

"The governor."

"The governor?"

The trail of cars left with the troopers leading the way, clearing out traffic. Booker made his way to the semicircle of reporters. Two of them were smiling, watching Booker set up his camera gear. His phone hummed.

"Booker . . ."

Claire Stanley was on the other end. "We're hearing the governor made a surprise visit at your news conference. Something about a twelve-point plan to pay teachers more money. Big stuff Booker, tell me what you got."

The next few seconds seemed like four years. Booker spoke low. "I missed it."

"You what!"

Booker kept thinking about that old phrase, 'You're only as good as your last story.' His hands suddenly got cold as an Iowa winter morning. All of Claire Stanley's words sounded like one long word, all slurred together like a slap across his face. "Ya-gotta-be-kidding-me!"

"I'm sorry, Claire. I was only a few minutes late."

Stanley yelled. "Late, my ass, what were you doing?" A few moments paused as Booker did not answer right away. Stanley's voice came back down to calm. "Okay, we're gonna do this. I'll make arrangements and get the governor's comments from a state-wide video feed. You get ready for the noon and front the story from there. Check your computer and pull up the information and talking points from wire services. You got that!"

"Okay. And I'll look for anyone here for reaction sound."

"If they're still there. And Booker, when you're done today, come see me."

"I will."

Clendon Davis was now standing next to Booker. Davis had a wide smile. Every tooth in his mouth was exposed. "Screw'n up again, Booker? We all wondered why there was no one here from good ole reliable on-the-spot Channel 27. Booker, you're really showing your intern how to do things right."

Booker had work to do. A lot of information had to be gathered in the next ninety minutes.

9

When the top of the noon hour hit, Booker was right there with the other reporters, with the same information, as though he was on time, right from the start.

Even though he wasn't.

In the time leading up to the noon newscast, he was able to get the governor's sound clip and plenty of associated information. The teacher's union rep was still there, so he recorded some reactions to the announcement. And he got the groundbreaking video of the new mall and what it would do for new jobs from video feeds. The process was ugly. Booker thought his story matched the other stations.

On the way back to the newsroom, he apologized to the intern. "I should have listened to you and made the trip to the park in the afternoon."

By the time Booker finally sat down with Claire Stanley, she had calmed down. He came out of the meeting with another warning. No more mess-ups. Stanley explained she covered for him. The big-wigs didn't know he missed the governor. He owed her, big time. Again.

Sitting in his newsroom cubicle, Booker wrote the information for the newscasts for what was commonly known in the news business as a VO. Short for voice-over. Booker provided the information on the day-two coverage of the body parts found in the park. No other station did a full report, just a short VO like Channel 27.

Before he left the news station, he caught Grandhouse before she left. "You said before you wanted to learn from me. I'm sorry, but I let you down today when I missed the governor."

She cracked back. "You firmly believe there's more to the discovery of body parts and I agree with you. They should have let you do a day-two on it."

"Maybe so, but I had an assignment and I almost blew it. Learn from my mistake, intern."

She laughed. "I won't be an intern forever. One of these days I'll be right back here as a GA."

Booker shook her hand. "General assignment. I think you'll make a great GA reporter. Are you back tomorrow?"

"Yep. They can't keep me away."

"Take care."

Booker went home and found Demetrious was not there. On the way, Booker stopped at his favorite restaurant to get a Caesar salad with extra chicken and no croutons. A glass of red wine and an NBA game rounded out his evening. His thoughts kept going back to Clifton Park and the pile of human flesh left to rot in the Florida sun.

10

David Napston banged his hand on the table and closed the laptop. A few seconds later, he opened the computer again and did all the normal checks to figure out where the email came from. There was no URL in the corner. He decided he would not get anyone involved to help him search for the sender. Not now. This was too sensitive.

He prided himself on having everything in order. All of his appointments he kept himself, no need for a secretary. Everything in its proper place. Bald for years, Napston rubbed his hand over the top of his scalp and formed the courage to look at the video on the laptop one more time.

He started the video.

The angle was wide, then the person shooting the video zoomed in and he could clearly see his own face. He was in his car, the Volvo, windows down, parked under the shade of a banyan tree. He was hidden, safe to do what he was about to do.

He raised a clearly marked bottle of Vodka and pushed it to his mouth. This was no sip. He gulped it down, enjoying every drop. Napston leaned back in his car seat and let the breeze fill up the inside of the car. Then, once again, the video showed him raising the bottle, pushing the Vodka toward his mouth.

Satiated.

On the vid Napston smiled. He was the man who usually went about his day doing everything proper, always by the book. He tossed the empty Vodka bottle onto the grass. The car started up and Napston drove toward the building.

The secret photographer got video of him driving off then panning down to the bottle. Some shaky video followed as it showed someone walking to the bottle, picking up the bottle with gloves, and letting the camera zoom in to give the impression fingerprints would be found. A current edition of a newspaper was thrust into the picture frame. The camera moved back to the building where Napston was headed, clearly identifying the sixteen-floor structure.

Then black.

There was a message along with the video:

IF YOU DECIDE TO RUN WE WILL DISTRIBUTE THIS VIDEO TO ALL THE PROPER AUTHORITIES, INCLUDING THE ETHICS COMMITTEE, ALONG WITH THE ACTUAL BOTTLE. DO NOT, REPEAT, DO NOT RUN AGAIN. DROP OUT. YOU HAVE TWENTY-FOUR HOURS TO REPLY.

Napston hit the desktop again, only harder. There was one last sentence from the sender. The message hinted there were seventeen additional videos just like this one.

More than anything, Napston hated to be told what to do. He always was the one doing the ordering. He was in charge. This was different.

He had to figure out what to do. Just as he was about to look at the video one more time, there was a knock at the door. A large man appeared and leaned into the large office.

"They're ready for you, sir."

Napston straightened himself up. "Thank you. I'll be right there."

He reached for the piece of clothing on the hanger. Napston remembered the day he first got it. All the years of college, all the work, the studying, all for this moment. He felt the material, tried to produce a smile, but could not.

He put on the garment.

A black robe.

Napston walked down the corridor and went through two security doors before reaching his destination. When the last door was opened, a room of people were already there, including two rows of lawyers.

His big bailiff addressed the gathering. "All rise! Judge David Napston presiding."

11

One year earlier

A soft wind pushed past the seventeen palm trees lining the driveway. The end of a perfect day was about to turn bleak. Before Janet Kemper parked her car, she heard the first few raindrops hit the hood of her just-polished Porsche. She was now in a hurry to get inside the house and wasn't able to use the garage. The entire space was filled with all kinds of items leaving the three-car garage packed. She kept telling herself she needed to get rid of things. Kemper was able to do that with her louse of a husband. Some mere things in the garage shouldn't be a problem.

Once out of the car, she took two steps and the sky unloaded. Raindrops the size of pennies pelted the walkway. Both her hands were full and she couldn't hold an umbrella. A white-silver streak of lightning tracked across a dark sky, followed by a body-shaking boom of thunder. Rain was coming off the roof like someone was tossing buckets of mop waste. She made it to the front door and put down her purse and four bags of groceries. Everything she was wearing was soaked. Her clothes stuck to her body by the torrent of droplets. Behind her, the palm fronds whipped and swayed at the whim of the strong winds. She opened the door and expected to hear loud music coming from her daughter's room.

There was nothing.

Kemper yelled out, "D.K., you home?" There was no response. Putting the groceries away would have to wait. Her fifteen-year-old might be sleeping, she thought, since the teen called her to say she was homesick. "D.K., you up there?"

Kemper reached to turn on the light. They did not come on. She hit the light switch three, four times. No lights. She went to another room. Still, the lights would not come on. A shock wave of thunder rattled the table lamp in the dimly lit living room. Kemper looked down and saw her hand shaking. Fear and concern rose up from her gut. All she wanted to do now was get to her daughter's room and just check on her. She used the light of her cell phone and took one step at a time, making her way up the staircase toward D.K.'s room. It was the first door on the left. On the second floor, here too, the lights would not come on in the hallway. She was breathing so hard, the air in her throat now came in quick bursts. Her natural breathing was way off. She got to the door and managed to whisper, "D.K.?"

Kemper aimed her hand toward the doorknob. She held it there for several seconds. She turned the knob. Kemper cracked the door open a few inches. As she opened the door, more of the room was exposed to her. D.K.'s desk and chair were there. On the wall were photographs of friends and favorite singers. No D.K. yet. She opened the door some more. Now she could see the wood floor and a couple of stuffed toys D.K. kept since she was a small child. Next came the twin bed. The headboard was stacked with five pink pillows. D.K.'s color of choice. The door creaked. Kemper kept promising herself to put some oil on the jamb.

She stepped into the room.

Kemper moved her cell phone light from right to left. D.K. was sitting in a chair. Her hands looked like they were held behind her with something. She was blindfolded. A tear rolled down her cheek from under the blindfold and she looked beyond scared.

"Come all the way inside," a voice said. He was wearing gloves and a black balaclava covered his face, head and ears. His left hand covered D.K.'s mouth.

Kemper froze. "Who are you? Let my daughter go right now!"

The voice gave another command. "Toss the cell phone on the bed.

Now!" A large knife eased out from his side and the blade was placed nice and snug against the teen's neck. D.K. trembled as the cold blade touched her skin. "You say one thing I don't like and you'll be responsible for your daughter's blood all over this floor. Now go to the desk over there and sit down."

Kemper looked at her cell phone now resting on the bed covers. If she could figure out a way to reach it and dial for help.

"I said, sit down!"

Kemper moved as slowly as she could. She was trying to size up everything in her head, while thinking of any weapon she might use once she got to the desk. All the pens were gone. No pencils. The desktop was cleaner than normal. Her daughter's cell phone was not there. Her most immediate concern was D.K. She didn't appear to be injured. Based on an estimate, Kemper theorized the figure was at least six feet tall. When he reached out, he was wearing plastic gloves. All his skin was covered with camouflage face paint, even around his eyes, so she wasn't able to exactly determine his ethnicity.

Kemper tried to stay calm. "What do you want? Obviously, you've been waiting for me. I can give you money."

The male voice was even toned. "The request is simple. So simple, we can have all of this wrapped up in no time. You're on the board of Songjust Industries, correct?"

"What do you want with them? There's nothing my daughter can do for you. Just let her go and both of us can talk this out."

His voice was harder now. "I ask the questions. I'll ask just one more time and if you don't answer, it's not going to be pleasant to watch." He took his left hand and grabbed D.K. by the head, lifting up her chin so the knife blade had more skin exposed for a good cut.

"Okay! Yes, I'm on the board of Songjust. Been in that position for six years."

"And you are about to move into the CEO position? Something you've been aiming for all this time?"

"Where did you hear that?" In a flash, Kemper thought about what he said, that he didn't want to hear questions. "Yes, yes, I've been working hard for this position and I have applied and it looks good."

The voice was back to calm. "You will tell them by email and letter that you are no longer interested in that position, that you thought it over and this would not be a good fit for you."

More than anything, Kemper wanted to ask more questions. Why would they stop her from moving into the number one slot in the company? One look at D.K. and she knew she would have to comply.

"I will do as you ask. I will take back my application."

"Good. You will send the email in exactly thirty minutes. Now don't think about going to the police or some nonsense. We've been watching you for a long time. You go to the gym three days a week, mostly in the early morning hours. You make a monthly trip to your nail salon and get yourself done up. Your daughter's school is the most prestigious in the county. Her driver gets her there exactly twenty-five minutes before class starts. We know the route he takes. Janet Kemper, we know when you take a shower, what you watch on TV, when you go to bed, and the three times the gardener stayed a bit longer here than normal. Your bank account number ends in 5998. We can perfectly match the way you sign your name. We know everything about you. Don't even think about going against this. We will kill your daughter in front of you, then make your last moments the worst ever. Turn in the paperwork. Send the email. Get this done. And you will never hear from us again. Now, is that a yes from you?"

Janet Kemper never sweat unless she was in the gym, but now runny beads of perspiration were coming off her forehead in lines of sweat. She felt cornered and was out of options. "Yes, I'll do it. Just don't hurt my daughter."

"Ah, thank you. We knew you would see things our way." The man moved just a bit to show one more piece of persuasion. A gun was strapped to his waist. "Now, there are a couple of things left for you to do. First, look in that desk drawer and pull out the blindfold." He kept the knife at D.K.'s throat.

Reluctantly, Kemper reached into the drawer. A blindfold was there.

"Now, put it on. You're almost home free."

Kemper pulled up the blindfold and placed it against her face and eyes. There was a Velcro backing. She pulled it tight so he could see she was following his orders.

"That's good, Janet. Now, remind your daughter she must not say anything to her friends. Nothing. Not one word. And no mention on social media. We will be watching. You don't want D.K. to get you both killed. Now, face the wall."

Kemper turned in the chair. She was facing the wall and listening to everything she could. If she so much as heard a whimper of pain coming from D.K. she would tear off the blindfold and do what was needed to at least try and save her.

She sat in the chair for several minutes. It was quiet. Kemper called out to D.K. "Danetha Kathy, you okay?"

"I'm okay, Mom. I'm alright. I think he's gone."

Kemper yanked off her blindfold and rushed to her daughter's side. She pulled down D.K.'s blindfold. A full-on hug wrapped both of them in arms tight, holding in an embrace. Kemper kissed her daughter a dozen times. "Did he hurt you?"

"No. I didn't hear him 'cause I had the things in my ears. I was at my desk and he came up behind me. I never saw his face. Then, he put a blindfold on me like yours. Mom, I thought I was going to die." Another tear made its way down her cheek. The cell phone was gone. After a check, D.K.'s phone was also missing.

She kissed her daughter again. "You're not going to die. We'll be just fine."

"Are you going to tell the police?"

"No, Danny, darling. No police. And you're not going to say anything either. Please promise me you won't say anything to anyone. Not ever. I think it's time for us to move. Everything is going to be just fine." She kissed her another ten times.

D.K. started to cry. Her body was shaking uncontrollably. Kemper grabbed her daughter's face and held it in her hands. "Look at me. Look at me! I've got money put away. We sell the house, package up everything. Money is no problem. What we have to do is leave and reorganize. You hear me?" D.K. settled down. Kemper wiped down her cheek until the tears were almost gone. "You are D.K. Kemper. We'll get through this. And yes, we will keep it quiet. You pack your bags right now and we leave here, is that clear?"

D.K. nodded. "I love you, Mom."

"I know. We'll eat on the road. We're taking off right now. I'll shut down everything from another city. All I want you to do is pack a suitcase. I'll arrange a cleanup of the house. We are leaving."

Kemper kissed her daughter two more times. As Kemper left the room, D.K. pulled out two suitcases. She gathered up her pink pillows. They would go in the car.

12

Wednesday morning, Booker got his Cuban coffee and started his usual routine of working the phone, looking for news stories. The producers left him alone this morning, putting him on what was referred to as breaking news. If anything happened, anywhere, he was first up. Halfway through reading the newspaper, Booker saw Grandhouse. He found out she was there at four a.m., finding out everything she could about the early-morning crew.

Booker got the keys to the van, gathered up his camera and gear, then headed to the exit.

"Leaving without me?" Grandhouse had a half-eaten donut in her hand.

"Aren't you ready to go to bed? You were up early."

"Naw, I'm ready to go. What are you working on?"

"I'm on breaking news. Nothing yet. I'm headed to somewhere near downtown and wait. No trips today to the other crime scene."

"Can I come? The desk knows where I'm going."

"No problem."

Once out of the parking lot, Booker headed near downtown, then parked. And waited.

Booker's cell phone rang. An UNKNOWN caller. He picked up.

"Hello . . ."

"Are you alone?" The voice was female. Low in tone. "Is this Booker Johnson and are you alone?"

"I can be. Just a second."

Booker got out of the van and walked a few yards. "Who is this and how did you get my number?"

"That's not important right now. What's important is I have information about the scattered body parts found in the park."

A bevy of questions peppered Booker's thinking. "Information you've shared with the police?" Booker tried, but he could not place the woman's voice.

"No police. Just you. I'm not going to give you my name."

"How do I know what you're going to tell me is accurate?"

"The body parts were scattered near the water, all chopped up into tiny pieces. No ID. No name."

"You could get that from the newspaper." Booker was looking for an angle to identify the caller.

"I know who the person is, or rather was. He was a friend of mine."

"Who was it?"

"Ah, not that fast. First, are you interested in what I'm telling you, 'cause if you are, we can continue this at another time."

"How do I call you?"

"You can't. I'll call you."

"So far you've told me nothing."

"How about this. You know Holiday Park? Under the third bench as you enter the park, I will leave an envelope. That envelope will contain much information. Not for the police. For you. I want my friend's killer caught."

"And what time will this envelope be there?"

"One hour. Don't be late or it will be gone."

"I'll be there."

Booker started driving north and headed for Holiday Park. He only let the newsroom know what direction he was headed, not the phone call. He wanted to check it out first before sharing anything with Stanley.

For him, the cities of South Florida were not so many streets and avenues. For Booker, areas and places represented past events of misery, theft, and death. He drove past the home where a woman, tired of her husband's assaults, killed him and kept the body in a freezer for two years. A power outage gave way to smell and the police were called. He drove near the spot of the barricaded subject, who finally gave up after thirty-seven hours. Booker came close to the intersection where four cars collided two years earlier. Four cars and not one driver was belted in. They all died, except a baby in one back seat survived. He looked down the block where a grandmother cried on Booker's shoulder after she felt responsible for her grandson hanging with the wrong people, until one night he died in a drive-by shooting. Booker consoled her as much as he could. All terrible memories, yet they were now stuck, embedded in Booker's thoughts as he crossed from one side of the county to the other, the result of a voice on the phone.

Close to thirty minutes passed in travel time to reach Holiday Park. Just like most days, in the morning hours, there were few, if any, people there. Booker drove into the park and stopped.

He looked all over, scanning for any cars. Anything.

"What are we doing? You on another mission, Booker?"

"This time you can't talk about this at the station. At least not yet. Is that clear?"

"Okay . . ."

Booker spotted the third bench as soon as he got there, opting instead to just watch the spot and see if there was any activity before he approached. Fifteen minutes passed.

Nothing.

He turned to Grandhouse. "Stay here."

Booker walked toward the third bench. He surveyed and checked out everyone near him. A man and a woman were walking a dog, moving away from him. Far off to the left, a person was getting into a car with a couple of bags. Booker was basically alone.

He reached the bench and looked around, again, for anyone following him. He sat down and reached under the bench.

A large envelope was taped to the slats.

Booker pulled it up and decided to open the envelope back in the van. As he left the bench, he kept looking for anyone who might be scoping him out. Finding no one, he made it back to the van and closed the door.

Grandhouse stared at him, wide-eyed. "What is this, some spy stuff?"

"Again, no word of this back at the station until I can figure out what's going on."

She could not take her eyes off the envelope. "Does this have something to do with the body?"

"Maybe." He opened the envelope. Inside, he found a photograph. He put the photo to the side and thought about what just happened. "I can't believe someone contacted me this way."

"What?" Grandhouse took her attention from the photograph.

"I'm sorry." Booker picked up the photograph.

In the picture, a man was walking out of a bar. The name on the outside of the place was NAME DROPPER. There was nothing else, no name, no information, nothing. Just a guy walking out of a bar. He studied the photo for at least a minute. "I know where this is, never been inside."

Grandhouse leaned back in the van seat. "This is all a bit weird, isn't it?"

"Very weird. All I can tell you is I don't know what this means. And nothing, I repeat nothing, goes on the air until I can confirm something. Right now, it's just a bunch of nothing." He held the photo up to the light. "Well, almost nothing."

He put the envelope away. Over the next four hours, Booker drove to two car accidents, a small fire in a house, and a lost child who was eventually found three doors away.

The van was returned, camera put away, and Grandhouse promised to keep things quiet. Booker walked out the door with just one thing on his mind. A trip to the Name Dropper.

13

Name Dropper was blocks from the Atlantic Ocean, close enough to smell the blend of sea brine and body lotion. The place looked out of place with the area. Paint colors here were Florida peach and beach sand. The Name Dropper had four handcrafted doors made of metal. If this were downtown Chicago or somewhere in the Northeast, the front of it would fit right in, yet here it just seemed out of place.

Once inside, Booker found a quiet surrounding, much too quiet for a bar at sundown. He sat at the bar, holding copies of the photograph inside an office folder.

"Whatta-ya-have." Her tattoos ran the length of both arms. The eyelashes were big and exaggerated, yet fit her face nicely. Booker spoke up rather than make her think he was staring at the tats. "Just sparkling water and lime."

"Wow, should I make that a double?" She had a half smile. "Just kidding. You could be recovering. I shouldn't joke." The drink came right away.

Booker took a sip. "I'm trying to figure something out, maybe look for someone. You're here in the afternoon?"

A long black curl of hair fell over her left eye. The right eye never stopped staring at Booker once he asked the question. "You try'n to hit on me? 'Cause I just met you what, ten seconds ago?"

"Let me show my cards. I'm Booker Johnson with Channel 27."

"I thought you looked familiar."

Booker kept going. "If you don't mind, I have a photograph I'd like to show you."

The watchful, quizzical look returned to her face. She pulled three glasses from a bin and started cleaning them. Booker took the photograph from the folder and placed it on the bar.

She took one look.

And dropped two of the glasses, just catching the third.

The smash of glass on the floor was loud enough for a side door to open and a man emerged. He was muscular, even with a shirt on. Seconds later, he was at the bar checking on her. His fingers squeezed into tight fists. "What's going on? Dani, you okay?"

She pointed to the photograph. "He's got a picture . . ." She couldn't finish.

He looked down at the photograph. "Where'd you get this?"

"Do you know him?" Booker decided to get in some important questions first before the exit door became his only option.

"He's our brother. He disappeared two years ago. Been looking for him ever since." The man behind the bar could not take his eyes off the photograph. "I remember this day. Said he was working something big. Couldn't talk about it. I just thought it all sounded shady. There was the promise of a lot of money. We tried to make him slow down. Check out this company, which he would not identify."

Without any proof or backup information, Booker was reluctant to make any connection to the body in the park. "No idea what he's been doing recently?"

"My name is Ronark. My sister Dani. You have to tell us, where did you get this photograph?"

"It was just passed on to me. I'm following up."

He was visibly upset by the answers from Booker. "Following up? On what? Why exactly are you here?"

"I think the best thing is for you both to contact the police. They can fill you in. Ask for a Detective Jensen. Tell her you spoke to me. I can't tell you any more than that, mainly because I don't know any more."

Upset grew into anger. He came from behind the bar, pointing a finger at Booker. "You come in here with this and you don't have a reason why?"

Booker eased toward the door. "Please check with her. She can help you."

Dani grabbed the photograph. "We're gonna keep this. We always thought he was in some kind of trouble, but he'd never talk about it, then he just disappeared."

"No problem. It's a copy. Again, contact the detective." The only thing on Booker's mind was not indicating their brother might be dead. That was a job for the police, not him. He had a family connection. That was enough for now. Booker turned to leave. Before he was all the way out the door, she had one last message for Booker.

"And so you know, his name is Greg. Greg Tally."

14

Thursday morning, Booker was assigned to get video of an old fly-over next to the I-95 Expressway. The state was putting in a new one. Once he got his VO, he was on breaker patrol again. He called and set up a meeting with Detective Jensen. No intern, just Booker. He met Jensen outside a coffee shop.

All the resentment toward him was still there. "This brother and sister called me, Book. It would have been nice to get a warning from you first, but I'll look into it." She kept checking her watch.

"Gotta go?"

"One, I shouldn't be here. I got tons of stuff to do." Her tone softened. "I'm beating you up too much. Where did you get this photograph?"

"Can't say yet. Wouldn't even consider this a source. I really don't know. Just that this is supposed to be your vic. I told the family to contact you. Obviously, I can't say anything on the air until I hear from you."

She moved in the direction of her car. "I have to be somewhere. I called PIO and they're aware. Any new information will come from them. The siblings volunteered to give DNA for a comparison, so we should know something soon. There is a big rush on this."

"Okay."

"And Book. Don't contact me anymore. Just talk to the PIO."

"Clear."

There was purpose in her step. Booker watched her walk away and his degree of respect for her only grew. He just wished he could take back the day of exposing one mistake she made.

Booker made it through his Thursday with little effort. He did a live hit for the four p.m. newscast, showing traffic all blocked up due to an overturned box truck. Doing live TV by just himself was tricky and, in some cases, dangerous. Once he set up his tripod and camera, got in the live signal back to the station, fed video, and dialed the phone number to hear the newscast in his ear, he was all set to stand, by himself, in front of the camera. In one recent case, a reporter who was working by herself was struck by a car while live on television. Booker waited for his cue in his earpiece and he started talking.

He got back to the station, put away his gear, and finally got back to an empty apartment. Still no sign of Demetrious. There was a fresh pile of clothes in front of the second bedroom door. It would be nice, Booker thought, if he could just leave a note on what he was doing. He could see some qualities in Demetrious that belonged to the mother they shared. Still, part of Demetrious was an unknown, like who was his father? They would have to have a real talk.

Booker leaned back in his chair, and just as he got ready to bite into a meatball sub, he got a phone call.

"Booker . . ."

"Hey, it's Claire. Turn on the TV. We just got word from the PIO. That lead you gave us has paid off. They identified the victim in the body parts. What's his name, Greg Tally. It's confirmed."

"That's great."

"The story is all yours tomorrow."

While Stanley was giving him the information, Booker also looked at an incoming text. "Hey Claire, I'd like to work tonight."

"Tonight?"

"Yes. The other stations all have his name, but they won't have this. The family just contacted me. They want to do a sit-down interview. Just me. Tonight. I'm coming back in."

15

Kamden Starling greeted Booker at the station. Starling was the nighttime assignment editor, the guy who sent crews on their journey into the night. Three crews in all. They were already out the door and gone when Booker walked into the newsroom. Tall and possessing a DJ's voice, Starling shook Booker's hand. "I gotcha covered, Book. Van's all gassed, your camera is on the desk over there, and the night team thanks you for the story."

"Thanks, Kam."

"Just call me the black giant. You need anything, just holla."

"Got it."

"What I don't have is a photographer. You're by yourself. My guys are on breakers all over the place."

"No problem. I got it."

Booker arrived at the location. Greg Tally's brother lived behind the Name Dropper. The place was a three-bedroom deal with one bedroom on the ground floor, two on the second level. Booker, by now, had figured out how to carry the camera, tripod, backup battery, and microphones by himself. The living room was small but adequate. "Come in, Mr. Johnson."

"Please, you can call me Booker, or Book, either one."

"Okay."

There was redness in his eyes, a weariness that came with dealing with a death in the family, loss and sorrow. His whole demeanor was different. "Can I get you anything, Book?"

"Naw. Just let me set up the gear, I'll go over a couple of things and we can get started."

"My sister, Daniella or Dani, will be here in a couple of minutes."

On the wall behind Ronark, Booker saw a long row of family photographs. He recognized Greg in four of them.

"Sorry I'm late." Dani Tally wore all black. Not quite goth, but close. Her eyeliner was black, probably more than the usual. The tats were covered by a long-sleeved blouse, black with a white collar.

Camera set up, Booker clipped lavalier microphones on both of them. "Okay, I'm recording. Both of you have talked with the police?"

Ronark settled into the chair. "Several times. We just want some answers. Who would want to do this to him? We don't understand it."

"He wouldn't hurt anyone." Dani's eyes bored into the lens. Booker kept a wide two-shot, with both of them in the frame. "It's been years since we last saw him. No contact, not even on birthdays or holidays. We miss him. And now he's been taken away. And this was brutal." There was anger in her words.

Booker pointed the camera at Ronark. "We didn't know Greg. Tell us about him, the things the public would want to know about Greg, about why he was loved by you both."

"When I think about it, I think he was always trying to leave. We lost our parents years ago, so we've been on our own. We own the place, but Greg took off. For college and elsewhere. He was a great person. Someone who would help you if you needed it."

Dani took a different approach. "I want answers." Her voice was firm. "I want to know what happened and why. We're not going to rest until we get that, the people responsible for his death. It was horrible. Just know that we're not going to rest. Ever!"

Booker asked, "Where did Greg go to school or college? Was he working?"

Ronark looked agitated. "Well, he tried working at the bar, but it didn't last. He went to some Broward College classes, studied government, and stopped. But he knew a lot of people. I mean, he had contacts. If we needed a new supplier, Greg found him." He stopped, as if he was saying things that might hurt his business.

"And he left on good terms with everyone? No enemies?"

Dani rolled up the sleeves on her blouse, revealing all her tats. "Far as I know, he was good with everybody. But remember, we haven't seen him for a long time."

A few questions more and Booker was done with the interview portion. He moved his tripod and photographed all of the pictures of Greg, along with several more Ronark provided. They also gave Booker permission to use two home videos of Greg. An hour passed and Booker had all the information and video he needed.

Dani shook Booker's hand again. "Thanks for leading us to Detective Jensen. She was great about everything."

Booker left four business cards on the table. "If you think of anything else, please contact me. This will be on the eleven p.m. newscast, so I've got some work to do."

Booker was out the door, headed back to the station. An hour of editing, a bathroom check to make sure he looked right, and Booker was in front of a stationary camera in the newsroom, ready for his live hit at 11:01 p.m. Booker was the lead story. He told South Florida about Greg Tally, used the video interviews on what the siblings told him, and asked the question of why he was killed.

16

Just after Midnight, Mikala Williams parked her car outside the address she found in the text message. The message also said to come alone. Three of the streetlights were out and she found herself bathed in darkness. More than once, she wanted to turn back and go home, but this, she reasoned, was too important to ignore.

She found the correct door and stopped to examine the place. There were three warehouse bays, all of them looked empty. She soft tapped on the door.

Nothing.

One more try. She knocked, waiting for an answer, and the metal door swung open to a large empty room. The floor was covered in dust. She worried about working up her allergies.

Fear was building up in her so much it was hard to take the next step. Still, she had to answer in person and follow the message of the text.

"Hello?" No answer. She walked into the room and felt small. The ceiling was high and the framework of the attic was uncovered, the metal ribbing going across. One bulb in the far corner supplied all the light for the space. It was time to leave.

"Mikala ..."

She stopped.

The booming voice kept her frozen in place. "You can't leave yet. We haven't finished our business."

She stood still. Everything inside her being told her to turn and run. Mikala looked for the source of the voice and found no one. She backed up three steps, moving closer to the door.

"Mikala, do you know why you're here?"

"Because of what happened?"

"Yes."

Her voice found a bit of strength. "But we finished all that. I did my part. That was what, three years ago?"

"Yes, you did your part, but what about now?"

She tried to place the exact spot of where the voice was coming from. Too difficult with all the black corners of the room.

"What I'm doing now has nothing to do with that."

"Oh, but it does."

She remembered the voice. The same low-pitch, even tone of someone who sounded like he plucked wings off a butterfly and laughed about it all. "I'm not doing anything."

The voice had an edge to it and stayed in the shadows. "You are the leading candidate for the CEO of the newest and biggest firm that just moved here."

"I did what you wanted back then. I'm not doing that again."

"Oh, but you are Mikala. You see, that position is not destined for you. That position will go to someone else."

"I've got money. How much do you want? More than anything, I want that job. You can't stop me."

"Now, now, Mikala. You will tell the company you are no longer interested in that position, that you are fine just where you are, and you're backing down. You got that?"

"Please don't do this again."

"We have to keep promises."

"I'm not going to quit. I have earned the position."

"Mikala, look to your right."

In the corner, a light came on, revealing a large tarp over something.

"Keep watching Mikala." The tarp was pulled away and a wrecked car was now visible. The front end of the auto was smashed and the driver's side door was crushed. "You did this, Mikala. Remember?"

"Why are you showing me this?"

"This is the car you hit back then. The driver died. We kept your part from the public. And we managed to steal the car, complete with the paint of your car all over it. Our little insurance. Back then, you accepted the position we had for you in exchange for keeping this quiet. We changed the narrative of what the police found, so you were in the clear."

He was right, Mikala thought. She had checked the newspapers, TV, everything. There was no mention anywhere of her taking off that night. Taking off and leaving a man to die. She never found any account of his death, but she saw the blood. The injuries were enough to convince her she was in the wrong. There was too much to protect. She got away with vehicular homicide and she didn't ask questions. Mikala had bargained with the merchants of death.

She ran a small office of sixteen employees, made the company line grow, and built the establishment into a multimillion-dollar business. Her work became the focus of several articles. She owned both a two-year-old silver Maserati and a new Jeep for weekend trips. The night of the incident, she also owned two speeding tickets, a suspended license, and a glove compartment with a few parking violations. And if checked, there would be the noticeable amount of alcohol in her system. If she could take back that night, she would. The CEO position was so close.

"Why are you doing this?"

"Because the position you want has been promised and paid for by someone else. Not you."

"And if I don't want to go along?"

"I want to be clear about something. If you fail to comply, we will make sure this vehicle is discovered by the police, with all of your fingerprints when you came over to check it. You were a hit-and run driver, remember? We cleared away the car and Mikala, the body." The light over the car was turned off.

The voice was low and evil. "Now run along, Mikala. Do as we say. We will be watching."

She turned to the door.

"And one last thing. And please take this to heart. If you don't do as we say, or say anything to anyone, after the police arrest and humiliate you . . ."

Her bottom lip trembled.

"We will kill you."

17

By the time Booker Johnson reached the assignment desk Friday morning, he'd heard the words, 'Nice work,' fourteen times. Claire Stanley was the fifteenth. "So, you stuck with your gut and pulled out a story. More than once on this one."

"Thanks." Booker looked around as if waiting for an assignment of a news conference or run to cover an accident. Stanley was patient, waiting until she caught his attention. "Word from the big boss. You don't have to be a one-man crew anymore. You can go back to the regular world of working with a photographer."

Booker thought for a moment. "I'm fine by myself. I'll keep what I got."

Her smile evaporated. "You sure? Whole lot easier working with someone. Make it easier for you to do live shots."

"I'll stay a one-person unit, if that's okay."

"Sure. If that's what you want, but it's just you."

Booker stepped away from the scanner noise. "Ya got anything for me?"

"We had our morning meeting. They want you to stay on the Tally murder. It's all yours."

"There's nothing set up. I can't promise anything for the noon newscast."

"That's okay. Keep doing what you've been doing. Keep digging. If you get anything, let us know. For the immediate future, you're on this one story."

Booker nodded a yes and went for his gear. He had a few things to follow. The Tally siblings gave him the last known address for their brother. He could start there, and later he wanted to make a quick stop at the courthouse. A Judge he respected might be stepping down.

After loading the camera into the news van, Booker headed for the Greg Tally location.

His phone rang. "Booker..."

"Hi, it's Lacie."

"Hello, intern. What's up?"

"Hope you don't mind, but I did some checking on Greg Tally online. His social media stuff."

"Whatcha got?"

"He was posting stuff on Facebook up until two years ago when he just stopped. Found a few pictures of him with people and got a few names. I can text you the information."

"Thanks. Good work. Anything else?"

"Yeah, as soon as I heard the name, I jumped on the computer and my phone. Good thing I did because someone wiped all his social media accounts. He was busy on IA, I'm sorry, Instagram. He was big on Twitter and, for a short time ,on Snapchat. There's a lot of stuff."

"Let's do this, are you at the station today?"

"Actually, a day off, but I can come in."

"I'll meet you later for lunch. I'll send you a text. We can talk then."

"Great."

"And Lacie, thanks."

"No problem."

Conversation over, Booker stopped in front of an apartment complex. Nothing fancy, just a three-story building with little landscaping, a tiny parking lot, and no pool. When he got out of the news van, Booker looked toward the second floor. Greg was supposed to have a rental there on the east side of the building. From what he could tell, the apartments all looked rented. Three knocks on the manager's door and a woman opened it about one inch. "If you're looking for a place, we're all booked right now." Her hair probably saw a comb four months ago. Booker took a step backward to hopefully make her feel at ease.

"Not looking to rent. I'm Booker Johnson with Channel 27. Did Greg Tally still live here?"

"Who?" She thought for a moment. "Oh, I remember him. He was on the news. The police already been here. And no, he didn't live here. Left a long time ago. Didn't even get his security deposit, but that's okay since he left without paying the rent."

"Any forwarding?"

"I wish I knew. He just left."

"Okay, thanks."

Booker backed away and walked back to the van. Anyone given the job of noticing things for a living always kept a keen watch on everything in and around. From the time he got out of the van and went to the apartment, he had the notion someone was watching. A gut feeling that kept him out of trouble.

He noticed someone watching him from across the street, then ducking behind a building. In the van, Booker quickly set up his camera to record through the front window. He then got out, locked the door of the van, and ran toward the area where he saw the man.

No one was there. He scanned the parking lots and the streets and saw no one there. All while he was searching, he had to keep a close eye on the van and the extremely valuable camera. Then, Booker turned around and saw a figure running to a car. Booker tried to catch up but the man got into the car and drove off, laying down burned streaks of rubber. Booker got back to his camera, turned it off, and transferred the video to the editing deck.

Booker got out his reporter pad. The man was about his height, probably 180 pounds. He jumped into a blue Honda with a Florida plate number. Booker froze the video and wrote down the number.

He called the assignment desk.

"Hello, Booker."

"I need a favor."

"Go . . ."

"Can you look up this plate?" He repeated the numbers twice.

"Ya want to stay on the line or call you back?"

"I'll wait."

Four minutes went by. "I got'm Book. I'll send you all the information."

"You get a name?"

"Sure. Whispis Dulan."

"You have time to work up a profile? Any criminal background, business ties, home, protective orders, I want the works."

"I'll put it on the list. Just kidding. You'll get it in about twenty minutes."

"Thanks."

There was one thing that bothered Booker. Rumors. He considered them nothing more than lies based on lies. This rumor, however, was about someone he knew and respected his work on the bench. Judge David Napston. Someone told someone and then someone left a message for Booker that there was a rumor Judge Napston might reconsider his run to stay on as judge.

Booker headed to the courthouse. One more stop before meeting Grandhouse for lunch. In fifteen minutes, Booker was going through the check-through lane at the courthouse. Everything in his pockets went into a basket. All bags were checked and by machine. Cleared, he made one stop first.

Bond court.

Every morning, court bailiffs posted a list showing the names of those arrested overnight and the previous day. The defendants would face the bond court judge and find out their fate on whether they could post bond. Every TV newsroom worth some salt would send someone over to check the list. Reading the list would take less than five minutes and could yield the name of a lead story. Booker checked, and this time, the list did not show any potential news stories. He headed for the courtroom of Judge David Napston.

This was a good time to check. Just after the noon break. The morning hustle of juries being escorted through the hallways was over. There were just a few moments of calm. Booker spotted Judge Napston's bailiff, Sandra McKerry. The first thing you saw was her red hair. She kept a mellow even temperament until someone got out of line in the courtroom. The voice then turned to controlled thunder and her muscular arms could snatch you up quick.

She had a smile for Booker and a confused look on her face. "We don't have any media-strong cases. You need something?"

Booker bored right in without the small talk. "Is the judge stepping down?"

"Now, Booker, you know I can't say anything, even if I knew."

"Can I see the judge?"

"Pretty bold today, aren't 'cha?"

"I just wanted to hear it from him."

"He ain't talk'n that much, I can tell ya that. Gotta go, we got a jury coming in."

"Take care, Sandra." Booker decided he would try another way, later in the day. Or sometime soon.

A thought kept bothering Booker. He never got another phone call from the mysterious woman who told him about Greg Tally. His cell phone let him know he was getting a phone call.

"Booker . . ."

The always-calm-under-pressure voice of Claire Stanley. "Book, we need you to back up three other crews. Federal Highway near the county line."

"Three crews? What's up?"

"We got three dead, maybe more. Another three going to the hospital. I'll text you the address. Go!"

18

When Booker pulled up to the scene, he spent almost three minutes looking for a parking spot. The place was a drug house. Booker angled his van next to another Channel 27 vehicle. When he got out, camera on his shoulder, he looked for another reporter to get directions on where he could best fit in.

Everything was chaotic.

Two people were on the ground, lifeless and appearing to be sleeping. Paramedics and one police officer were trying to wake them up, shaking, shouting at them, anything to make them move. The rescuers, police, and paramedics were wearing protective gear over their faces to protect them.

That's what fentanyl could do. Too much and the body wanted to drift into sleep and then death. Getting too close could also be deadly for people trying to revive the drug users. The two on the ground were in the in-between world of the here and the dead beyond. Off to Booker's right one woman was yards away. Her crying was so loud and piercing, Booker flinched each time she wailed. Finally, she was moved to the police car, where she could be questioned.

The area near the drug house was eerily quiet.

Booker only heard the sounds of police and fire crews moving about professionally and with purpose to save as many as possible.

Shouts of "get Narcan" were heard. Booker got video of the drug being sprayed into the noses of the two. More shouts to wake up. One started to move. The other needed a second spray of Narcan. Her left arm twitched, then she began to open her eyes. When she woke up, she started slapping the arms of paramedics. They moved her to a fire rescue truck. Booker was getting all of his video from a long distance, as this was a possible hazard to anyone too close.

Booker counted eight fire rescue trucks and more than two dozen police units. When one of the fire trucks got ready to leave, Booker fired up the camera and got video of the unit moving out, lights and sirens. The police had a pool of reporters locked down in one spot. A command post was set up some sixty yards from the house. The command post was not where Booker wanted to be since he would just duplicate a Channel 27 crew's angle already in place. He moved in and around the back of everyone until he got a full-on view of the house.

The single-story building had all the windows blocked with newspapers. There was moaning and crying peppering the air. Booker started videotaping a person on the ground being worked on by paramedics. She didn't look good. He tried to shoot the video in a way to hide her face. Police officers were going in and out of the house. He was recording it all. Booker overheard a PIO telling the large group of reporters there would be an update in twenty minutes. He called Stanley, gave her an update on what video he had so far and if he was needed to report.

The answer was no, just keep shooting video.

The Channel 27 crew consisted of Merilee Yang and photographer Sam Drewhill. According to Stanley, they would handle the news conference. Channel 27 was breaking into regular programming and providing live coverage. The plan was to stay on the air live until the PIO spoke then go back to regular programming.

Booker kept a watch on police movements. With his camera, he zoomed into the back of the police cars. He got video of three people who were being detained. He made it a point to keep track of them. Back at the station, those on the assignment desk were probably going through tax records to see who owned the place. Once they got a name, they would check for previous arrests or if the person was known in the community.

He got video of another fire rescue truck taking off with another victim. Then, video of a fresh fire truck just arriving to back up the others. By his count, Booker saw eight people being treated, three in custody and perhaps two others still in the house. The entire street was lined with police tape. Booker walked back to his van, got the equipment ready, and fed all of the video he had recorded. Once that was done, he got another spot to set up his camera. Beyond the tape, a crowd was growing. He could never understand why anyone would bring children to a crime location where death had occurred. Still, there they were. Young ones and teens, all gawking at what was unfolding. Booker moved, as best he could, to a spot overlooking the back of the house. He was the only reporter there.

Booker trained his attention on the back door. Sixteen minutes later, a man was brought out in handcuffs. He walked, head down, not resisting. A police car moved to the back and the man was put into the car. Booker had the only video.

Again, Booker went through the motions and sent the video back to the station. When he looked over at the group of photographers, the PIO was giving a statement. While they were busy with that, Booker looked for any witnesses.

He found one man looking disgusted. Booker aimed his camera at the ground. "You live near here?"

"Yeah, three doors down. I knew this was going to happen."

"Why do you say that?"

"All kinds of cars coming and going. I reported a few times, but the police can't be here all the time. And then today." He pushed his hands down into his pockets.

"Okay if I ask you a question or two?"

"Not on that camera." He tugged on his Miami Marlins hat.

"What if I aim the camera at the ground? Don't need your name."

"I guess that would be okay."

Booker aimed his camera at the sidewalk and eased a microphone toward the man. "You live near here. What's your take on what you're seeing?"

"I'm sorry to see people hurt. I really am. Don't understand why they use that crap. I've seen all kinds of cars coming and going. They need to do something and do it now."

Booker asked him two more questions. The first answer was the best. No others wanted to speak, so Booker moved toward the pack of reporters to find Yang, the reporter. Her long black hair went down her back. She had just signed off, turned around, and saw Booker.

"Thanks for helping us, Book. Heard you got all kinds of stuff."

"No problem. You need me anywhere else?"

"You seem to be doing just fine by yourself. It's starting to calm down. Thanks for your help."

"Again, no problem. I'll text you with a list of all the video I shot."

"Thanks."

Booker sidestepped another reporter. "What's the breakdown?"

Yang checked her notepad. "So far, four dead, six others in the hospital. This was some kind of party thing. They apparently got word out that drugs were in. Three being questioned and one arrest. Details coming later."

Her forehead scrunched down into tight rows. There was a look of concern on her face. She kept her voice down so only Booker could hear. "You should be the one out here with the lead story, not me."

"Thanks. I'm working my way back. They offered me a photographer but I turned it down."

"Like working by yourself?"

"So far. Look, I'll get a few more pieces of video, feed it in, and I'll be off."

"Take care, Book."

In this case, Booker thought, Yang was the best choice to handle the story. Yang had been a reporter for Channel 27 for the past nine years. She had wise eyes, sized up things quickly and, had a smooth on-air delivery. With her experience, Yang could have been in New York or L.A. She had the ability to deliver gritty, just awful news and yet her demeanor on air made a person feel like everything was going to be okay.

He smiled at Yang and peeled away from the group of reporters. There were a few more things to photograph. The crime techs were in the house and in the yard, bagging up evidence and taking photographs. Booker got video of them doing their work. He panned slowly, left to right. Detectives had covered up the license plates of every car on the property. In doing so, reporters were not able to get the tag numbers.

Booker zoomed in on an object and stopped.

He froze.

A feeling of panic ripped through him. He looked down and saw his right hand had a slight tremble. A ton of questions rammed through his thoughts, all based on what he found on the worn sidewalk leading to the front door of the house. In all of his years covering a multitude of events, Booker never felt this close to being pulled into a story. He stopped recording, looked at the object, and squinted at the sun to make sure of what he was seeing.

There, on the ground, Booker saw a bright red gym shoe.

19

Booker fought off panic and looked everywhere for Demetrious. Yes, the shoe might belong to someone else, yet Booker was convinced Demetrious was here or had been. Booker looked over the location four or five times. No sign of Demetrious. He stared into the house. From what he could see, everyone was out of the building and the crime techs were about to take over.

He called Demetrious.

Voice mail.

He sent him a text and an email. Booker checked all social media platforms for any sign of him. No Demetrious.

Booker got permission from the assignment desk to leave the scene and he drove back to the station. His explanation was he wanted to hand deliver and import the rest of his video. In reality, Booker went into an edit booth, closed the door, and started examining all the video from the overdoses. Fortunately, the crews got there from the beginning. Booker slowed down and froze the video to study the faces of all those being worked on.

He did not see Demetrious.

Booker also could not find the red gym shoe in the video. He researched his own video, scanning the wide shots of the house, looking for the shoe.

The shoe was right there, from the moment Booker arrived.

So, where was Demetrious?

He texted two reporters still at the scene to send him any names, if they were released by the police. The move was just a wild play since there was a slim chance police would release the names right away. Booker determined no one else was wearing those familiar red shoes.

Four p.m. Booker got permission to leave for the day. He hustled back to the apartment. Soon as he walked in, he saw it on the floor.

A single red gym shoe. Left foot. The one at the scene was for a right.

And no Demetrious.

He called Demetrious again, making it five times. No answer. More text messages. Still nothing. Booker got into his car and drove to the online coffee shop where Demetrious looked for job postings. He asked the manager if he had seen Demetrious. Yes, but that was very early in the morning. When asked if he knew where Demetrious might be now, there was a long pause. The manager was studying Booker as if he was trying to determine his level of trust.

"He's my brother and I have to find him. Now."

"He might be . . ." The manager paused. "I shouldn't be saying this. Could get both of us in big trouble."

Booker pleaded. "I've been in here before. I'm trying to help him. Now, if you know where he is, tell me."

"You might check out The Brick."

Booker wasn't sure what he was going to do once he reached the place. The Brick was a name given to a housing project with drug dealers who run the collection of four low-income buildings. The official name was Sunrise Manor, like it was some upper-crust country club. The Brick was a better name. Each building had a skeleton of standard South Florida concrete block. On the outside, some of the original planners got the screwy idea to use northern-style red paver bricks on the outside. Instead of stucco. The buildings looked hot, even in the coolness of a Florida winter. This was the summer.

Booker parked his car.

From a first-floor apartment, curious young eyes watched him. Booker felt like the eyes of a hundred people were boring into him. Then, above, he saw one, then two tiny things hovering above him.

Drones.

Gone were the days of kids riding on bicycles to check him out and alert others. They could just track Booker's movements with a hovering protection system. The floating dots in the air stayed seventy feet above Booker. He looked around for any sign of Demetrious and wondered if this was where he would hide away at times. In some of the windows, there was a tiny reflection coming back at him. More cameras, stationed in various windows. Booker imagined a full network of surveillance cameras watching the complex.

Three of the buildings looked perfectly livable. Outside the main door of each building, there were rows of flowers. Someone went to the trouble of making the space nice. The sidewalk looked like it was routinely swept. Inside, families with below modicum budgets were probably doing the best they could at the moment. Honest middle-class families, some with single parents, worked and lived here. Not so much for the second building called Number 2. The main doorway had no flowers. Booker recognized at least three hard cuts in the door from previous bullet shots. There was an apparent attempt to sweep the sidewalk, which was dotted with dried vomit and a few old blood stains. Any flowers here died a long time ago.

This was the right door.

Booker did not plan on going inside any of the buildings. Without a name or a destination, only trouble resided in those hallways. He did what he wanted to accomplish, just stand there. If Demetrious was here, he would surely know because word would get back to him.

A large man emerged from the second building, headed directly for Booker. There were two scars on his arm and he wore a knit cap.

"Don't know you. We ain't got nuthin' you want. You can get in that car while you still got it and git."

"I'm Booker Johnson. I'm look'n for someone."

He followed the man inside the apartment building to an open door. Booker hesitated. "Follow me," the man said. There was a hard edge to his voice. Booker went inside. A hallway led to an apartment. The apartment was almost empty. Clearly, no one lived here. The room had other purposes Booker didn't want to question at the moment.

The man turned to leave, leaving the door open. "Wait here." He left.

Less than a minute later, Demetrious walked into the room, now wearing black gym shoes. He looked upset. "What are you doing here?"

"Me? I was at that place with all the drug deaths. You were there, am I right?"

Demetrious showed no reaction. None. "Don't talk about that here. Let's go."

Booker followed him out the door, down the graffiti-filled hallway, and into the sun-bleached courtyard. There were no words spoken, not even when Demetrious got into the car and they were seven blocks away.

Booker almost pulled the steering wheel off the car. "What are you doing here? And what were you doing at that place this morning?"

"I can't talk about it."

"Demetrious, I thought you might be dead."

"Not me," he shouted. "I don't do that shit."

"Then what were you . . ." Booker took it down a level. "I'm just glad you're okay."

There was no conversation the rest of the way. Booker decided he would try again when the moment was right. When they walked into Booker's apartment, Demetrious picked up the red shoe and started to throw it at the wall, then stopped. He tossed the shoe into the garbage bin.

He turned to Booker. "It's hard to explain what I was doing there. But it was a favor I owed someone."

Before Booker had a chance to ask a question, Demetrious went into his room and closed the door. There were four slices of cold pizza in the fridge. Booker sat in front of the television but never turned it on. He just gnawed on the pizza and waited for Demetrious to come out of the room, but he never did. Booker called Stanley to see if he was needed back at the station and got a thank you for helping.

20

When he woke up the next morning, Booker walked to the kitchen to make a meal and saw the second bedroom door was open. Demetrious was gone. Booker had a slew of questions for him. Why was he at the drug house? What was he doing in the Brick? Booker showered, scrambled two eggs, and scraped them into a plate, next to a pile of cut-up cantaloupe.

For Booker, Saturday morning meant cleanup and some shopping. The weekend went quickly. Usually, he tried to stay away from the news on the weekend, then paid close attention Sunday night in case some story might be passed on to him come Monday morning. Booker knew a lot of attention would be centered on the overdose deaths. Fentanyl-laced marijuana leading to deaths would still be the top story unless another catastrophe took its place.

Booker spent the afternoon in the gym, walking on the treadmill and doing some light lifting. He did not see Demetrious the entire weekend.

On Monday morning, Booker decided he would wait to send another slew of text messages to Demetrious later in the day. When he reached the station, two reporters had been doing follow-up reports on the drug overdoses since the start of the 4:30 a.m. newscast. The 9 a.m. dayshift would pick up the story after a number of angles that would be discussed in the morning meeting. They kept Booker out of the mix for now. Breaker patrol would be his first assignment while he continued to work on the Tally murder.

Booker read the three most active news bloggers. All of them had a story about Tally with old information. One blogger also had a long piece on the overdose deaths. Booker read the articles and saw nothing new in any of them. He kept going.

There was a truck-car crash on the Sawgrass Expressway. Booker was assigned. Grandhouse was told to stay behind at the assignment desk and answer the phones. Booker was by himself again. He headed south on the interstate, passing Atlantic Boulevard. The accident was less than two miles away. Booker was absorbed in his thoughts. Any conclusion about Demetrious at the drug house did not sound good. And in the Tally case, what was he doing those two to three years when he went missing? What was his connection to the sultry female voice on the phone? How did she know about Tally? Why was he killed?

Booker was not ready. A box truck crashed into his driver's side, causing Booker to almost lose control of the van. The hard crunch against his driver's side door caused Booker's hands to momentarily leave the wheel. He had to act fast, or the van might veer off into the next lane. Booker regripped the wheel and held on tight. He tried to see who was driving the box truck but it was too late. The truck smashed into his van and again knocked his left hand off the steering wheel. He was driving with just his right hand. When he tried to straighten up the van, the truck would not let him, actually forcing him to drive straight toward a V-shape of sand-filled barrels. Booker was also concerned that the truck collisions might cause the airbag to deploy. A quick check showed there were no other cars behind him. The danger was straight ahead. If the barrels did not stop his van, he could go over the concrete barrier and drop ninety feet down to busy State Road 84. In this area, the Sawgrass Expressway was built high over the other road.

The driver of the truck knew what he was doing. This was all timed so that he could line up his truck and pile drive Booker's van through the barrels, and force or push him over the embankment, to his death.

Booker did all he could to stop the van. Both feet down on the brake pedal. The box truck moved off, kicked up in speed, and rammed him again and again. Booker did not dare look to his left. He just wanted to concentrate on what was in front of him.

The left mirror broke off and became road debris. Every time the truck crashed into him, Booker thought the impact might break his leg. The windshield was a mishmash of light and dark with the sun darting through shadows. For now, the windshield held. A degree of panic swept through Booker thinking he might hit a car to his right and cause them to have a problem as well. He was bouncing around so much, he couldn't get a clear view on any traffic next to him on that side.

He crashed into the barrels.

The news van was slightly turned when it hit and some of the force of the crash was blunted. The sound was enormous. Metal hitting solid objects. He had a face full of airbag.

When Booker looked up dazed, the barrels had stopped his forward progress. He did not go over the edge. The windshield was now a spiderweb of broken glass. Booker peered into a cloud of hot misty water from the radiator and reservoir. His hands were frozen on the wheel. Movement was almost impossible. There was ringing in his ears and his right arm was sore from hitting something. Booker couldn't open the driver's side door, so he crawled across the console. When he managed to crack open the passenger side door, Booker did a check of the equipment. The camera was still locked in a cabinet. A driver was asking him questions but he couldn't hear or understand all the words.

And Booker was angry.

Someone deliberately drove him off the road. Paramedics arrived and six times Booker refused the need to go to the hospital. He swore he was okay. Three Highway Patrol units were there. One did the investigation and the two others blocked off traffic and kept drivers away.

Then, Channel 27 showed up.

Booker was now part of a story.

Yang and her photographer were there. The intern Grandhouse got out of her personal car. "You alright?" There was deep concern in her voice.

"I'm fine. I'll be sore tomorrow, but I'm okay. Man, you guys got here fast."

Traffic on the Sawgrass was building up. In Florida, anything could slow down traffic. Everyone always had to stop and see what was going on. In ten minutes, the road would be clogged.

Yang's photographer shot some video, Yang got a short interview from Booker and she took off for her main assignment, the follow up on the overdoses. The police had released the names of those who died and Yang contacted two families who said they wanted to talk. Since she was already past the crash, her journey forward was not slowed down too much.

Booker knew his crash would be a small part in the news wheel. Something called the twenty-second VO. This would be a first for Grandhouse. The producers let her write up the story. After she was finished, two producers showed her how to improve the wording. The written VO was passed on to an executive producer who did the final version and inserted the copy into the 4:30 p.m. newscast to be read by the anchors.

Booker and the station kept the driving-Booker-off-the-road allegation to themselves. For now.

For Booker, soreness became his new best friend. Everything on his left side was sore. He had aches in his back and lower left leg. The pain rocketed up his side and settled in the back of his neck. None of which did he mention to anyone. Booker only wanted to stay on the story.

Even Demetrious contacted by text. When Booker checked his phone, the short message said:

HOW U DO-IN

Booker texted him back he was do-in great. When Yang arrived at the crash, she and her photographer had taken possession of the camera. It would be returned to the station later. The van itself was probably totaled. There was a lot of damage to the driver's side and the chassis looked like it was bent. Booker was still in a bit of shock. He replayed in his mind how the box truck moved into his lane, hitting him repeatedly, and then moved on.

A hit-and-run.

Booker was notified he had a visitor. Detective Jensen. She had her usual detective pad and her look was serious.

"You okay?"

"You're the twentieth person to ask me that." Booker thought for a moment. "Sorry. I'm feeling fine, just sore. I'll be walking like a zombie in the morning. Thanks for asking, though."

She pulled out her pad. "I volunteered for this. Usually, the traffic guys would be here, but I wrestled it from them. I need a statement from you. I want to be clear, the Highway Patrol still has the lead on the crash. I'm only here to see if this is related to, let's say, other things."

"No problem."

Booker gave her the rundown of everything that happened. All the details. Leaving nothing out. Booker stopped. "I don't want you to put this down yet 'cause I don't have any proof." He rubbed the small of his back.

"Someone tried to kill me."

Roanna Kounce, the traffic reporter, walked up to them, a worried look on her face. "I have something you need to see."

21

Kounce sat at a console with two computer screens. The setup she used to view traffic crashes and street traffic. Inside her office was Booker, Stanley the assignment editor, Detective Jensen, and behind her was the news director, Ken Diven. Kounce held her finger over the play button.

"I searched all the traffic cameras and I was able to find Booker driving on the Sawgrass Expressway." She hit play. They all saw the news van moving at a steady pace down the road along with dozens of cars. "Now watch," Kounce said. "On Booker's left, a box truck moves up, slow at first. See that?" She pointed to the computer monitor showing the truck moving up like a shark in the water.

The small group closed in around the monitor. Kounce said, "Then the truck does this." Booker and the others watched the driver turn his truck directly into Booker's lane, hitting the news van. Watching it all on video caused Booker's left side to hurt. Kounce continued her play-by-play, "He wasn't satisfied with just hitting Booker one time. He kept hitting him."

Then, the crash.

The news van turned just slightly to the right, then careened into the V-pattern of barrels. Booker's van kept going a bit and stopped. The van came to rest about twenty yards from going over the embankment and a nine-story drop to the ground below. There was a small yelp from someone in the back. It was Grandhouse.

Diven spoke first. "Is this road rage or something else?"

Booker turned away from the computer. "I think this has everything to do with the Tally murder."

Jensen was busy writing notes. "I need a copy of that tape. And I'll make sure FHP knows about it as well."

"You got it," Diven said. "Booker, if you want, we can hire a guard for your apartment."

"I appreciate it but I'll be okay."

Diven didn't seem convinced. "You sure?"

Booker rubbed his left leg until the soreness was gone. "I won't stay at my apartment tonight or tomorrow. I'll find a place."

Stanley didn't say anything, however, her jaw was chewing gum at a quick pace.

Diven started for the door, speaking to Jensen. "If you need anything else from us, let us know." He was gone. Kounce got on the phone to get the process going to make copies of the crash. Grandhouse moved back to the assignment desk along with Stanley. There was just Booker and Jensen.

"When you figure out where you're going to be, let me know. I can get a unit to swing by a couple of times." Jensen seemed like she wanted him to say yes to the idea.

"Thanks, but I'll be fine. I know you're busy. I'll text you if there's anything off." He stopped her from leaving. "There was just one thing about the truck crashing into me."

"Yes?"

"I know we didn't see anything on the video and you can check it for yourself but in that quick moment, that flash of a second when I looked over at the driver, I could have sworn he had something on his hands."

"Like what?" She was poised and ready to write something down.

Booker said, "I could swear the driver was wearing black gloves."

"Black gloves. You sure?" She made a note of his comment.

"Well, I think they were black gloves. It was all a blur. Just happened so quick."

"Thanks, Book."

Jensen closed up her notebook and made for the other side of the news-room and the exit. She turned back twice before leaving. Booker offered up a weak smile.

He was all set to sit down and go over everything on his mind about what happened. Booker was ready to plan out the next move, and follow up on one or two stories. Just one thing could stop him.

Human resources.

Anna Colon was waiting for Booker at his desk. He was ready for the speech. "Okay, Booker, how come you're not at the hospital being checked out?"

"Like I keep saying, I'm fine."

"Not by me, you're not. I know you're the aggressive type but as of this moment, you're not doing anything more for Channel 27. Worker's comp. You go get checked out and you can't come back here until you have a note signed by the doctor. Is that clear?"

"A doctor's note?"

"I said, is that clear?"

"Clear. Doctor's note. Signed. Got it."

"I'm going to stay right here until I see you leave the building and the parking lot and go to the ER or your doctor's office." She finally smiled.

Booker Johnson's day was over.

22

Demetrious Moreland entered building 2 in the complex and waited for instructions.

He was at the Brick.

While families lived in the other two buildings, the second building belonged to the gang. One by one, as families were scared out, the contracts were given to only gang members and their women. Building 2 was now the hub of everything going on at the Brick. Everything wrong. The place was run like a kingdom.

Two people approached him. One, he knew from way back. The other, not so much. The familiar face was big, almost six-five with a short beard and a left arm full of scratches that never quite healed. On his right cheek, there were two teardrops on his dark skin, which to Demetrious, the teardrops could mean anything from murders committed in prison or in the street. Demetrious didn't want to ask. The second one was a woman. Mixed race, her hair was in long braids. Her arms were muscular, and the few times Demetrious was in contact with her, she never ever smiled.

He never knew her name. The teardrop man went by one name.

Strap.

A .45 pearl handle was tucked snugly into his pants. Demetrious could also tell the bulge in the pants cuff of his left ankle was most likely a second, smaller go-to weapon.

"He's waiting for you," Strap said. He led the way through a long hallway of graffiti. Behind him was the woman. They made a turn into an apartment. There, a large hole was busted through, allowing two apartments to become one large living area.

They made their way to the other side of the room.

Strap held up his hand, meaning stop.

Demetrious stood, staring at the large human before him. He was amazing in the fact he had no markings on him, no tats, no battle scars. The man was wearing a clean short-sleeved white shirt, silk tie, and pressed pleated trousers.

All the times Demetrious ever stood in front of him, the well-dressed man never opened his mouth. Strap always did all the talking. He turned to Demetrious. "What happened?"

Demetrious spoke. "Like I said when I was here before, they were definitely selling product that had your brand on the package. But that wasn't your stuff anymore. This stuff was stepped on with fentanyl. I was about to buy some, like you asked me to do, but people in the party room started to fall down. They weren't moving. Started turning blue. Overdosing. I had to get out of there. I started running. Left a shoe."

The man with the expensive tie took it all in, staring at Demetrious.

Strap said, "So, you didn't bring anything back? We needed to see it for ourselves."

"From what I saw, this was your original product. High-grade weed, but they added stuff. I never got a chance to buy any. Too much went down."

Strap went over to the man with the tie and whispered in his ear, then turned back to Demetrious. "Can you identify the people selling?"

"Yes." He paused. Then, "I think you can send someone else in just to be sure, then you can—"

Strap was yelling. "You don't do anything! You don't decide anything. You just do what we tell you to do."

Demetrious tried to show he was not shaken. "I've done what you asked me. I don't want any part of this anymore. You can get someone else. I'm done."

The man with the tie just looked at Demetrious. Hard. There were still no words coming from him. A solid minute went by with no one saying anything. Finally, the man in the clean shirt motioned for Strap. More whispers. Strap walked up to Demetrious. "Just one last thing. We need you to point out the people."

"You know where the house is, you don't need me anymore."

"This one last task is on your tab. And you will be done."

Demetrious looked at the man in the tie as if pleading for this to be over. There was no response from him. Before he was allowed to leave, Demetrious made one last statement. "I know you must be nervous. People died after using a product they thought came from you. You're worried that the word on the street is your stuff killed people, when you had nothing to do with it. And you don't want more to die. You don't sell fentanyl. I know that, but the people out there, they don't know that. If the police track all this back to you, this is a very bad thing. Your other drug lines, the coke and meth, might suffer. I'll do this last thing and we'll be even. You got it! We'll be even. And I'll show them to you only if you promise you won't kill them. I don't want to be tied to that."

Strap smiled. "We can't promise anything."

23

After telling everyone he was going to a hotel room, Booker instead stayed at his apartment. Bravery or stupidity, he decided to rest up and do some digging at home. Dinner was a fast-food rush. He spread out sheets of paper on his desk and began a computer search on the name Whispis Dulan, the man Booker spotted outside the apartment where Tally once lived. He had all the information given to him from the assignment desk.

He also had a formal letter from his doctor, assuring everyone Booker was fit to return. He scanned the letter and emailed it to the HR department. A paper copy would also be given in the morning.

Booker winced from some pain on his left side. He found out there wasn't much information on Dulan. Those on the assignment desk discovered that Dulan was once a busy lobbyist, then he was a publicist for a short time. From all accounts, Dulan worked by himself as a public relations firm. Booker checked Florida's SunBiz.org website for more. Sunbiz was a great spot for information on businesses in Florida. Dulan's contact information of address matched the info he had in front of him. Beyond that, Dulan's existence was an empty canyon. He wasn't active on social media sites, and there didn't appear to be a business location. Nothing on Facebook or Instagram. Two phone numbers attached to his name were disconnected. The man was now apparently off the grid. A priority for

Booker was finding out more since he was convinced Dulan was tied to Greg Tally. And right now, any connection to Tally, Booker thought, was tied to the driver of the box truck that hit him. Clearly, there wasn't enough solid proof to say anything on television. For now, Channel 27 just said Booker was involved in a hit-and-run crash. Nothing more until there was proof of something.

In the morning, Booker planned to visit the locations of Dulan's home addresses. Somewhere, somehow, somebody knew him. Booker was able to find where he went to high school and looked up the phone number to the alumni association. The number was added to his to-do list. For now, Dulan was not part of any information shared with Channel 27. Not until he knew more about him and could make a solid connection.

11:10 p.m. Booker wasn't worried about Demetrious but there was no contact with him since the small text message. He started to text him, then changed his mind.

The station sent him all sixty-seven seconds of the crash video. Booker watched the video over and over. The windows to the box truck were heavily tinted, so no view of the driver. Watching the news van come so close to the edge of the embankment just made Booker want to keep working all night until he could come up with some names and some answers.

Booker stopped his research and pulled out some photographs of Misha Falone. He needed her now. She was always good at listening to his TV news exploits, hearing about the stories. Some gruesome. Then, she would offer her own take on what happened. The talks calmed Booker, kept him settled. All that was missing now for months. The walks with the dog were memory-building moments he now treasured. He could always dream about her. He went back to the research.

Just after one a.m., Booker turned out the lights. Still no Demetrious.

24

Before Booker had a chance to say anything, Claire Stanley again proposed a photographer would work with him. Once, this was an option. Today, Tuesday, there was an order. After the crash, management wanted someone with him. He was assigned to Kip Dominguez, a twelve-year news veteran. Booker sat down with Stanley and gave her a rundown of what he wanted to do, starting with tracking down this guy called Whispis Dulan.

Her face was a study in skepticism. "Shouldn't you be doing something on your crash?"

"I will. But I have to track this down." Booker thought about the word crash. A solid do-not-cross-this rule existed at the station that no one, no writer, reporter, or anchor would ever refer to a collision between cars as an accident. The more accurate description, until the police call it an accident, it was a crash. Plain and simple.

Channel 27 was still very much involved in the overdose deaths. Yang was able to track down parents and friends. Heart-grabbing interviews led the newscasts. Another reporter did a story on the effects of the drug on the body. A third reporter found the drug house itself was under investigation after a spate of code violations.

Booker checked his work email. Dozens of people contacted him to see if he was okay, including attorneys who work at the courthouse and three local police departments. He would answer them on his phone. For now, he had to get out the door.

Dominguez was on his second cup of coffee. He sat in the news van waiting for Booker. "Are we in the noon?"

Booker said, "No. No noon newscast for now. We're just exploring."

"Gotcha." Dominguez was set to drive off, then stopped. "So, where are we going?"

Booker gave him the address. Dominguez drove while Booker went over notes and answered emails. They had worked before on dozens of stories.

Whispis Dulan lived on a cul-de-sac. His home was a single-story affair with tan roofing tiles. Booker decided to have Dominguez near him, with a camera, and leave the camera on the ground. Let Dulan know Booker was more than willing to just talk first.

Booker knocked. No answer. The place was quiet. He leaned a bit and looked through a window. No movement. Booker knocked again. When the result was the same, Booker left a Channel 27 business card on the door with his number.

Then, Booker started knocking on neighbors' doors.

People must have been at work. No answer for three homes. Before he reached the fourth location, a woman came out into the street. She looked retired. "He ain't there. At least I don't think so."

"I'm Booker Johnson. Channel 27. When was the last time you saw him?"

"It's been months. At first I think he used to stop by late at night and pick up his mail. Then even the mail stopped. The place has been a ghost. The grass got too long and the homeowners association was probably gonna get on him. Someone cut the grass and baby, other than that. Nothing."

"Thanks." Booker handed her a business card. "If you want, if you think of anything or he comes back, let me know."

"Okay." She turned to go, then stopped, and snapped her finger. "Mystic voyage runner."

"What's that?"

"It's a long shot. I saw it once parked in his driveway, but he moved it."

"His what?"

"His house trailer. You know, a small mobile home."

There were just two trailer parks in the nearby area. When Booker checked the first lot, it was full and no one new moved in for at least the past twenty years. The second lot had a new section of spaces rented by the week or month. Booker took a chance and they drove to Sunlot Vista.

Dominguez drove around three times and did not see the dusty car Dulan was driving the day Booker spotted him. An enormous banyan tree gave shade to nearly an acre. Parked just behind the tree, Booker found his missing car.

The blue and green trailer was there, just as the neighbor described.

Dominguez parked the van next to a row of benches. "How do you want to play this?"

"I'll approach him. No camera."

"You sure?"

"Either he talks or he doesn't, but I'm not going to force anything."

"I'll be right here."

Booker got out and walked the forty yards to the door of the trailer. He knocked. There was a muted sound like someone moving or shifting weight inside the mobile home. Booker knocked again, then stepped back a few feet so Dulan could see him.

"Whispis, this is Booker Johnson, Channel 27. I just want to talk. There's no camera on you."

The door popped open.

Whispis Dulan had the smallest set of eyes Booker had ever seen. He was wearing too many clothes for South Florida and he looked like he was about to run away at any second. He spoke in low volume. "Inside."

Booker ducked his head and entered the mobile home. The space was clean. Not even a piece of dirt anywhere. "Were you a friend of Greg Tally?"

Dulan blinked his small eyes a few times. "I'm not saying anything on camera. And when you leave here, I'm going." He looked out the tiny windows, checking the parking lot. Dulan turned back to Booker and looked him straight on. Hard. The small eyes looked larger and Dulan looked like he might take a bullet at any second. "Were you followed?"

"No, I don't think so. Who is after you?"

Dulan swallowed. "You have no earthly idea what you have stepped on. You need to turn around and forget you ever saw me."

"What did I step on?"

"Death."

25

Booker stayed put and did not move. "I'm not afraid. I'm here to get at the truth."

"You might be a fool. Ya know, I saw that crash on TV. They were coming after you." He looked out the window again. "And they're not done with you."

"Just who is 'they'?"

Dulan sat on a couch. He let out a sigh and for just a moment, his shoulders sagged. "There were many times I wanted to contact somebody in the media." He rubbed his chin, eyes at the ceiling of the mobile, then back to Booker. "The thing is a few of us broke away and we were running."

"Running away from what?" Booker was going to gently press until he got an answer.

"We were part of something. Something bad. And a few of us broke away. I knew it was time to come clean."

"Is it okay if I interview you?"

Dulan sat, deep in thought. "I really want to but I don't know. It might be too early."

"I can put you in silhouette. Keep your face in the dark. Won't use your name. If we need to, we can change your voice."

"Sounds good. I just need to think about it."

"Can you give me some hint on what you wanted to come clean about? What was the group doing?"

"Not yet. Here's what I want to do. There are two others. We want to come clean but we don't think it's safe yet. I will get in touch with you very soon. I promise I'll do something on camera."

"As soon as I leave here, you're going to leave, correct?"

"Yes, and I don't want you to follow me or the deal is off, I'll never speak to you."

"Here, take some of my business cards. My cell number is on the back. Call me anytime, 24-7. I'll be ready for when you want to talk. Until then, anything on what the group was doing?"

"Okay, Booker. I just feel guilty 'cause we changed lives where we should have left things alone."

"I saw you in a photograph. Looked like you were working."

"I'll tell you this much. When I saw you at the apartment, we had a place. That was our safe location. We could hide stuff there. I still have a key and I think the apartment is still there for us to use. I just have to be careful."

"And Greg Tally?"

"You have to go. Please go. I promise to get in touch with you."

"Do you have a number you can give me?"

"I'll give you an email but no number."

He told Booker an email and it was jotted down in a reporter pad.

Dulan ushered him to the door. "Now go. I have to move."

Booker walked out into the Florida sunshine. The news van was in the same place. Booker started walking. He reached the van and instructed Dominguez to stay put, do not follow. Seconds later, Dulan got into his dusty car and threw a small bag into the back seat. Then drove off. When he got to Booker's news van, Dulan stopped the car and let the window down.

Booker opened the door.

"Just one thing," Dulan said. "We want to say something. I promise. Just let me talk to them." He drove off in a peal of spinning tires spitting rocks.

26

Moments after Dulan drove out of the park, Booker got a call. "Hey Book, ya got anything?"

"Let me guess, the producers want something or they want to move me to another story."

"Exactly."

"I'm headed back to the station. See you in a few."

Seventeen minutes later, they pulled into the parking lot. Booker went to his desk and Dominguez went into an edit booth. Stanley looked at him like she wanted to send him out the door to cover some spot news or an announcement. She approached him. "So, we talked it over. You have a bit more time. I'm guessing there's nothing we can put on television right now."

"Correct. Everything is in the works."

She smiled. "I'm gonna trust you, Book." Stanley left.

Booker rolled over in his mind the entire conversation with Whispis Dulan. To say he was hiding something was an understatement. He was joined by Grandhouse. "What's up, Booker? You still sore from the crash?"

"I'm fine. Listen, can you make sure I've got all the video or photographs from your social media search of Dulan and anyone else?"

"No problem. You should have them."

For the next half hour Booker and Grandhouse printed out the very limited amount of photographs of Greg Tally and Whispis Dulan from anytime they were on the Internet. The photos were spread out on Booker's desk. He knew that at any moment, if there was a fire or a shooting somewhere, he would be called on to go check.

"What are you looking for?" Grandhouse was sipping some coffee and staring at the array of photographs.

"Not sure what I'm looking for. I just want to examine all of these." There were a few photos of Dulan. One picture caught Booker's attention. Dulan was standing in the background, surrounded by a group of people, and they were all staring at a woman in the center.

"Who is that?" Grandhouse put her finger on the woman's face.

"In the comments, there is a name."

Booker stopped and pulled out his cell phone. He sent a text message to Demetrious, asking him if he was okay. Two earlier texts went unanswered. If he did not respond, Booker would have to go look for him. He put the phone down.

Booker again made a phone call to check on the apartment complex where Dulan claimed there was a safe house. The woman Booker met in the manager's office told him the place was newly rented. No more Tally, no Dulan. Booker kept thinking, a safe house for what? Clearly there was a more direct connection to Tally but it wasn't clear yet. Everything was quiet. The investigation into Tally's death was publicly cold. He knew Jensen was obviously moving on every lead she could find.

In his checks, Booker also took a few minutes to search into the dealings going on at the Brick. He pulled up articles written in the past few years, all of them negative. There were arrests but no convictions. Witnesses changed their statements. Things happened and no one wanted to come forward to testify. There were police searches with no result. The occupants were on the police's radar, yet there wasn't much to show for their efforts. Booker didn't like knowing his brother was someone involved with the place, no matter how small.

Before him, on his desk, he added another five sheets of printed information and a couple more photographs from the Internet. What he found made him curious. There was a woman he and Grandhouse found in their searches who had an interesting past.

Dominguez and Grandhouse both stood by Booker's desk. The photographer rubbed his stomach. "Is it lunchtime?"

Grandhouse stared at Booker as if she knew lunch would have to wait. He pointed at the photograph of the woman and this time, he pressed his own finger on her face.

"Whispis Dulan said something to me that I can't forget. He said, 'We changed lives where we should have left them alone.'"

"Hmmm and what did he mean?" Grandhouse asked.

Booker gathered up his phone and notepad and again pointed to the photograph. "Maybe the one person who can answer that is her. We need to catch up to Mikala Williams."

27

"You promise you won't kill them." Demetrious Moreland leaned back in the rear seat of the SUV and wondered if he should just run. The driver and front passenger remained silent.

Across the street and down three houses, a trio of people stood outside. Two men and a woman. The men, one black, one white, and all of them looked addiction lean. They appeared nervous. The woman caught your eye and held your attention.

She had meth face.

Her forehead had two sores. There were a few more on her cheeks that looked like scabs. She kept turning around, eyes darting left to right, like she was suffering from paranoia. Then, she would put her hands in her pockets and at times reach up to scratch a sore. All of her body movements told a story of not being able to stand still.

Strap, in the driver's seat, kept his eyes on the three targets. "Is that them? The folks who fucked up our shit?"

Demetrious started to nod and realized that he had to speak up. "Yeah, that's them."

The woman in the passenger seat tensed up and Demetrious could see her shoulder and back muscles tighten into thick lines like tie-rods under the skin. He found out she had a name. Abrafo, meaning warrior. For just a moment, she pointed to the three in the street. "You mean those folks right there just let people die in the street? Did nothing?"

Demetrious had a sliver of anger in his voice. "They ran off as soon as they saw people start to drop."

"I'd like to drop them." Strap adjusted a bit in his seat.

"I pointed them out. Can we go now?" Demetrious turned from angry to anxious.

Strap pulled up a camera and started taking pictures. "Not yet. We sell other products, coke 'n stuff, but this is the one last thing we did not want to stop selling. The weed. I mean it's legal in a lot of places. But street weed is still king. Now, these animals go and mess that up. With our stuff!"

They sat in the car and watched the whole operation. A car would pull up. Meth face stepped to the door. A few words were spoken, only Demetrious was a bit too far to hear. She signaled with a finger or two fingers, probably indicating which drug was being purchased. The purchaser pulled into the driveway. One of the two other males handed something over. The car backed out and left. Deal done.

"You got one last thing to do." Strap put away the camera. "Ya gotta buy some stuff."

"Why me?" Demetrious had his arms waving, punctuating each word.

"Cause you never bought anything the last time you were here. The only thing we got is your word that you saw something. That ain't good 'nuff."

Abrafo cracked her knuckles. "We need proof. Then you're free. Your debt is paid."

Demetrious put his hand on the door handle. "I'll go with just one promise. You don't kill anybody. Otherwise, I stay in the car."

"Like I said," Strap turned and looked into the eyes of Demetrious. "I can't promise anything. Now go!"

Demetrious got out of the car. The trio was working out of a new location. The house where the deaths occurred was boarded up. He walked down the street, not looking at any faces, not making eye contact with anyone. He just wanted to score and go. Demetrious expected these people to be a bit skittish since the police would love to locate them and make a connection to the overdose deaths. And Demetrious was walking, not in a car.

Meth face took a considerable amount of time before she realized Demetrious was close to her. She jumped a bit, then settled down.

In the SUV, Strap watched and took pictures. The photo business was not discussed. He didn't know, maybe the pics could be used in some way in the future if Demetrious got cold feet. Strap hated to act like a snitch but business was business. He couldn't hear what was discussed between the woman and Demetrious. He could see that once upon a time she had a beautiful face, possible model quality. Not anymore. Methamphetamine had a way of boring into the body and taking over, replacing gorgeous with ugly. In the camera lens, when she spoke, Strap saw tooth decay, cracked lips, and two broken teeth. The rims of her fingernails were caked in dirt.

She held down two fingers.

One of the other men went to a bag stashed behind a bush. The face motioned for Demetrious to go to him. All three stared at him like he might be carrying a weapon. Getting ripped off was always a high probability.

Demetrious exchanged his money for the package. Strap snapped away. Less than thirty seconds later, Demetrious was back in the car. He handed the stuff off to Strap. He immediately examined the purchase.

"Yeah, this is our marking on the wrapper. And we'll get it tested. You did good, sir. Thank you very much."

"Then let's go." Demetrious was the only one wearing a seat belt.

Strap eased back, then pulled out, made a U-turn, and drove slow down the street. He seemed pleased with himself for getting the drugs.

Demetrious made an observation. "You got this stuff. And you can show it to him. But you're gonna have a problem explaining one thing."

"Explaining to the boss? What's that?" Strap asked.

"Somebody is supplying them with our wrappers and maybe our pot. If there's fentanyl, that could be from your supply as well. From what I can see this has been going on for a while. A solid supply line. They don't look like the geniuses who could pull this off alone. And that stuff just doesn't come out of thin air." Demetrious looked back at the three drug dealers, then back at the two in the front seat. "They had help. A lot of help. From someone inside. You've got a mole."

28

Booker Johnson stared at the two-story Caanrip Industries building. They had remained outside the place for almost twenty minutes. Dominguez was sitting in the driver's seat, resting with the camera on his lap.

Booker looked at his watch. "I called and they told me she was out to lunch and would return soon. She should be back any minute." He had the photograph to help spot her. Another fifteen minutes passed. A woman parked a green sedan and got out.

It was Mikala Williams.

Dominguez was out of the van before Booker could even turn the door handle. Together, they walked a quick pace to catch up to her. Booker was prepared to ask her about Whispis Dulan. That's all. It was just an inquiry, nothing more.

In his years of reporting, Booker Johnson was completely surprised on a story four times. Two times during a live broadcast, with Booker holding a microphone, a person came up to him asking a question. In both cases, Booker merely moved to his right a few times and kept talking. The person finally got the message and backed off. Another time a car crashed just over his shoulder and part of the incident ended up live on television. A fourth time, Booker was stranded out of the country on vacation and a major story broke. He called in and was immediately assigned to work a worldwide news story. During his extended stay, money resources were running low. He finally finished the story and got out, but the experience remained with him to this day.

This would be another surprise.

"Excuse me, I'm Booker Johnson with Channel 27 News. I just need a moment to ask you . . ."

"I knew you'd finally catch up with me."

"Are you Mikala Williams?"

"My name is Mikala R. Williams and I don't care if my life might be in danger. I'm taking a stand. I've been holding this in my heart for too long and I'm ready to let it out."

"I'm sorry, I'm not clear what you're talking about. I just want to ask you about your possible connection to . . ."

"I know. The car crash. The death. I don't care about any threats anymore. I want to come clean."

Booker looked back at Dominguez. Yes, his camera was up and recording. "The crash?" Booker tried to rely on what he found in her background check.

Williams took a deep breath. "I didn't mean to kill him. It was raining that night. When I'm finished with you, I'll speak to the police."

"Before you go on, I want to let you know we are recording this . . ."

"I don't care. The truth has to be free. I know what I did and it's time to talk."

"Danger? From who?"

There was a pause. She was sizing up the situation. Booker could tell she was weighing her next few words. "Mr. Johnson, there was a time I would have run from you and that camera. I'm done running. My will is as strong as my coffee in the morning. I hit that car that night and someone was injured."

When she talked, her right cheek formed a dimple. Both her fists clenched as her words flowed. Booker thought about what she was saying and she scored low on his BS meter. From what he could tell, his gut told him Mikala Williams was speaking the truth. There was a pure honesty coming from her, a sincerity he knew would come through on television.

Booker took a chance. "I went over your files. You've had a DUI arrest in the past. And a suspended license violation."

"That was me before. I've changed. And with that change, I very much believe in step number eight. Time for me to make amends."

Booker inched closer to her. "You graduated with honors, after getting into college at the age of sixteen. I read that your ideas changed the way your company handled the flow of information and that moved you up the ranks till you made CEO. And now you just recently stepped away from a change in position. Another CEO position?"

"You've been doing a lot of reading. Yes, I changed my mind and decided to stay where I am, that's correct."

"Why?"

"I hit a car just over two years ago. I was drinking that night. A lot. And with the rain, the car just came out of nowhere. I hit the car. There was a person inside. I looked in, saw that I could not help him and I left."

"No witnesses?"

"That's the strange thing. My cell phone rang just when I got out of the car. A voice on the phone kept telling me to leave, that someone would clear it up, clean it up, something like that. I was so messed up, I don't know exactly."

"And that happened?"

"I just had that recent drunk driving arrest. I cleared that up. But I knew after this injury, I'd be going to jail. And I wanted it all to go away. I followed the directions from that phone call." She stamped her right foot on the pavement. "But that was the old me. I'm facing whatever comes my way. After that night, I got sober. Clean ever since. And it's time for me to clear up what I did. My company, I think, will stand beside me. In fact, I know they will."

"Did you find out who was on the phone?"

"No idea. Just a voice giving me instructions. It was all very strange, but in that moment, I wanted to be free."

"And the person in the car, you got a good look at his face?"

"Yes. Till the earth stops moving, I'll always remember that night. It's frozen in my memory forever. Every indication was he was dead. That I killed him. I have nightmares because I didn't do anything, that I left him there to die. I have to talk to the police. That voice on the phone kept telling me to leave. That I was at fault, that he knew everything."

"But you remember the face of the person in the car?"

"Oh yes! Like he was right here in front of me. I see that face in my mind every night. I'm haunted by it. So much blood. All I have wished for is to replay that night. Don't have any drinks, don't get in a car. Just one night to do everything all over again."

Booker again played a hunch. He took out a photograph from his pocket, unfolded it, and showed it to Williams.

She shuddered, then put her hand over her mouth. When she lowered her hand, a small tear formed in her right eye. A tear that was quickly wiped away. "No crying today. Where did you get that picture?"

"Why?"

"That's him. That's the man I killed. I need to speak to the police and his family. I was drunk and killed him."

"Mikala, you say this happened two years ago?"

"Yes."

"The man in that photograph, his name was Greg Tally. And until a few days ago, he was very much alive."

29

The interview lasted almost ten minutes. Dominguez would cut it down timewise after Booker wrote the story. The words and images would probably last ninety seconds on TV. In television talk, it's what's called a package.

Booker had to explain what happened to Claire Stanley three times before it all sunk in. Then, he had to speak with the executive producer, the person responsible for everything seen and heard on a newscast.

The EP, Kevin Foster, was grumpy at times, but always fair. "So, your package will run a buck-ninety, right? Nothing over. We've got a packed six."

"No problem." Booker was talking and looking at video in the tiny edit suite in the van. "Yeah, and I need a favor. Can you get Claire to check out this alleged accident?" He gave Foster the exact dates and location.

"I can take care of it," Foster said.

"Before I air anything, I need to get some response from Greg's family. And I don't want them to see this until I speak with them first."

"That's fair. Is that your next stop?"

"Yes. We're packing up now and heading to the bar."

Mikala explained she did not see any news coverage of Tally's death.

She never saw his picture flashed on TV because television was not part of her routine.

The decision was made to leave Booker out of the five p.m. newscast and save him for the top of the six. Lead story. That would give Booker time to speak with Tally's family and possibly get back to Williams if there was a follow-up.

Traffic was unusually easygoing and Booker got to the Name Dropper bar within twenty minutes. More than anything, Booker wanted to tell them in person, not on the phone, about their brother. And he definitely didn't want them to hear something on the news. He wanted to tell them firsthand.

After getting the word that Greg might be involved in something shady, it was Ronark who spoke first. "He kept talking about some deal and that he might come into money. We didn't question it. And then he disappeared on us."

Dani sipped on a glass of water. "If he was into something bad, someone made him do it, that's what I believe."

Booker kept his pen poised, ready to write. "I'm giving you the chance to say something, if you want."

Ronark kept rubbing at an imaginary spot on the bar. "We didn't know anything about what he did. This is all new to us."

"We just find him dead after years of searching for him and now he's supposed to be this bad guy?" Dani took a glass and threw it against the wall. Shards of glass shattered on the floor like sprinkled diamonds. "Someone put him up to this!"

A full minute went by and no one uttered a word. Booker let it all vent. He left Dominguez in the van with instructions to come in only if Booker gave the signal to get the gear.

Dani wiped some water on her pants. She looked angry enough to boil the water off her body. "I know my brother. He just would not do anything like this. You say he pretended to be a victim in a crash? If he needed money, he knew he could come to us."

Ronark backed her up. "He worked here at the bar, made a lot of money on tips. We were all shocked when he was gone. It just didn't make sense. But she was sure it was Greg?"

"Yes."

They both declined to speak on camera. That was enough for Booker. He got a fresh twenty seconds of video of the Name Dropper bar and headed back to the corporate headquarters of Caanrip Industries. While Dominguez set up for a live picture, Booker got in touch with Mikala Williams. She came downstairs and met Booker.

"I've been on the phone with my attorney." Her look was stern. "We're headed to the police station in the morning."

Booker was busy writing notes. "I do have something to tell you."

She looked anxious. "Okay."

"We did some checking. Apparently, the car you ran into that night was stolen."

"Stolen?"

"If okay, I'd like to get your reaction to what I'm about to tell you."

"Alright."

Dominguez got his camera, checked the lens adjustment, and signaled he was recording. Booker extended a microphone. "What we've found out is police think you were the victim of a fraud. A fake accident."

"He was playing dead?"

"They had you believing you injured or killed someone, when in fact, it was all a ploy. And they used this fake to do what?"

There was anger in her eyes. "I removed my name from a position I wanted. That was the price I had to pay."

Booker said, "The man you identified in the car was found murdered."

"What?" Her eyes moved from side to side, as if not believing what she was hearing. "They got me, got me bad. But that night, I was so full of drinks I would have believed just about anything."

"This voice, you remember anything else about it?"

"No. Just that recently, I got a message to meet someone at a warehouse not too far from here. When I got there, they again demanded that I again refuse a new position, that it was promised to someone else."

"Recently?" Booker asked.

"Yes. And they showed me a car, all smashed up. It brought back all those terrible memories of what happened."

"The car you hit that night was later recovered by the police, burned in a field. The car you saw recently had to be another car. The police want to speak to you, but I'm told they have absolutely no record of a crash that night. No injuries and no deaths. You are not facing any charges."

"You're sure?" The tear started to form again in her eye. "You know I kept thinking about that night that somebody put something in my drink. Not a roofie, I heard of those. But something else to push the drinks I had. Make me even more tipsy. But you say I won't face any charges?"

"I'm sure. The police will be contacting you. You were the victim of fraud."

30

Booker Johnson stood in front of the office building. He was ten feet from Dominguez. Two extremely bright lights were pointed directly at Booker. The lights were mounted on tripods. Behind him, Dominguez had another set of lights aimed at the building. In his right ear, Booker had a molded earpiece tucked firmly into place. The earpiece was connected by wire going down his back to a device about the size of a deck of cards. The small device was able to pull in the audio sound of the newscast and, just as important, the voice of the producer.

"I can hear you," Booker said.

In his ear, Booker heard, "Your package runs one minute forty-five seconds. The outcue is 'I'll never do that again.' We come to you live in two minutes."

Booker gave a thumbs-up to the camera. Back in the Channel 27 control room, the producer was watching Booker on a monitor. In fact, there was a panel of several monitors on a wall.

After a commercial break, Booker was given the fifteen-second warning. He heard the anchors speaking the lead-in and an introduction to Booker, called a toss.

When Booker heard his cue, he started talking. He brought the audience up to speed on the Tally investigation, then said there was a major break in the case. Mikala Williams. He tossed to his edited video package and waited for it to run. When the package was over and he heard the words "I'll never do that again," Booker spoke to the camera.

"Williams will now speak to the police. She wants to clear this up, but from what Channel 27 is being told, she is not facing any charges. But they do want to know more about the incident that happened two years ago. Reporting live, Booker Johnson, Channel 27 news."

Booker stood still until he heard the words, 'You're clear' in his ear. Dominguez shut down the camera and started to pack up. "Nice job, Book."

"Thanks."

Booker was especially careful about what he said about Greg Tally. He let Williams identify Tally but he did not accuse Tally directly of carrying out the fake crash. He would leave that up to the police. He got word from the PIO that Brielle Jensen would be watching.

Throughout his news story, Booker was fixated on a few things. One, he wanted to question the person who got the CEO position two years ago in place of Williams. Booker also wanted to know about the male voice on the phone who talked to her.

Williams approached him. "We changed up. We're meeting with the police tonight. Please don't say this on TV but they seem very concerned after I told them I was threatened when I went to the warehouse. I might get some type of police protection."

"Be careful."

"Thanks, Booker. And thanks for letting me clear my conscience."

BOOKER AND DOMINGUEZ packed up and traveled two miles to the location of the warehouse Williams mentioned. It was almost seven p.m. Yang was already there with a photographer.

So were the police.

A warehouse door was open and Jensen could be seen walking around the place. From where he was standing, Booker thought the inside was empty. Still, a forensics crew was there looking for evidence.

"Place looks empty." Yang stood off to the side. "They've been in there thirty minutes and so far, they've come out with nothing. I think they're going to wrap up soon."

"Thanks. Take care."

Booker and Dominguez returned the van and put away the camera equipment. Booker left a few details with the folks on the night assignment desk. He headed home.

HE COULDN'T MISS IT. On his way to the apartment, Booker drove past the drug house. There were lit candles everywhere. Hundreds of people stood in silence to honor the memory of the people who overdosed. Flickering flames and quiet stares. They all faced the front yard, where most of them fell. The home was still boarded up. A red crime tape covered the door-knob. A police officer sat in his cruiser, probably assigned to watch the place and make sure no one disturbed a crime scene.

Booker got out of his car and checked the faces. Some of them held up photographs of the victims. Camera crews were on the other side of the gathering, getting video. The photos showed smiling faces, taken during happier times, when there were no drugs, no stealing money to buy grass laced with fentanyl. A girl of about eight years old placed a bouquet of flowers on the ground. The bouquet was just one of dozens of arrange-ments all layered in a makeshift memorial. One person held up a sign. DO NOT FORGET THEM.

Booker stepped back and got into his car. He turned off the radio and drove home in silence. When he stepped into the apartment, he went to the fridge and looked for something to put in the microwave.

The door to the other bedroom opened. Demetrious walked out. He was dressed like he was about to go somewhere.

Booker stopped what he was doing. "I haven't seen you for a while. We need to talk."

31

Demetrious looked like he was in a hurry. He was dressed in all black. Reluctantly, he sat down.

Booker rubbed his tired eyes. "Where have you been?"

"So, you're my guardian now? I don't have to answer to you. I go my own way. My way." He slapped his right thigh, hard.

"Right now, your own way is my apartment. I'm a bit concerned about you."

Demetrious started putting on a pair of workout gloves. The gloves had the fingers cut out. "I'm fine."

"Fine. Have the police talked to you?"

Demetrious pulled up the gloves, nice and snug on his hands. "They don't know anything about me. And even if they did, I wouldn't say anything."

"Please, Demetrious. I know you've been going to the Brick. That section of the place is not good. I looked it up. There are tons of articles. It's run by a guy named Caston. Roland Caston. Sometimes just called Ro. He's been arrested four times."

"And no convictions," Demetrious added.

"Yes, no convictions. Witnesses just seem to change their story or later on refuse to testify. These were all drug-related charges. The guy is no good and from what I hear, he's dangerous. Hanging around a guy like that is no good for you."

"Why, you worried it might somehow affect you, Mr. TV man? Are you all worried about your public image? Your image. He's been there a long time and no one has ever made anything stick on him. He's free today, walking around all presumed innocent."

Booker gripped the arm of his chair. "This guy is probably tied to dozens of drug investigations. He may have tampered with witnesses. He's tied to meth, cocaine, and other drugs flowing in and out of South Florida. There's a rumor that he doesn't say anything, just sits there while his minions do all the talking and all the dirty work. That way his words won't come back to haunt him in a courtroom."

Demetrious spoke so low, his voice was barely heard. "He'd be fine. Just fine."

"What?"

"I said, he would be just fine."

Booker started to get up, then sat back down. "When I got a call from my mother."

"Our mother," Demetrious cracked back.

"Okay, our mother, she asked me to take you in. I did that. I never heard one word about you before that. And she didn't want to answer any questions. Just take you in. Where have you been all this time?"

"It's a long story." Demetrious sat back in the chair. "I've been in boarding homes. Spent a lot of Christmas nights with a few presents but no family. Not even our mother."

"Where was she then?"

"It's complicated. I didn't want to bother you at first. She insisted I get to meet you. Spend some time with you."

"You're here, but we don't do much together." Booker rubbed his eyes again. "Part of that is my fault. I need to make a place for you in my life. I mean, you're staying here."

"I did get a job by the way. I got a job."

Booker was all smiles. "Great."

"Assistant manager at the Internet Café where I spend too much time. They invited me to apply. I did and I start next week."

"That's fantastic." Booker's smile went away. "But you could really mess that up. If you keep going to the Brick . . ."

Demetrious was shouting. "The Brick, the Brick, the Brick. Is that all you can think about? The Brick?"

Now Booker was standing. And pointing. "If you only knew what that place was doing. And the guy at the center of all that is a potential felon. A dangerous man. Someone you really need to stay away from."

Demetrious was now standing. Eye to eye. "Well, you need to know something. That dangerous man you keep talking about? The man running the Brick? That man is my father."

32

Booker sat back down. "He is your father?"

"Roland Caston, the silent man, the maker of the Brick. The one who never speaks, the man arrested several times. Yes, that Roland Caston is my father."

"But your last name is Baker."

"I had my last name legally changed as soon as I was able. I didn't want to be associated with him."

"How did—"

"What's the connection to our mother? Your father was happily married to mom. She never talked about this?"

Booker said, "Never."

"Your father was away for a bit. Months on a job. While he was away, Caston started hitting on her. Small stuff at first and she always brushed it away. Somehow she got in her head that Caston was this smooth, flashy dude. That he was all everything. He kept at her, kept at her, until one night she let her guard down. And they had a very brief affair. Next thing you know, she's pregnant with me. You were probably around thirteen months old, I'd guess. You wouldn't remember him coming over. Mom pushed Caston out of her life as soon as she learned more about him. But I was this little reminder of the affair. No matter what, she wanted to keep the baby.

Your father knew something was up right away and he wanted out. He took off again."

Booker was shaken. "Mom never said one word about any of this. I just know she was a single mom."

Demetrious looked intense. "You see, I'm the one responsible for breaking up your family."

"Well, it wasn't you. She let Caston in. All of this falls on her. You just happened to come along."

"When I was born, I was passed around. The money came in for me to go to some great schools. But I never had any parents to show what I was doing. By arrangement, our mother stayed out of my life."

"What arrangement?"

"What our mother was trying to do is get back with your father. In order to do that, she swore she would not bring me into the picture. That meant Caston paid my way. But what happened was your father eventually could not do it. Just the thought of me out there somewhere was too much. And the whole thing just fell apart."

Booker remembered. "I knew she was trying to get back to him. I heard them yelling on the phone. My father left and I never heard from him again."

"You ever try tracking him down? I mean, he is your father and wouldn't you want to know what happened to him? I know I would."

"I almost did twice. With my job, I have the ability to track down just about anybody. But I never did that. But why did you come back? Why are you here?"

"I stayed away from Caston. I became Demetrious Baker and that was it. I'm here because of something that happened three years ago between our mother and him."

"Why didn't you tell me all this when I first met you?"

"Cause it wasn't time. I'm just grateful you helped me out, driving to job interviews."

The phone calls to his mother were made every week, no matter how busy Booker might be or what he was doing. They texted often and she always wanted to know what was going on in his life. She was out of state and didn't make it to South Florida that much anymore. It didn't matter to

Booker. He always went to see her. What got him so riled internally is why she never said anything about Demetrious before. Not until now. He could understand not saying anything about Roland Caston. Once she got to know him, her world must have been destroyed and she couldn't pull all the pieces back together. Booker wanted to call her right now. He looked at his watch and decided it was too late. He would call her tomorrow.

Booker took another long study of Demetrious. They both had their mother's eyes. Same sympathetic smile and demeanor. Demetrious had the height, although Booker was a healthy six-feet-plus. All the while he was listening to Demetrious, he kept thinking why his mother never told him about a brother? Why the secrecy. Booker was a man gifted with the talent to be given secrets. In his reporter life, all kinds of once-hidden information was passed on to him. He had scores of exclusives. People relied on him to listen to their inner worlds and hand-deliver them to Booker. Yet, his own mother never disclosed one of the biggest secrets in her heart. Another son.

"Okay, Demetrious. You still haven't answered my question. If you hate Caston so much, why are you here?"

"I can't answer that right now. I'm working on it and at some point, I will tell you because it involves both of us. Just know, that the reason I'm here is because I owe Caston and I'm paying him back."

"Owe him? For what?"

Demetrious walked out the door.

33

Whispis Dulan leaned against his car and pressed the cell phone to his ear. "I know, I know. We're not supposed to call each other. That was the agreement, but this is too important. Is everybody on the line?"

He waited for a response. "I'm here." A deep rumbling voice came through clear.

"And I'm here." His words were distinguished.

Dulan checked around him. He was in another park and far away from listening ears. "The safe house is no longer an option and we all need to figure out how to get to the money."

Rumble voice cut him off. "Forget the money. We all agreed to break away. They found Greg but they're not going to find me."

The distinguished one agreed. "You see what they did to Greg? We're next. This has to be our last phone call together. We just go where we go and damn sure don't tell each other where we're going."

Dulan looked at the bags on the back seat of his car. He thought about the RV he had to leave behind. Too slow. He had to travel fast. "What about this reporter?"

"He can't help us." Rumble voice's heavy tones seemed to fade then come back strong.

Dulan gave in. "Okay, if you think so, I'll leave him out of this. I left you both his business card in the PO box."

"Got it," Distinguished said. "Won't use it, but I got it."

Dulan had more instructions. "When we're done, toss these phones. No one contacts each other anymore. No one goes after the money shares. That's done. What we did is what we did. There's a reason we broke away from the group. Greg had the right idea. I just didn't think we would be killed if we wanted to leave."

There was remorse in the voice of the distinguished one. "The money made us what we became. And right now we know too much."

34

Ben Olson, the rumble voice on the phone, checked his watch. Just past 5:30 p.m. He had everything ready to go. He parked his everyday car at the airport, kept his face away from cameras, and literally walked the long distance out of the airport complex, all the way to a public bus. There, he got off near his home and entered. The place was warm. Very warm. All electricals had been turned off. No power and no cable. Everything was shut down. One suitcase was by the rear door. He grabbed the suitcase and thought about setting the home on fire, then changed his mind. Just leave quietly, he thought.

A stolen car was in the garage. The bag was tossed in the back seat and he drove off, nice and smooth. He wore a flesh-toned mask to ward off facial recognition, however, that shouldn't be a major problem since he was not going up the I-95 Expressway or the Turnpike. He took Federal Highway north. The trip would be a lot longer with a million stoplights, but he didn't mind. Many miles down the road, he would drive over to the middle of Florida and take a tiny highway north.

Inside the car, he had maps of New York State. Although he wasn't going to New York. He kept driving, with the fear of being caught pushing him forward. Olson didn't plan to stop. If he needed to pee, he would pull over, do what's needed in a jar and keep moving. Then toss the contents out the window. He wore gloves but he didn't care. When he was done the car would be torched anyway. He patted the contents of something in the pocket of his flannel shirt, just in case he definitely changed his mind about the entire thing. For now, he kept driving.

Everything was arranged. He arrived at the motel located four miles outside Orlando. This would be his so-called stop for the night. The room was prepaid, done by someone who posed for him, put money on the room, and kicked in extra cash to have a key waiting in a certain location. The motel was picked for a reason: the surveillance cameras did not work. When he got into the room, he took off the gloves and Ben Olson touched everything. He picked up the gloves, grabbed the remote and tossed the sheets around. Olson plopped on the bed and gave himself four hours to rest.

For a bit he could not sleep. Too much going on just outside the extremely filthy window. He heard scattered noises outside and bits of conversation. Two lovers arriving in separate cars and leaving an hour later. One guy stood outside his room smoking because the woman inside the room didn't want all the smoke.

Then, he had a visitor. A brown dot crawled up the wall near the bathroom. A giant Florida roach. Olson didn't have the energy to get up and smash the thing so he just let it continue on its journey up and around the bathroom door. He closed his eyes.

Just past five a.m., his phone alarm kicked off. For Olson, it was time to leave. He could easily drive anywhere in the United States. He had been out west many times before and he knew that part of the country well. Olson just had to get rid of the stolen car, get a legitimate ride.

He had no smartphone and no burner phones. Not one. The stolen car was missing the catalytic converter. As far as he could tell, the old wreck had no GPS locating software. They didn't know his face, the car would be burned.

Ben Olson was free.

He had escaped the group. No more stories to hide about Greg. A smile pushed across his face. There would be no more calls to get involved in schemes to circumvent careers. Getting dirt on people was one thing. What Olson had engaged in was illegal and potentially dangerous. A small bit of a good consciousness grew into a giant ball of guilt and he wanted no more.

He could have gone just about anywhere.

Instead, he got in his car and drove to a preplanned spot near a dump. There, he set the car on fire. He made sure the maps were outside the car and could be found later. The flames licked the outside of the roof. Inside, the seats gave off a terrible smell. He picked up his suitcase and walked to a bus station. He opened the suitcase and took out a bus ticket. The destination was South Florida.

"I can't leave," he said to himself.

He sniffed to see if there was any car fire smell on him. No. He burned everything without gasoline and stayed back from the smoke. The plan was to make everyone think he was headed to New York. Another part of the plan was simple: leave a ton of DNA at the dump of a motel. People could describe the car he drove. A car now burning to a crisp.

On the bus ride back south, he found a place by himself and went to sleep. His life was burned with the car. Driver's license, social security card, anything connected to him was gone. Now in his pocket was a new man. New name, new passport, new everything. He was ready to go. Ben Olson was gone.

The trip down was a lot longer than the four hours going up. There were stops to make. When the bus stopped in South Florida, he got out, grabbed his bag, and almost bent his body in half, leaning down and away from the surveillance cameras. He was wearing a wide-brimmed hat. A half mile later, he found another car. Legit. Not stolen. He tossed the bag in the back seat and drove to a different location. The place was a townhouse on a cul-de-sac. All of his moves were planned out months in advance. The key was placed under a rock on the side of the house. He walked in, threw the bag on a couch, and kicked off his shoes.

He was done traveling.

Just before getting some sleep, he thought he heard something. Ben with the new name walked to the back door and looked through the small glass windows.

Nothing.

He was sure he heard something. While he was in the kitchen, he was enamored with the plates he picked out for the place. He was still operating without a phone. A new burner was on his to-do list.

His head snapped around in the direction of the front door. He heard it again.

He ran to the front door. No one was there and silence enveloped the house. "I'm hearing things," he said to himself.

Throughout his dirty dealings, he never owned a weapon. Maybe he should add gun to his to-do list. He stood in the middle of the living room and waited to see if the townhome produced another strange sound.

He looked around for something to use as a weapon.

A hand grabbed him by the back of the neck and tossed him forward with so much force he crashed into the wooden coffee table. After hitting his face, he rolled off the table and came to a heap on the tile floor.

He looked up.

The man was wearing black gloves. A Glock G40 was strapped to his hip. The weapon was big and imposing. "All that travel. It didn't matter where you went, we would find you."

Olson pleaded. "I didn't tell anyone anything. Nothing. No one. I'm ready to come back."

"But you left. You ran off just like Greg. We have to make you an example of why you can't leave the group."

Olson's hands were shaking. "I'll do anything. Just let me live. I can do everything I did before and more. Just test me. Anything."

"Too late." Olson had only heard about this man. Rumors of a handler, someone who carried out assignments from higher up.

"And to think," the figure tightened up his gloves. "I lost you in Orlando. You took off and I didn't see you leave. If you kept going, you would have made it somewhere. I thought you got away and that wouldn't be good. But then we remembered you just bought this place. I thought you might double back. And you did." The man with the gloves moved in on Olson, picking him up like a small bag of groceries and running his body forward until he smashed Olson's face into a wall. He wouldn't let Olson fall to the ground, holding him up like he was squeezing the neck of a bowling pin. "I followed you all over the place. Damn near wore me out. But the running is over."

Olson tried to think of anything to save himself. He checked the room for a weapon. Before he could get to anything, he had to break free from the monster holding him.

"You're about to be part of a message."

"Just let me go. I never told anyone about, you know, Apex."

"You just told me." The grip on his neck got tighter.

"Let me go, please."

The gloved man said, "Not gonna happen. You should have kept running when you had the chance."

35

Booker's walk into the newsroom Wednesday showed little pain in his steps. After three jokes about him needing a walker to work again, Booker was back at his desk and ready to follow up on a number of things. He read the newspaper online before work, and now he took a moment to read what the bloggers were saying. One online post reviewed the new positions being filled in the prosecutor's office. Another blogger commented on the possibility of a row of trees being cut down near Federal Highway. The trees had a long beloved history and the blogger was making that point known. The third blogger, called himself Rich the Revealer, wrote about the lack of an arrest for the murder of Greg Tally. Rich said there were questions to be answered and what was the state of the investigation?

Booker shook his head. The police never talk about the so-called state of the investigation. Not to anyone, until it's over. Not even to Rich the Revealer.

Just as he was about to try and move up to the assignment desk, he got a call from the other side of the newsroom. It was Claire Stanley. "Okay, Book. You're on the sidelines today. And before you complain, that's an order."

"But I . . ."

"No but I about it. You're inside. That's from the boss. One, someone tried to kill you. Two, you still look like the Dolphins used you for a practice dummy. Just work from the desk. Go over your stuff. We'll talk later. Okay?"

"And that's an order?"

"Order." She hung up.

Booker took out a sheet of paper and started making a list. First, he called the Florida Highway Patrol PIO and asked if there was any update on the crash. The spokesman explained that cameras showed the box truck got off at the very next exit, made a couple of turns, and vanished. They are looking for the box truck but fear it might be stashed in a warehouse or garage somewhere. Or destroyed. Next, Booker called to check on Mikala Williams. Her office said she was away and they did not have any other information. Booker surmised she could be under some form of police protection. She showed courage to come forward. All of these phone calls and contacts Booker was making would be put into an email going to Stanley and the producers. Booker just wanted to let them know what he found.

He got a visit from the HR department just to check and see how he was doing. Once satisfied, she left and Booker went back to business. He made six more phone calls and answered twenty-nine emails from the general public, as many people were concerned about him. Booker glanced at his watch. Eleven a.m. He was just about ready to think about lunch when a frantic Claire Stanley quickstepped it to his desk.

"Just got a call from the police. They want you there." Her jaunt caught her a bit off guard as she was finding the air to push out the next sentence. "They asked for you specifically."

"Me? Why?"

"They didn't say why, just that they asked if you could come to the scene."

"Scene?"

"We're sending two crews, putting up the helicopter and we're on standby to maybe break into programming."

"All that?"

"Booker, we're not sure what we got going on. We just know the police say they have a dead body and they want you there."

"On my way."

36

Booker and Dominguez parked and saw the assortment of news crews already there. The sun was unrelenting. Florida in the summer. People stood under the shade of two banyan trees. The reporters, police, and crime techs were all exposed to nature's withering scorch.

All the attention was centered on a site not more than twenty yards from Booker. Merilee Yang and photographer Sam Drewhill were up ahead. Drewhill had his camera on a tripod. With them was Grandhouse, who looked like she needed a chair to sit on.

There was a lot of crime tape. The scene was big and since the police were trying to keep people away from the main location, they really had no choice.

Three crime tech vans and four police cars blocked the public's view. There was also a canvass wall stretching perhaps twenty feet. The whole scene was near an area mostly used as grazing land for a few cattle, miles from the coast and on the county's west side. For now, Channel 27 agreed to a request from the police and did not put the helicopter in the air and over the scene.

Booker finally reached Yang and Drewhill. "Anyone saying anything yet?"

Yang looked at her photographer and Grandhouse, then turned to

Booker. "We were one of the first ones here. Before they had a chance to put up all this crime tape. We couldn't shoot anything at first. We had to wait. But we did shoot a bit for in-house use only."

Under self-imposed news rules, Channel 27 and all the other stations did not put video of exposed bodies on television. It just wasn't done.

Booker took out his notepad. "What did you see?"

Yang hesitated at first. "We didn't quite know what we were getting into when we got here. The station called and we just ran out here. But we didn't expect to see . . ." Yang stopped.

Drewhill took a step back from his camera. "I got out and I was just about to put the camera on sticks." He looked at the intern. "I mean the tripod. I put out my sticks and I saw him, or rather he saw me."

"What?" Booker put his pad down.

Grandhouse the intern spoke up. "We saw him staring at us. His eyes were open, looking down the road at any car that might approach."

"You okay?" Booker studied Grandhouse.

"Yeah, I'm fine. This is stuff they don't talk about in class."

Yang said, "He was leaning against the gate leading to the cows. As far as I can see there are no cameras out here. And no lights. At night, this would be a very dark place."

Drewhill cut in. "You could clearly see the bullet wound to the head, between the eyes."

Yang's voice had a tone of anger. "This is one sick person. He wanted to make a public spectacle with this."

"Have the police talked yet?"

"Not yet," Yang said. "We're supposed to get a briefing in about an hour."

Booker checked his watch again. "Possibly during our noon newscast. Where do you want us?"

Yang looked around. "For now, just get some perimeter shots. You know, the usual. See if anyone saw anything, which I doubt. At some point, Sam and I will be moving to the command post where they will give the news conference. While we're setting up for that, just be some extra eyes in case there's movement anywhere else."

"No problem."

Yang motioned Booker to step away from the crews and the intern. "Book, Claire told me. The police want you here. Any reason why?"

"No idea. Do me a favor, any way you can pull me up some video of the victim. They have everything covered up right now."

"Sure. I took a picture off Sam's video with my phone." She handed her cell over to Booker. He took a long look at the face, then used his fingers to expand the picture.

Booker handed the phone back. "I've never seen this guy before. I have no idea why they asked me to come here." He moved toward Dominguez to begin the search for any witnesses. Booker got an email from the station. Photographs of the victim were beginning to show up on social media. A cold-blooded move, thought Booker. Keeping his microphone out so people could see he was a reporter, Booker walked outward from the immediate crime scene, looking for anyone who might have seen a car or anything.

The cow pasture where the body was found was next to a busy two-lane road. On the south side of the road, there were perhaps eight to ten houses. Booker started the trek down the sidewalk. He was looking for two things: witnesses and any doorbell camera video. Maybe someone got vid of a car driving by. When he knocked at the first three houses, no one answered. He kept going. In the front lawn of the fourth house, two little girls were playing outside. Booker heard a woman's voice call the girls back inside. He got a shaking of the head from the mom, meaning she did not want to talk. Booker moved on. He was striking out.

It was almost noon and Booker had nothing to give to Yang for her report. He moved back to her. Drewhill, her photographer, had a two-microphone setup. He had one microphone for Yang and he had the second microphone propped up at a podium fifteen feet away.

Since Yang was fixed in place, Booker and Dominguez stood ready for anything that happened elsewhere.

Exactly at 12:01 p.m., reporters from three different TV stations started to give their reports to a live audience. The noise level increased dramatically with three reporters talking over each other.

Booker checked his phone. A PIO would be talking to reporters at the microphone stand in exactly fourteen minutes. The message came from

Claire Stanley on the assignment desk. Booker watched people in front of their homes. One by one, they were standing and watching. One home looked empty. Lights out. The reporters were now finished, for the moment. Once a PIO stepped in front of the cameras, Yang would be on again. The PIO was young, couldn't have been on the force for many years. Carol Clipper, hair pulled back, walked up to the microphones and waited. Two of the photographers asked her to say a few words so they could get a good volume level of her voice.

"Mic check. Mic check. My name is Carol Clipper and we will start in one minute."

All three photographers worked the controls to sharpen their focus in the camera lens. They were ready. Booker knew the routine. Rather than have Yang talk first, the anchors would do the lead-in, and the TV audience would only see Clipper.

She started. "My name is Officer Carol Clipper. At approximately 7:27 a.m., we got a call into our 911 call center of a male, possibly deceased, here at this location, just east of Samiack Road. Paramedics arrived, determined the victim was deceased. At that time, this matter was turned over to the homicide unit. We will not be giving out a lot of detail other than the next of kin has not been notified so we will not be giving you a victim's name at this time. I can answer a few questions."

Yang jumped in first. "Do you have a suspect at this point, and any indication what the victim was doing here?"

"There are no suspects in custody at this time. As to what he was doing here, that is part of the investigation."

A question from Clipper's right. "Is this connected to anything else?"

"Again, if there is a connection, and I'm not indicating there is one right now, that's part of the investigation."

Yang raised her hand. "Any word on what type of weapon was used? Knife? Gun?"

"Once we get word back from the medical examiner, we can say more, but we can tell you the victim suffered at least one gunshot wound." Before another question was pitched her way, Clipper kept talking. "We would ask the public that if anyone saw anything, please contact our tips line. We know that someone was posting pictures of the crime scene and putting them on social media. We would ask that person to come forward. We just want to ask a few questions. That's all I have right now. We will update you with an email later today." And with that, Clipper was done.

The live feed was over.

A woman with a gun on her hip was making her way toward Booker. She walked past the U-shape of tripods, past the curious faces of reporters. Brielle Jensen had a notebook pad tucked into her pants. She made a direct walk to Booker. Before he had a chance to say anything, she had him follow her out of the collection of media, until she found a piece of shade. She stood in the dappled light.

"I was told police wanted to see me. I'm here."

"I probably have three, maybe four questions and we're done." She was all business. "I'll leave it up to you but I'm going to ask you something and for now, I'm asking to keep it off-the-record. At least for now."

"I'll try. What's the question?"

"Does the name Ben Olson mean anything to you?"

Booker thought for a moment. "Olson. Ben Olson. No, I don't know that name."

"That's interesting," Jensen said. "We can't name him as identified yet, but we think the vic is Ben Olson. And he has your business card in his shirt pocket."

37

Booker had that surprised look on his face that surfaces on rare occasions. He always wanted to be so informed he was hopefully, never surprised.

Until now.

"I looked at a picture of your victim. I swear, I've never met the man," Booker said.

"Okay thanks." Jensen appeared done. "If you keep that name to yourself for a few hours, I'll confirm it to you and the world later." She turned and moved through the onlookers. Somehow, Booker thought, this had to be connected to Greg Tally.

He took another long hard look at his surroundings. He didn't tell Yang yet, but the video still of the man who could be Ben Olson was looking at something. Booker returned to Yang and the rest.

"Whatcha got Book?" Yang kept her voice down so the other reporters could not hear her.

"Not a lot yet. But after looking at that video of the victim, I was thinking." Booker and Dominguez picked up their search for a witness. There was a line of houses. All of them had what looked to be an acre of land. Each house was different in style and color. Booker liked that because so many communities were cookie cutter with houses the same, color the same, trim alike. Not here.

Booker looked for dogs first. One thing he always did was to raise his hand in a greeting to let people know he was there and to acknowledge they saw him. If the pleasant greeting was not mutual, Booker could move on.

The house had a three-car garage. Inside one section of the garage was a 1957 Chevy. Long before Booker reached the front door to knock, a man came out. He was wearing jeans, which covered up a message on his shirt. His well-worn construction boots clopped on the sidewalk as he approached Booker.

"Can I help you?"

"I'm Booker Johnson, Channel 27 news. I was wondering if you saw or heard anything last night?"

"Yeah, heard lots of stuff. Some bullfrogs out back and around nine, the cicadas got really loud."

A grin reached across Booker's face. "Besides that, you hear anything like someone in trouble?"

"I thought I did. I'm a light sleeper."

"Okay if I ask you about that for a comment?"

"Okay."

Booker raised up the microphone. "They found a victim not far from here. You see or hear anything last night?"

"I thought I heard a car come creeping down here sometime after four or five am. I have no idea if that had something to do with it. I'm too far away from the corner to hear much of anything and I like it that way."

"Did you investigate it at all?"

"Naw, I kept listening to see if there was any other noises, but it stayed quiet. Went back to sleep."

"Thank you." Booker put down the microphone. Dominguez shut down the camera. Booker started to ask for his name, but he waived him off. No name is just fine, thought Booker.

The man looked like he almost never left the place. The top of his head was starting a bald spot and his nails looked like they were never cleaned. He pointed to his front door. "You see that?"

Booker followed his gaze to the front door. A shotgun was propped up against the wall by the door. The man was smiling so big, all of his teeth were exposed. "I got plenty more like that. Anyone comes here with bad intentions will leave face down."

"I understand. Thanks for talking to me." Booker and Dominguez left. They returned to Yang. While Dominguez downloaded his video, Booker explained what he had in terms of an interview. Yang was thankful.

Booker again wanted to look at the video of the victim, spreading the picture with his fingers. "I've been thinking about this." Yang and Grandhouse leaned in. Booker continued. "He was shot twice. Once in the head, once in the chest. Heart and mind. He was sitting looking across the street. Or, at least in that general direction. What if he was forced to look that way?"

Now, all of them started looking away from the body scene. Booker wanted to point, then did not want to draw attention to what he was doing. "The thing that is across the street is that house. I knocked on doors and there appeared to be no one home. What if this home is important to the victim? What if . . ."

Grandhouse started to shout, then whispered. "He lived there."

Booker picked up his cell and called the station. While he was doing that, he gave some directions to Dominguez and Drewhill. "Start shooting video of everything. The house across the street, the road leading up to the house, VO of everything down the street."

"Claire Stanley . . ."

"Hey, it's Booker. Do me a favor and go online and look up the property tax ownership for the address I am about to give you."

"Go ahead, I'm ready."

"One-six-nine-four-four Samiack Road." Booker could hear her clicking on a keyboard.

"Well, I've got it. From what I'm reading, the house belongs to an Olson. Ben Olson. Does that help?"

"Thanks Claire. Yes, it does. Thank you."

Yang couldn't hold back anymore. "What does it mean? I think I heard her say Ben Olson."

Booker was quick. "Don't say that name anywhere just yet. Next of kin hasn't been contacted. Just hold it." Booker looked around. "We got enough video of the neighborhood? The next move should come any moment now."

Grandhouse put her hands on her hips and looked around. Police officers surrounded the reporters with a demand. Pack up and move back. Grandhouse put her hand up to block the sun. "Why are they moving us?"

"Because of these guys who are arriving now."

A large police truck pulled up and parked. Booker started to help Dominguez put away the gear. "That folks, is the bomb squad."

38

Rather than move TV crews out, the police just made sure everyone stayed in place. The police and the bomb squad checked out the place Booker originally pegged as having no one home. The whole procedure took just over thirty minutes. In the air, the station's helicopter, with a police okay, was getting video and sending a feed to the station. Yang and Booker watched the chopper video in the van. They got a good layout of the property and the backyard.

There was no swimming pool. The backyard was spacious, with what looked like a shed. Nothing about it stood out and Booker turned his attention to the front of the place. The Channel 27 helicopter moved back and flew away from the area.

"Something's up." Booker turned his vision away from the TV monitors and toward the front walkup. A bomb squad member was at the mailbox, which was located on the swale in front of the house. The bomb unit obscured all views of what they were doing. A thumbs-up was finally given and a bomb unit member was seen carrying some type of device from the mailbox. Both Drewhill and Dominguez were shooting video of the entire thing.

Yang said it first. "Well, that was interesting. Something was in the mailbox."

"That's it." Booker looked at the victim scene, then to the mailbox some fifteen yard away, across the street. "I can't confirm now, but I'm seeing a terrible scenario." He pointed to one side of the road, then the other. "My guess is this. The victim was forced to watch as they put something in the mailbox. The last thing he saw was a bomb being placed to hurt someone close to him. But who?"

Yang checked her notes. "There was nothing in the records about another person co-owning the property. Could be he was expecting someone to come home. Maybe a parent, a girlfriend, who knows?"

"And that someone would be killed as soon as they went to the mailbox." Booker wiped down a line of sweat from his forehead. Yang was on the phone with Claire Stanley. After seven minutes or so of conversation, Yang addressed the group. "Okay, so the producers want Booker and I on the story. We are leading the five. There will be an umbrella lead, two in the box, with the helicopter used for the umbrella. At the end, I'll do a live reporter toss to Booker's package. Booker will come out live on the tail only. When he is done, the control room will go back to a double box for Q and A. The feedroom will make sure there are no mix-minus problems. And then we're done."

"Got it," Booker said.

Grandhouse whispered to Booker. "I didn't understand any of that."

"No problem." Booker explained, "An umbrella lead means the anchors will talk about a range of details all dealing with this murder and another top story. Two in the box simply means showing two reporters on TV standing there, waiting to talk. Yang will introduce my story or package and I will talk live at the end."

"Thanks. And what is mix-minus?"

"When you have an earpiece, sometimes the sound you hear in your ear can be delayed half a second or a second and what you are saying comes back in your ear. It is very, and I mean very distracting. That's why you see reporters pulling their earpiece out of their ears on TV. They will try to make sure that doesn't happen."

"Thanks."

Yang and Booker started writing. Yang would do the main story and Booker would do the neighborhood angle and use the sound clip he got earlier. Both crews and Grandhouse were also looking for something else. If Booker was right, then someone might be arriving at the home where the bomb was found. Another update was coming sometime after five p.m. Again, that update from Clipper would be shown live.

Booker noticed several police cars were located at the entrance of the road. The TV crews were locked in place and now only local residents were allowed in. If his hunch was right, Jensen was busy looking for the person or persons who were expected to show up at the home.

The helicopter was back.

Just as the helicopter was arriving, Booker got on the phone to send it away. "Hi, it's Book. Tell them to move the copter back for awhile. The PIO is talking in a few minutes instead of five p.m. All that chopper noise will be too hard to hear her. And, we'll be sending you the live feed of the newser so you can put that on our website. Thanks."

Booker sat in the shade of the van. Dominguez was putting together the one minute fifteen-second package. Yang, however, was in a holding pattern. Since she had the main portion of what happened, she had to wait until the news conference to get all the latest details. Booker sat, watching the mailbox and thinking. He also did not know how Olson got his business card. Just as promised, Clipper walked up the arrangement of microphones early.

Clipper waited until she got the attention of everyone. The live signal was being sent through Channel 27 to the station website. Thousands across South Florida would be watching. Clipper leaned in just a bit toward the mics. "I just wanted to give you a quick update. The medical examiner is here. At some point, we will conduct an autopsy. I can tell you that we have identified the victim as forty-eight year old Ben Olson. Mr. Olson lived at an address across the street. You saw our bomb squad unit there and we did find a device. Just what type of device and exactly what we found is part of the investigation. We expect to open the road in about ninety minutes. I won't be taking any questions at this time but just two things if I can. First, we are again reaching out to the public. If you saw or heard anything that might be related to this case, even if it's a small detail, we urge you to call our office. You can also use the tips line. Second, the next update to the news media will be by email." She left the microphones.

A few questions were still tossed at her and Clipper kept moving on. She was done.

Once Clipper finished, Booker was free to look for other aspects of the story. Yang, however, had to stay locked in position. Drewhill would have to get video of the body being moved by the medical examiner. Booker was also free to get a quick bite.

"What do you want to eat?" Booker had his pad out and he was ready to write. "I'll bring you more water and I'm open for what you want." He wrote down a sandwich wish list for the three, Yang, Drewhill and Grandhouse. Before Booker could eat, he would bring them some food first. Dominguez and Booker stopped by a fast-food place and placed the orders.

His cell phone rang. It was Claire Stanley. "Okay Book, you ready? Once we heard the name Ben Olson and confirmed an address we went to work."

"Whatcha got?"

"Well, Olson, from what we can determine had two pervious arrests. Small stuff. One for loitering. Another for bad checks. In both cases, they were nol-prosed."

"Charges dropped by the prosecutor."

"Exactly." Stanley continued. "Since they were not considered felonies, there is no mug shot. He owns the house where you are now but he is listed as owning two condos. Other than that, he is not active on social media. None of the major ones at least. He did do some work for a public relations firm but I called them and they said he left them two years ago. He has a blank hole in his life."

"Sound familiar?" Booker was busy writing down notes based on her information.

"You mean Greg Tally?"

"Yes. Both of them dropped out of sight. We now know or at least suspect Greg was not doing stuff considered legal. I don't know about Olson. One thing is very clear, someone is eliminating people. And they are being very public about it. This killer clearly is not happy. And the problem is the killing might not be over."

"I think you're right. Anything you need from us?"

Booker put away his pad. "No. Just send me the locations of those condo addresses. Not sure if we have time to go by there. If he's connected to Greg, they moved in secret. Did you get a read on whether anyone else was living at his location here?"

"No. Nothing."

"Okay. Thanks Claire."

Conversation over, Booker delivered the food to the others. He gave Yang a full rundown on the information from Claire Stanley. Just as he finished, Stanley sent out an email to everyone on the news side. Now everyone had the same info. This was done in case anyone else picked up the story, they would have the background information.

Booker checked his watch. Two p.m. He had a few hours to do some checking.

39

Demetrious Moreland again found himself in the back seat of the SUV. Strap turned to him. "Look, you don't have to be here. Ya might want to get out now."

"I just want to make sure you don't do something. You know what I mean."

Strap turned back to his three targets. "I'm gonna find out what I need to find out. If I need to do some pain, then that's what I'm gonna do. You have a problem with that?"

Demetrious opened the door. "Just remember what I said." He got out and started walking away from the car. Two houses and an empty lot later, he found a watch spot behind a tree.

Strap and Abrafo rolled up slow in the SUV. She got out and tried to look submissive. Hard to do with her size, heavily muscled arms, and shoulders full of tats.

The young woman on the sidewalk saw Abrafo and took a step back.

"We just want a piece of the good stuff. You sell'n right?" Abrafo had one thing going for her. She did not look like police.

"We ain't got nothing right now." The woman was clearly nervous. Behind her, the two others inched closer to the hedge they loved so much. Besides their drug stash, anything could be within reach.

"Just stop right there mofo." Strap pointed his .45 in their general direction. When meth face glanced back from staring at Strap, she was also looking directly at a gun held by Abrafo. Two weapons aimed at the three dealers. Strap eased slow and easy out of the car like he was honey being poured from a jar. "Now here's what we're gonna do. You two get in back with my friend. Your lady here, she gets to ride up front with me. Is that clear? We're gonna take a ride. And don't even think about running. This bullet faster than you ever be."

From where he was hidden, Demetrious could see the men were still thinking about making a move. Bad idea. Strap would cut them down before the next thought came into their heads. The men reluctantly did as told. They got into the back seat. Strap watched them move into position. Abrafo watched the girl take the front seat.

Abrafo aimed the gun toward the girl's face. "Just do as he says."

"What's this about?" The girl said. "We're just running a business. Why y'all got to mess it up?"

Strap laughed. "We messed up? We got a lot to talk about."

Demetrious watched all of them pack into the SUV. Now, it was his turn to be nervous. What happened next was out of his hands.

STRAP DROVE DIRECTLY WEST. Active neighborhoods and busy streets melted away until he was facing US 27 and the Florida Everglades. The woman up front in the car got more agitated as he drove away from what she might consider would be safety nets. Strap slowed down and pulled off the highway onto a small parking lot. This was the location where fishermen launched their boats. Right now, there were no people, just the animals.

Strap's voice was forceful. "Everyone out!"

At first, no one moved. The power of the gun meant they would eventually leave the comfort of the SUV. With no engine running, they were alone with the sounds of the Glades. There was a very soft rustle of cattails not too far away. Every now and then a fish popped the surface of the green-black water. They all knew what was out here. They saw the news stories. The Glades were overrun with Burmese pythons. Thousands of them. Alligators were already here. Mating season had passed, yet they would still be just as hungry.

The woman looked down at the ground like she was about to step in some poo and couldn't figure out where to place her feet. The men didn't want to stray too far from the car.

"Git on over here." Strap used his gun to wave them into position. "We're gonna have a little talk." They all moved closer to the water. Strap kept the gun low and against his hip so a truck driver rolling down US 27 might not see too much. "Out here I don't need to bury you. I just jack you up a bit, git you nice and bloody, and put you out in that water. How does that sound?"

All three captives showed puckered-up faces like they were about to eat something terrible. Strap pointed to the surroundings. "All my creeping friends here would love to say hello and have you for dinner." He laughed hard. Then, the smile was gone. A bead of sweat rolled down his forehead and stopped on his face near a teardrop tattoo. "Now, I don't care who talks. But somebody is gonna talk. And you're gonna tell me who has been giving you the wrappers and product you been selling. Where are you getting your shit?"

No one talked. All three seemed to close their mouths shut. "Okay," Strap said. "One more time. I'll ask. And if I get that silent crap you been giving me, then someone is gonna take a bath out here and never come back."

Two vultures flew by, black bodies, looking heavy in the soft breeze. Abrafo moved next to Strap. Now, two guns were again pointed directly at them. "You heard him," she bellowed. "Who is your connection?"

Strap tapped his gun. "I got death here. You three been sell'n stuff that got four people killed. You stepped on it and when you did that, you made it lethal. All of this can be traced back to the wrong people. To us. And we're gonna correct that right now."

The taller one looked like he was ready to talk. "If we say something, we . . ."

Strap yelled at him. "We, what?"

"Then we die."

The pearl handle glinted in the afternoon sunlight, making the weapon look bigger than it was. "Let me sweeten the pot." Strap's smile widened his face. "You talk and we keep driving north. We git on the 27 right there and keep going north. We put you someplace else, far far from here. Because as far you sell'n here, business is closed. Closed for good."

The taller one said, "He warned us you might come after us. He said he would protect us."

"Shut up fool!" The shorter one admonished him.

The .45 smashed into the short one's face sending him sprawling back-ward. He landed hard on the rough gravel surface. Blood was lined down his face.

"Got you good, didn't I?" Strap looked like he was deciding if he needed to swing again. "Got that good blood flow going. You almost ready for them gators and pythons. They could just swallow you whole."

The wounded one touched his cheek. He got back up. Strap moved in toward him. "You know how gators eat? They don't swallow up right away. They roll and drown you first. Then they stuff you up under the bank for a bit and let you git real soft and mushy. Just right. That's when they come back for the meal. You make one more bad move and your next landing spot will be the water."

No one volunteered to offer any Information. Abrafo changed tactics. She stared at the woman. "Ya know, I'm in touch with the best crystal around."

A change came over the twenty-something. She had a half smile and revealed some of the greenish teeth. "You do?"

Abrafo tried to close the deal. "Meth is not my style but you, I bet you can tell the real deal. And I've got plenty. Just waiting for you."

"You do?" Twenty-something was just about all in. She was beyond enticed. Abrafo figured the street sales with the two males probably kept her from selling her body.

"I got the hookup. And it's all yours. You don't want to pass on this stuff. You need this stuff. You want this stuff." Abrafo should have been a used car salesman. "You know you want it. Come git it girl. Just say the word. Give me some knowledge. Who gave you the stuff?"

The shorter one started to open his mouth as if to stop her from talking. A .45 moved within four inches of his face changed his mind.

"Okay. I'll tell you." She was itching her left arm. "You say you can move us out of here? Put us in another city?"

Abrafo lowered her gun. "You got it, sweet cheeks. Talk and the meth is yours and we move you all on out."

"Okay. I'll tell you, but you're not going to believe it."

40

Booker sat in the van reading all the news accounts he could regarding the death of Ben Olson. His five p.m. time slot to go on television was an hour away. Since the noon newscast he had visited both condo locations supposedly owned by Olson. No one, at either location, remembered or knew him. Booker found himself back at the original scene. A lot was cleared away. The body of Olson was gone and at the morgue. Most of the crime tape was taken down and the road was reopened. All of the live trucks and reporters were parked in new locations along the wide swale.

The move gave new angles of where everything happened. The producers also had a different setup. This time, Yang would do a live report at 5 p.m. and then she would tease Booker's story coming up at 5:30 p.m. Booker was only needed in one newscast. The change also meant he had a bit more time to prepare. He was now a follower of the Rich the Revealer blog post. Booker read how Rich was upset and angry the police were, as he put it, moving too slow on the Greg Tally murder. And now, there was another death. Rich the Revealer questioned why there were no arrests and pretended to mount a public outcry on the police investigations. There was a lot of yelling through the Internet, however, Booker thought there was nothing revealed in the column. Calling out and pointing fingers without proof didn't fly with Booker.

Booker moved on.

These were moments he hated. After the noon newscasts, all of the TV stations were at the same starting point. All three had just about the same amount of information. All had a lot of the same interviews. With the five p.m. newscast looming, did Booker do enough to get all the information he could get and be ready? Did he miss something the other stations might find and put on the air before him. He was late getting the name confirmed on Greg Tally. Did Yang miss anything? When the newscasts started, every producer, reporter, and news director in South Florida would be fixed on watching to see if one station had more than the others. Missing a key angle somehow was not pleasant. Someone would have to answer to why a fact, an interview, a key piece of video might have been missed.

Booker did not like the minutes leading up to five p.m.

He did everything he could to be ready. While Yang reported, Booker watched a competitor station. They had everything, including the interview with the man who saw a car. Someone tracked him down. Just past 5:30 p.m., Booker stood in front of the camera set up by Dominguez and told his viewing audience about what he found. He detailed the neighborhood, showed his interviews and his package, including the video of the bomb squad locating something in a mailbox.

"Booker Johnson, Channel 27 news." Booker waited and did not speak or move until he heard the two words in his earpiece, "All Clear." Then, he moved. He walked up to Dominguez, who was breaking down all the equipment. "How late can you stay?"

The photographer thought for a moment. "I can stay but you gotta clear that with Claire Stanley. That's overtime big guy."

"Yeah, I know. I'll call her." Booker timed his call to her well before the start of the six p.m. newscasts because he knew they would all be watching and comparing. "Okay, Booker," Stanley started. "You're not selling me on this overtime request. We have to get Dominguez back. And you're not telling me anything that might result in a major swing in this story. Bring it home and start fresh tomorrow."

"Just two hours. Till eight p.m. That's all."

"That's more than two hours. He has to bring the van back and put stuff away. All that is on the clock."

"Okay. How about one hour. You got me for free. I don't get overtime pay and I never put in for a comp day. Just one hour."

"Okay, Booker. One hour." Conversation over. She was gone. Booker turned to Dominguez. "I heard it all, Book. You guys talk so loud, I think those cows complained. So, we got one hour, what's your plan?"

Booker left the scene. Only he and Dominguez didn't go very far. They pulled into a strip mall and waited to see if the other reporters left the story uncovered. Sometimes a nightside reporter would arrive and pick up the story. In this case, Yang and everyone did their six p.m. story and went home.

The place was quiet. Booker and Dominguez went back to the scene and waited. A police car was outside the residence of Olson. An officer dutifully sat and watched the place. Booker made himself known by parking off on the swale and not going door-to-door. All that was done earlier in the day. Booker was looking for someone else.

Forty-five minutes went by and there was nothing. Over a period of half an hour, a night sky reached up and across, pulling with it a blanket of stars. A few cars entered the road as people came home. Booker saw neighbors walk out into the night and share stories about what happened, probably what rumors they heard and what was seen on the news. Conversations over, they went back inside. The time limit for Dominguez was almost up. Booker had to head back to the station.

A faded blue Toyota pulled up in front of the police car. Even in the dark, Booker could see the car was in need of a paint job. A woman got out and before she could head to the house in question, the officer got out of his car and approached her.

"Get ready," Booker told Dominguez.

The woman was animated, waving her arms, pointing to the front of the house, the mailbox, the sky. After about ten minutes of listening to the police officer, he handed her a business card with some paperwork. The officer then called in to someone with his phone. More conversation. The officer got back into his car and continued to watch the house. She just stood there.

Booker and Dominguez walked up to her. He kept his camera aimed down, while Booker introduced himself. "I'm Booker . . ."

"I'm not ready for this. Not ready." Both of her eyes had tiny streaks of mascara from tears. "They're telling me I can't go into my house. I met with someone earlier and they told me about Ben." She stopped talking.

"Is it okay if we talk to you about Ben?"

"I guess so."

Booker started slow. Dominguez raised his camera and started to record. "We did not know Ben. What can you tell us about him?"

"Well, there were two Ben's. The good Ben and the distant Ben. The good Ben was kind. Took care of me." She wore a business suit of a blue skirt and a white blouse. The blouse had a stain on it like a napkin brushed against it. When she wasn't teary, Booker could see she probably had radiant eyes and let her hair get sorted by the wind instead of a comb.

"So, you two were close?"

She dabbed something at her eye. "I'll be honest with you. For a long time, all I saw was the distant Ben. He just wasn't around much. We were never married but we've been together for a long time. I heard about something on the news, called the police and right now, I'm the best thing he's got to a next of kin."

"From what you've heard from the police, any idea exactly of what happened?"

"No. Just that Ben is dead and they're looking for his killer. I wasn't even here last night. I was out of town. I sell houses, I'm a realtor. They tell me my mailbox was rigged with something. That's awful!"

"That's my next question. Did Ben have any enemies?"

"The police asked the same thing. I can't think of anyone who would harm him. He never said anything to me. But then, he hasn't been around for awhile."

"He hasn't been here?"

"At first, he said he was doing these jobs. He wouldn't say what kind of jobs they were exactly. But then he had money. Lots of money, so I didn't question it. Then, he was at home less and less, I asked him about it and he just wouldn't open up. Now this." She pointed to the house and the police car.

Booker threw out a name. "Have you heard the name Greg Tally?"

She shook her head no. "I haven't."

"Thanks. And again, your name?"

Dominguez lowered his camera. She pulled out a business card. "Greta. Greta Kenton. I've already been by the morgue. Identified him. That wasn't nice. I can't believe someone did that to him. Can I say one more thing?"

"Sure."

Dominguez was already recording. "What would you like to say?"

"You killed a good man. A good man. I want you caught. I don't know what happened or why Ben had to be killed but I want to see justice." She turned away from Booker.

Dominguez headed back to the van. Booker thanked her for taking time to speak to him and asked her one last question. He joined Dominguez, sat in the passenger seat while the camera was packed away in the lockbox. Booker got his cell phone and called the assignment desk. "Hey, it's Booker."

"I heard you asked to work late. Quiet out there?"

"No. Tell the producers I have a new angle for the eleven."

41

Reporters from all three stations working the night shift were assigned to the Olson murder. They were all lined up in front of a police satellite station. This would be the station closest to the murder scene. The thinking was no one wanted to set up and go live in front of a cow pasture or light up a quiet neighborhood at eleven p.m. The station gave everyone a chance to put up the strong lights for loud-talking reporters.

Reporters for the two other stations were twenty feet apart. They were expecting to see Jim Mason, the Channel 27 night reporter, who was with them all evening. All of them were rehashing video and interviews taken from the dayside. They had nothing new to report.

Then, Booker Johnson took Mason's place and stood next to the other reporters. They stared at Booker with worried faces. He heard a photographer say, "What's he doing here?"

One reporter pulled a cell phone to presumably call the station to find out if the police released anything new. Why was Booker Johnson at the station? Just being there caused a lot of angst.

Just after eleven p.m., Booker looked at a TV monitor and watched the start of the newscast. He heard the anchors do a brief rundown of what happened. Next to him, Booker heard the other two reporters talking about the same facts they were given much earlier in the day.

Then, in his earpiece, Booker heard, "Channel 27 reporter Booker Johnson has the exclusive details . . ."

"A worried partner of Ben Olson returned from a trip and found out the terrible news that her boyfriend of the past few years was a murder victim. She, like the rest of us, is trying to figure out why anyone would want to take his life."

Booker watched in the monitor and saw the interview he completed in the past hour. He also used a photograph she gave him, showing a smiling Ben Olson. The package ran about ninety seconds. Then, Booker was live again. "She is pleading for any help from the public. If you saw anything, heard anything, please call the tip line. Booker Johnson, Channel 27 news."

Booker heard the all-clear in his earpiece. He was done for the night. Finally. Near him, he saw reporters on cell phones trying to explain to someone how Booker got the interview. Even if they went to the murder scene now, Greta was gone. The station okayed all the overtime for Dominguez. They went back to the station and put away the van and the gear.

BOOKER OPENED the door to his apartment and leaned against it, tired and worn down. After the run-in with the box truck, he was still driving around his apartment building a few times in case someone was following him. And after driving around, he parked for five minutes or so, waiting to see if it was quiet. After the long day and night, he finally got inside his place around midnight. He had a chicken Caesar salad with him, with extra dressing and extra chicken. Booker didn't want to eat a heavy meal early in the morning, opting instead for the salad.

On the kitchen table, he found a long note from Demetrious. He explained he was working the overnight shift since the Internet Café moved to a twenty-four-hour operation. He would be back around seven a.m. or so.

Booker raked through his salad with a fork and turned on the television to stream a program. He didn't want to eat much, just enough to satiate any hunger pangs and head to bed. What he really wanted to do more than anything was call Misha. Somewhere in between the daily crush of news, Booker wanted to hear from her. He really wanted to see her, touch her face, smell the aromas she used to adorn her body. He missed everything about her. A glance at her picture on the shelf conjured up all kinds of memories. They loved strolling the beaches of South Florida, going to the Japanese Museum and Gardens in Palm Beach County, or picking out which restaurant to enjoy that week. Their favorite eating spots were on the Intracoastal. Now, they were just random thoughts on a lonely night. Booker went to sleep dreaming about his last embrace and wanted more.

42

Booker always called Thursdays pre-Friday. He did not want to wake up Demetrious by making noise in the kitchen, so he skipped cooking breakfast and decided to get something fast on the way. He already got an email from Claire telling him he could stay on the Tally murder or the Olson murder one more day, then he would be moved on to something else. Booker hoped to get off work at his normal time so he could sit down and talk with Demetrious. He still didn't understand why he owed something to a drug dealer. Especially since it might involve Booker's mother.

When Booker looked at the morning newscasts on the other stations, one of them managed to find and interview Ben Olson's partner. He walked into the newsroom with the aroma of an egg sandwich. The first stop would be the assignment desk.

"Morning Book. Thanks for working late last night." Claire Stanley didn't have much time. The morning meeting was about to start and she ran the whole deal. Like many newsrooms, an assignment editor would tell a group sitting around a table about all of the possible stories for the day. Stanley did this knowing at any second something could happen and throw all of the plans into the trash. After she presented her list, reporters, one by one, would pitch stories they were working on. Since Booker was already assigned to two murders, he didn't attend the meeting.

Stanley hit print and the copy machine started printing up the morning list of story ideas. "Book, you're still on your murders. If one of them has a development, you go with it. Clear?"

"Clear. I'll let you know."

"Can I help?" Grandhouse walked up to them holding a cup of coffee.

"Sure. Meet me at my desk." Booker moved through the lineup of desks until he reached his cubicle. Grandhouse pulled up a chair. "I've done a social media search about Ben Olson but he went underground a couple of years ago. I found some really old postings talking about doing some PR work. There were no pictures. He just kinda dropped out of sight."

Booker turned on his computer. "Sound familiar?"

"Like Greg Tally? Yeah."

"Right now, I have absolutely no evidence to connect them. At least right now. The one terrible thought that kept crossing my mind, and again I can't prove anything, is that the murders are connected. I'll check in with the PIO in a few minutes, but I've got to see if there is a connection."

"Everything points to that."

"Sure," Booker said, "but what proof do we have? We have to do some more digging."

Grandhouse continued to work on her laptop. Booker dialed the number to the police PIO. When he reached the office for Clipper, he was told she would return in thirty minutes. Booker put that task to the side.

As best he could, Booker was trying to trace where Olson was in the hours before he was killed. If the homeowner was correct, Olson was attacked sometime around eleven p.m. A check with residents turned up no surveillance video from a door cam. Fifteen minutes later, the gathering of reporters, producers, and Claire Stanley emerged from the conference room. People moved out in all different directions, fresh with assignments on what to do and where to go. She made a swing by Booker. "We just got word the parents of two of the people who overdosed are having a news conference. Yang will be there. The parents are putting up a sixty-thousand-dollar reward for any information and arrest. They want to get the people who sold their kids the fentanyl-laced stuff. You got anything yet?"

"Not yet. Still trying to contact the PIO and I might call Olson's partner. See if the police updated her."

"Okay, Book. Right now, you don't have a photographer. If you come up with something, I'll give you someone."

"No problem." Just as she left, Booker's phone rang. "Booker Johnson." The voice on the other line was Clipper. "Understand you're looking for me."

"Yes. Just checking in to see if there is anything new coming from the detectives on either Greg Tally or the Olson murder from yesterday?"

"Well, on Tally, I can say that they're following up on some leads. And on Olson, the only thing I can tell you is I can confirm we sent one of our detectives to the Orlando area."

"Orlando? On the Olson case?"

"Yes. I can't say too much but we are checking to see if Mr. Olson traveled to locations in and around Orlando and then made it back to South Florida."

"Can you say which locations?" Booker was pulling at his notepad.

"I'm putting together a press release. There won't be much in the statement 'cause we just got there and there isn't too much to say yet anyway. But if you give me, say, thirty minutes, I can give you what I can release."

"Thanks. I'll be in touch." As soon as he put down the phone, Booker walked off to see Claire Stanley. He gave her the rundown on what he was told, returned to his desk, and started to call a station in Orlando that works with them. After talking with an assignment editor up there, Booker found out they heard about something going on at a seedy rundown motel and they had a photographer there. And that there was a South Florida connection. Video would be coming soon. Booker then went back to Stanley so she could book satellite time to pull in the video from Orlando. Then, all of the producers were told about the new development. Booker could go back to the crime scene here and do a live hit for the noon newscast. This time, he would be working with another photographer.

Junice Coffee.

Booker had worked with her many times before and he considered himself lucky. Every reporter in the building wanted to work with Junice Coffee. Always professional and always prepared, Coffee knew when to turn the camera on long before any reporter gave her the nod to do so. And she had the knack for getting the money shot.

Once sent to a bank robbery gone wrong, Coffee figured out where the two gunmen were headed after they left the bank. She followed in her car, sirens wailing in the background, a police helicopter overhead. She did not back down and kept following them. The robbers made a hard turn, crashed their car, and started running. Coffee got out and started recording. The gunmen took up cover behind a row of cars, sending shoppers and bystanders running. Coffee did not move. The police arrived, set up a line blocking any escape, and tried to convince the men to give up. They did not. For the next twenty minutes the two sides exchanged bullets. Coffee found herself down in a shallow gully photographing everything, rounds firing over her head. She was the only TV crew for blocks. When the men finally gave up, Coffee was there to get the video.

The money shot.

For her efforts, she earned an Emmy Award for Spot News Coverage. The first of three for her. She walked up to Booker and tapped him on the shoulder.

"What's up, B.J.?"

"Junice, doing fine. They brief you on what we're doing?"

"Loaded up and ready to go." She looked at Grandhouse. "And your intern?"

"Well, there's no room for her in the van. She'll drive her own car and meet us there."

"No problem. She knows where to go?"

Booker picked up his cell phone and notepad. "She was there all day yesterday."

On the way to the cow pasture, Booker made several calls. He coordinated with the assignment desk in Orlando, and got more information. Reporters were sent to two scenes, one at the motel and a second near a dump site where the police were checking a burned-out car. The word at the scene was the car was driven there by Ben Olson. Crime techs were examining for possible evidence at both locations. The second call was made to Clipper to see what she could add to what info he got from Orlando. Booker started painting a picture of what happened, although much of what he was surmising was just conjecture that he could not say on the air until everything was confirmed.

"I think Olson drove up to Orlando and made everyone think he was headed somewhere, then turned around and drove fast back down here. Now, what happened here is still a question mark but he ran into someone who put two bullets into him." Booker was talking to Coffee, who was driving.

"I've been reading up on a lot of this, B.J., and there are still some pieces missing for me."

"For everyone. It seems like they are running away from someone. But who?" When they reached the Olson murder location, the two other TV stations already had crews there. They, like Booker, would be setting up for a noon live shot. The crime tape was still in front of the Olson home, along with the police car. There was no indication Olson's partner was there, so Booker did not go in that direction. Grandhouse arrived and looked around for some shade.

This was a moment where Booker had to think way beyond the noon newscast. As soon as the noon show was over, he had to move in another direction. Go after new angles and new interviews. No reporter ever wanted to stand pat and stagnant. Booker had to come up with an afternoon plan. One thing he had in his hip pocket was the information he gathered about the so-called safe house. He knew Tally once lived there. Checking on that location was put on his mental list of things to do. There would be plenty more video from Orlando so he would work things out with Claire Stanley to get more satellite time in the afternoon to pull in the video. He needed an update on autopsy information, so that was added to his list. He did not want to bother Olson's partner, yet he was ready for a call from her. The noon newscast was twenty minutes away. Booker stood where he would be in front of the camera.

Coffee studied him. "Honey, right now, you've got raccoon eyes. I've got to light you up."

She went to the van and brought back her light kit. Coffee placed two lights on stands, both facing Booker. She turned them on. Her setup would roast a chicken. The sun was a constant reminder of how hot it was in the summer. Still, Coffee was trying to eliminate the problem, even if Booker had to suffer with more warmth. When the sun was directly overhead, a person on television could get shadows under their eyes, hence the term.

Coffee examined him again and moved the lights even closer to Booker. She literally had to light him up about as hot as the fries in a fast-food bin. He could feel the heat. Booker was ready.

On cue, on TV, when he heard the intro in his ears, Booker talked about the case sprawling out of South Florida, to the Orlando area where detectives were tracing the last steps of Ben Olson. He went on to describe somehow Olson ended up back here and his demise. When Booker was finished, there had to be a break period for Coffee. Just as she finished putting away the gear, another Channel 27 van rolled up.

Merilee Yang got out and walked up to Booker, then ushered him away from Coffee. "I need to talk to you, Book. It's important."

43

Booker could see Yang looked like a person fighting through a stressful moment. Sometimes inner feelings still come through on a person's face, no matter the effort to keep outward appearances calm. She had a look he'd never witnessed before.

"What's up?"

Yang looked over at Grandhouse and Coffee as if to make sure they were not listening. "I want to say congratulations Book. It looks like you're no longer a one-man band. That's great for you."

"I know. Thanks. I wouldn't want that on anyone. Not in this major market. For me, it was a step down. Terrible, but I got through it."

She looked down at the ground, then back at Booker. "Well, I'm about to go one step down."

"Don't tell me . . ."

"Yes. When they moved you off that slot, they told me they are still committed to a one-man band pilot program, that this was a way to promote me, at least that's the way they phrased it. Promote me and save money at the same time."

"I'm sorry to hear that. Is there anything I can do?"

"You can't do anything. I worked in small markets before. I came from a situation where I did everything. They know that. What you can do for me is give me any tips. How did you do it?"

"I wasn't in that position long. Just days."

"Still, Book, anything you tell me would be great."

"First, don't let them get you down. What you don't want to do is let that deep feeling of disappointment show up on your face. Find a way to move on, keep a good attitude."

There was a small bend of a smile starting to form on her face. "I watched you. I saw what you did. You scored a couple of exclusives, got on a big story, and they moved you off the one-man stuff. I don't know if I can match what you did."

Booker watched Coffee get into the van's driver's seat. He could tell Coffee felt uncomfortable watching him speak with Yang. Grandhouse waited by her car. Today Yang was working with Dominguez. He too was sitting in his van waiting. Booker turned to make sure all of them would see Booker's face and not Yang's somber expression. "Just keep doing what you've always done. Work hard. They will see that. Keep your vision open for an angle no one else can get and go for it. Just show them the real Yang, the one who can out-report anyone in the street. If you feed them enough, they will get the message and put you back with a photographer."

"I'm just concerned sometimes about being by myself. Working the camera myself, setting up my own live-shots, it's a lot of work. My boyfriend wants me to find another job."

Booker kept up the assurances. "Before you do that, give it a try. Please remember, no matter where you go in that van by yourself, leave yourself a way to get out. You don't want to park somewhere and find you can't leave when you want to leave. Check out the streets and always have that escape route in your head. And if it looks dangerous, go live at a very public location, like a police department."

"Thanks."

"Did it sound like this might be expanded to other reporters?"

Yang did not hesitate. "Yes. I got the feeling they want at least two more reporters to start working by themselves. And that has the photographers worried."

Booker looked over at Coffee, then back to Yang. "They won't fire anyone. But what will happen is when a photographer leaves, they won't be replaced. All of a sudden, their budget has been cut by ten percent or more. I'm sure they would love that."

For the first time since she got out of the van, Yang looked like the old Yang. "Thanks, Book. You're kind of a leader in that newsroom. I appreciate it."

"No problem. Just be Yang, strong and a damn good reporter."

She turned and walked back to the van. Booker approached Grand-house. "Okay intern, you ready for some lunch?"

Grandhouse pointed the other way. "I'm headed back to the station to look at all the video coming in from Orlando."

"Don't you eat? You're gonna waste away to nothing."

"I'll be fine," she said. "We have to fill in some blanks before the other reporters do it first."

44

Booker and Coffee sat in the outside section of a sports bar. Booker had a Caesar salad. Coffee went with a fish sandwich. Both were drinking bottled water. While Coffee watched a sports update show on one of the fifteen TVs, Booker watched a recording of the news. He wanted to see the news conference of the parents who lost loved ones to a fentanyl overdose.

There were four of them talking, with the main speaker being the mother of a college student only twenty years old. The mom told the story of how her daughter thought she was buying street marijuana with a so-called touch of something to kick it up. The mom says her daughter had no idea the so-called 'touch' was fentanyl. A couple of times she broke down, letting the tears flow, causing her voice to sound hoarse by the end of the news conference.

Then came the anger. She was angry someone would put a lethal dose of anything into something and then sell it to the public. She and the others were asking and demanding for anyone to come forward to give information on the suspects. And they were willing to pay handsomely for such a gesture.

One hundred thousand dollars.

Booker thought the dollar amount would push anyone to pick up the phone and spill information. The newser ended with the police reminding everyone about the tip line, that they had extra people on standby ready for any and all info.

Booker put down his phone. He was thinking about Demetrious and The Brick. The whole connection between what happened and his brother being at the drug house was seared on his brain. Booker needed another talk with him to confirm or dismiss his own personal suspicions. But then, he thought, do what? If Demetrious was somehow connected, would Booker do a story on him? Give the information secretly to someone else? The whole idea was weighing on him.

He pushed his salad away.

"You're not hungry?" Coffee was pushing two French fries through a small mountain of ketchup.

"I'm just thinking about something." He sat there, watching the traffic yards away.

Coffee chugged on the water. "It's weird, isn't it?"

"What?"

"My name is Coffee but I don't drink any. Hate it. I'm only into water or red wine."

They both laughed.

Coffee got serious. "Thought you were gonna mention what's happening with Yang."

"You know about that?"

"Yeah, it's all over the station. Just like when you were made one-man. It stinks. If they try and reduce the photog numbers, that would be a bad idea. You don't have a story without the pictures."

"Trust me, I know." Booker made another try at his lunch. His break time was going by fast. He made another call to the police PIO. This time Clipper was in her office.

Booker had his questions lined up in his head. "Can you tell me about Orlando?"

Clipper cut him off. "Before you go too far, we can't say much about that. Yes, we have a two-person team in the Orlando area. We are following up on some leads regarding our victim, Mr. Ben Olson. As our team is still there and we are still gathering evidence, we can't say too much on what was found or discovered. What I'm trying to do is put together a few details to give everyone tomorrow morning."

"Does the department think Olson went up there then turned around and came back to South Florida? And was his car burned up there?"

"Police and fire responded to a vehicle fire near Orlando, yes. But we are not ready yet to make any connection to Mr. Olson. And before you ask, no, there's no update on the autopsy. We might know a part of the results by tomorrow, but as you know tox reports usually take three weeks. So, it will be awhile before we know the whole picture."

"Thanks. I'll be looking for your press release." Conversation over, Booker and Coffee were ready for the afternoon. He directed Coffee to drive to the apartment where he saw Whispis Dulan. The same place where Greg Tally once stayed. Again, he was playing a Booker Johnson hunch.

While they traveled in that direction, he called Grandhouse. Just as he listened to the second ring, he stopped the conversation. A notification appeared on his phone. This was an update from Rich the Revealer, the blogger. Booker pulled up the article. Most of the article centered on the investigation up in Orlando. In several paragraphs, there was no new information, just a rehash of everything that was on the news. Booker called Grandhouse again. "Hello, Booker."

"Anything new?"

"I watched the video. I am sending you a rundown of everything I saw, including two people identified as being from South Florida. I did not see Jensen. Before the police covered it up, the photographer up there got a quick shot of the license plate. I checked it and it came back to Ben Olson. I think he was trying to make people think he was headed away, then rented a car and came back."

"Thanks for the info. Any of the other stations have anything we missed?"

"No, everyone moved on to the parents of the overdose victims. I'm sure that's going to be the lead story this afternoon."

"Thanks."

Just as Booker ended the call, Coffee had arrived at the apartment building. She looked skeptical. "So, what are we doing here?"

"Just give me a minute. If I need you, I'll send a text. Be right back."

"Sure thing."

Booker wasn't sure what he might find. He was kicking himself because he did not get a phone number for the apartment manager. She was in and looked a bit haggard when she opened the door. "Well, you showed up and my doorbell hasn't stopped ringing."

Booker stayed out in the hallway. "Police been here?"

"Police six times. Crime scene folks twice, a couple of reporters, then the police again. And now you. I've seen you on TV since you first came here. You seem to bring trouble with you. What do you want now?"

Booker brought up a picture of Ben Olson on his cell phone. "You see this guy come around? Maybe go to that one apartment where Greg Olson stayed?"

She looked hard and long at the picture. "He kinda looks familiar, but I can't swear to it. Who is he?"

"Well, he's a murder victim. To be honest, I'm just playing a hunch here. Trying to see if this guy Olson ever came here or not."

"I'm not one hundred percent positive. I have to think about it." She stepped back as if she was about to close the door, then snapped off a question at Booker. "That picture mean a ton of folks are gonna come 'round again?"

"No, I don't think so. Just me. Thanks for your time." This time Booker took down her contact information and he left a few business cards. He was off back to the van. When he sat down, Coffee was all smiles. "You remember some neighbor back where they found Olson's body?"

"There was an older guy I met. He saw something around Midnight. That guy?"

Coffee stepped on the gas. "Buckle up, we're headed there now. Not him, someone else. Assignment desk got a call. Woman says she just got back from vacation. You left your business card on the door. Says she's got some surveillance video we should see."

"Let's go."

45

Strap appeared anxious, like a man ready to unload a lot of information and he was being held back. They were in the large room at the Brick. Abrafo was off to the side, doing shoulder roll exercises. The muscles in her back stretched like bridge cables. She was standing behind a figure who was seated in a chair. The man's hands were tied behind him and he had a small cut on his cheek.

"When's he getting here." Abrafo stopped stretching. She placed her hand on the neck of the man tied down and leaned down to him. "If they don't stop me in the next few minutes, I'm going to let you know how I earned my name."

Caston walked in. He was wearing a sky-blue dress shirt with the sleeves rolled up. His hair looked like he just had a fresh cut and there was a whiff of cologne in the air. He sat down in his big chair and stared at the man in the chair. After a minute, he motioned for Strap to come to him. There was a long conversation between them that no one else could hear.

Strap turned to Abrafo and the man. "He wants to know why you stole from us?"

For a moment, the man in the chair stared ahead like what was about to happen wasn't real. He bowed his head, then looked up at them. "I wanted to be like you?"

Strap walked up closer to the man. "You worked for him, and you worked for us. We never taught you to steal. You know that."

The man in the chair was in his early thirties. Almond skin, short haircut, slender build, and not quite tall as Strap. He went by the name Brim, since he was always wearing a hat. Today the hat rested in the corner smashed flat. Strap's eyes were blazing with anger, like he wanted to crush Brim into the ground. Instead, Strap walked to the hat, popped it back into its original form, and placed the hat on Brim's lap.

"What I'd like to do is cut your throat." Strap stood so he was blocking the man's view of Caston. "You stole drugs from us. Our lifeblood that feeds this family. You stole and then you put something with it that kills. You know we don't mess with the fentanyl. Look what you did. You sold shit and now it's coming toward us. You helped kill those people and now the police will come calling for us." Strap reached down and gently patted Brim's cheek. "That's why right now, we have to keep you clean. No more talk of putting you in the ground. You have a mission. And you're going to do this for us."

"Do what?"

Abrafo reached back to slap him in the head, and only a stern look from Strap stopped her. Strap smiled. "You have a mission before you, young man. We have to keep your face clean, your body free of injury. We don't want anyone to think we forced you to do something."

"Force me to do what?" Brim tried to angle around to look at Caston. "Force me?"

"First, tell us why you gave them our stuff? We promise we won't hurt you but we have to know why."

"I wanted to branch out on my own."

Strap's voice almost sounded calm. "Yourself? With our stuff? That doesn't exactly sound like on your own. That sounds like stealing, selling, and keeping all the money for yourself." He put his hand on his gun. "We know we should kill you."

The man called Brim started to plead. "Most weeks, I'm your best earner. You know that. Sold so much, you gave me more territory. I put a lot of money into the Brick."

"Ah, but you were also busy," Strap said. "We started checking things.

You've been shaving the loads. Getting a bit extra, taking a bit more for yourself. Selling it on the side to street punks. Going against the family."

Abrafo balled up her fist. She smacked her right hand into the spread open left, making a loud hitting noise.

Strap pointed to Abrafo. "See, she wants to hit you right now. But I'm stopping her because of the mission ahead of you. Oh, young man, you've got such an important role to play." Strap got down close to Brim's face. "In terms of dollars, how much did you steal from us over time?"

"It wasn't that long." Brim looked down again. He was talking to the floor. "I've done wrong, I know that. But I stopped. I can be your best earner again."

Strap gently grabbed his chin, lifting it up until Brim was staring directly at him again. "We figured it out, Mr. Young man Brim. We figured it out. I'm not going to dignify a dollar amount to you because it's tied to death. The fentanyl did not come from us. You know that and you did it anyway, making it look like it was our product. People have come to know our brand. Our drug. And you, young man, tried to ruin all that." Strap couldn't help himself. "Dealing in death!"

"I was doing exactly what you're doing. I'm giving people what they want."

Strap let loose with a long sweeping swing of his fist and just missed Brim's face by inches. "They didn't want death, you fool." He walked around Brim's chair until he was back right in his face. "You're going to do this. You're on your own. You did this on your own. And now you're going to do this for us. You are officially cut from the Brick. We don't know you. We didn't know anything about what you were selling. And that is the message you're going to keep."

Strap nodded to Abrafo. She pulled out her knife and cut Brim loose. The chair was pushed away. He stood up. "Just remember, you're going to do this for us. You're going to do this for yourself. And just think about it. If you don't do this, you know what will happen."

46

The woman was waiting for them when Coffee pulled up at the house. Down the street, at the Olson home, a police car was still there. Booker got out and walked toward the woman. "I understand you have something you want us to see? I'm Booker Johnson, Channel 27."

"Yes, Booker. I called your station. It's the only one I watch. Please come in. I'm Catora Miller. I have it all set up for you."

Booker walked into the house. The place was adorned with photographs on the walls. A small piano was in the corner. Three cats were running around. "I just got back. It's just me. Husband died four years ago. Went to see the grandkids. But I keep in touch with the news."

Booker noticed she had a surveillance camera on the door and another one in the front yard, pointed at the street. "How many cameras do you have?"

Catora laughed. "I have seven. They're all around the place. It's just me now and I wanted some comfort and protection. No more man around the house."

Booker followed her to a desk. She had a setup of two computer monitors. On one monitor, Booker could see the live signal from all seven cameras. Three cameras facing the street, one on each side of the house, and two cameras facing the backyard. Catora's face lit up with pride. "I got another whole setup of monitors in my bedroom."

Coffee stood off to one side, then rested her camera on the rug. Catora pointed to the floor. "You can see my video but don't put me on TV. No TV, is that a promise?"

"A promise," Booker assured her. "How did you find the video?"

"I heard about poor Mr. Olson. He was always around and I would speak to him, but then he just disappeared. Hardly ever saw him, going back some two years ago."

She brought up the video and played the sequence for Booker. "The car is only on one camera. What happened is the car drove up, turned around, and went back the other way." Booker saw the car approach. The time stamp was 5:09 a.m. It was difficult to see anyone in the car.

"Just wait," Catora said. "Right about here."

On the video, the car pulled up and a man in the driver's seat stared directly at the camera for a brief moment, then something caught his attention and he looked away. Booker wasn't sure but it looked like the other man in the car had something over his face. Behind Booker, Coffee was setting up her tripod, getting the best angle to record the video.

Booker said, "Can you play that again?"

"Sure." This time Coffee was recording. Both Booker and Catora stayed out of the way of the camera. In all, Coffee videotaped the surveillance vid four times.

Booker pointed to the monitor. "Thanks for sharing this with us. Now, here's the question. Do you recognize the man in the video?"

"Oh sure. That's Ben. I'm positive."

"And the other man?"

"I have no idea. Can't even see his face. His hands are down, so you don't see much. But for sure, that looks like Ben Olson to me."

"You don't have to, but last time, you sure you don't want to say something about Ben?"

"No. I just don't want to be on that thing, that camera."

"No problem. Once this is on television, the police will be calling."

"I already called them. They're on the way. Spoke to a woman. I think her name is Brielle something."

"Jensen," Booker said. "Brielle Jensen."

"One more thing. If we don't show your address and we're not going to mention your name, can we shoot some video from your yard, pointing the camera at the street?"

"No address, that's fine."

Booker thanked her a couple more times and left a business card. Outside the home, Coffee was busy shooting as many angles as she could from the yard. Then, with Booker driving and Coffee shooting video, they photographed four minutes of video through the windshield. Coffee also put the camera on the ground in the street and got more angles. Now, it was time for a phone call to the station.

After Booker was finished explaining everything to Claire Stanley, she was impressed. "Nice job Booker. Haven't seen that video anywhere. Normally, I'd say you would be the lead story but not anymore."

"What happened?"

"Not more than ten minutes ago, some guy turned himself in to the police and said he was the one who supplied the drugs, the marijuana-fentanyl that killed four people. We have to track down all the details on him, but supposedly, on the street they called him Brim."

47

Just one other news channel had a crew where Booker was standing. Two reporters on a murder follow-up. Booker stood waiting and ready for his intro. He knew it would be several minutes into the newscast. All of the attention was on the man called Brim.

In his ear and on his TV monitor, Booker watched the news coverage of the arrest. His real name was Kevin Brum. Channel 27 had three reporters on the story. The top of the newscast showed the three reporters on screen. Then one by one, they would do a live report. The first was the arrest. Brim just walked into the police department, asked for the detective handling the overdose cases, and waited.

The reporter said Brim had seven felony arrests, mostly for dealing drugs and assault. He had one conviction, served two years in prison, and was out four years ago. He managed to get the other cases dropped. With his criminal background, and with a possible second degree or manslaughter charge, getting a lower bond might be impossible. Booker studied the mug shot. No, he had never seen him before.

The second reporter, Yang, covered reactions. She had interviews with two of the parents who were part of the news conference. A bittersweet time that maybe justice was coming, and there was the harsh reality that a loved one was still gone.

A third reporter spent his time on the drug trade and about the explosion of illegal drugs on the street. A full nine minutes devoted to the arrest. After a commercial break, they would be coming to Booker. "Two minutes," he heard in his earpiece. He looked to his left to see what looked like an unmarked police car moving down the street toward the home of the homeowner with the surveillance video. He looked back at Coffee.

When Coffee was going to be outside for a long period of time, Coffee wore her original Marlins baseball cap. When Booker heard the introduction, he spoke:

"There is a major break in the murder case of Ben Olson, who was found yesterday shot to death just outside his home. Channel 27 has learned a piece of surveillance video just might give detectives a look at the killer."

Booker waited while the station ran his pre-edited video package. Exactly one minute and twenty seconds later, they came back to Booker. He wrapped it up with another plea to call the police tip line if anyone had any information. He signed off.

Booker started to help Coffee pack up the gear. He saw the other reporter on the phone, probably trying to explain why he didn't have the same video Booker used. He's going to have a difficult time, Booker thought, because he didn't mention the name of the person who gave him the video. If the station wanted to find it that night, they would have to knock on a lot of doors and see what happened.

When Booker got back to the station, he had to write a story for the station website. Claire Stanley, on her way out the door, stopped by his desk. "Hey Booker, another good get with the videotape."

"Thanks. We still don't know much about why Olson was in Orlando. Something for tomorrow."

Stanley put down her briefcase. "Anything new on Greg Tally?"

"Not a lot. We're waiting on a few things."

"Two things. The Highway Patrol called. They've had our van since your hit-and-run. They will return it tomorrow. Said it was checked for contact evidence, the paint from the truck. They're still checking."

"Anything on the driver?"

"Not yet. And one other thing." She took out her cell phone and checked a list. "Listen, this guy they arrested, the one tied to the overdose deaths. We were trying to get a read on where he got the drugs. We're not coming up with anything. There was one wild rumor that he was connected to a drug gang called the Brick. You ever heard of them?"

"Yes. I don't know much, but yes, I've heard of them."

She put her phone away. "Brum's attorney says this guy is going to plead guilty."

"Guilty?"

"That's what I was thinking. He's looking at a long haul in prison." Claire Stanley rested her arm on the top of his filing cabinet. "There's something not right here. This guy did everything he could to stay out of prison. Everything. And now he's more than eager to plead guilty. I think he's protecting someone. We just don't know who. Listen, Book, if you hear anything about the Brick, will you let us know?"

"Sure. And if I could, I'm asking a favor."

"I'm listening."

"Yang is a great reporter. I know what I have to say doesn't mean a lot, but putting her into a one-man band situation might not be . . ."

"Before you say anything else, that ship has sailed. And she might not be the only one. The boss is not hiding it."

Booker tried to make one last point. "Then, put me back on the one-man band. Keep her working with a photographer. I was doing okay."

"Forget it, Book. You're doing just fine. We don't want to slow you down. For now, you'll stay a two-person crew. Don't worry, Yang will be okay." She started to whisper. "I'm a manager so I'm not going to confirm anything but you've been here too long. You'll probably hear a lot of rumors that we're dropping sports from the newscast. Or the newsroom is shrinking, staff-wise. Until you hear it directly from me, ignore the rumors and keep going for the stories." Stanley picked up her briefcase and turned toward the exit doors.

Grandhouse immediately took her place and stood by the filing cabinet. "I heard everything."

"You're hearing the rumors too?"

She pulled up a chair. "Not just rumors. I know the audience for local news and news in general has been shrinking for years. Budgets are tight. I get it."

"So," Booker asked, "Knowing all that, you still want to get into this business?"

"One hundred percent yes. It's all I've ever wanted. I want to be a reporter. It's that important to me."

"Okay. See you in the morning."

48

Demetrious Baker stood in the outer room of the second building at the Brick and waited. He was there more than forty minutes and no one came after his initial entry into the place. Instead of the gritty, sometimes loud shouting one heard, there was quiet. There were no clocks anywhere, still Demetrious knew it was just after seven p.m. when he got there. His paid ride didn't want to come into the parking lot and Demetrious had to walk half a block.

Abrafo met him. There were no chairs, just walls of graffiti. She looked him up and down. "Thought you were busy, with, what do they call it? Oh yeah, work. What-chu need now?" She was wearing a cutoff shirt with a pattern of tic-tac-toe puzzles. The shirt was dotted in sweat.

"I just want to see Strap."

"Strap ain't here. Time for you to be gone too."

"What happened to the three people? I just wanted to make sure they're okay."

"We don't talk about such things here. You should know that. Trust me, they won't be selling around here anymore. They're gone."

"Gone like dead? Or—"

"We set them up in another state. They can be a problem for someone else."

"And the mole?"

Abrafo's face contorted into anger. She moved in quick and started to feel all over the body of Demetrious Baker. He tried to fight her off. The woman with the ripped muscles was too strong for him. She yelled, "You wearing a wire? 'Cause if I find out you're wearing something."

He finally broke away from her. "I'm not wearing a wire! How long you know me? I just want to make sure the person who sits in that chair in there doesn't get lined up for a murder rap because of your stupidity."

"We didn't do anything like that. They're just fine. Unless they come back here. And the mole is gone."

Demetrious asked, "Who was it?"

"Brim went to the police. Gave himself up."

"You sacrificed Brim?"

"He sacrificed himself. Listen, conversation over. This is Brick business. And that does not include you."

Demetrious considered his next move. He just wanted a quick word with Caston. He could be satisfied and leave, taking Abrafo's word as truth that the three were okay. Or he could try to get past her, seek the man in the chair himself and ask him directly. More than likely, she would smash him into the concrete, even though he had a blood tie to the top man.

One last try. "Let me talk to him."

"No way." The light workout of twisting Demetrious into a knot caused more sweat pops on her shirt. She looked like she was ready for a round in the ring.

"Well, can you at least get word to him, that I want to see him. Just for a moment. I'm not going to talk business. It's personal."

"You can tell me." She let the sweat just roll down her neck.

"I'm not telling you anything. Just let him know I want to see him. Any place, any time. Is that clear?"

"Clear as blood."

Demetrious waited for a moment to see if she would change her mind or if Strap would show up. A minute passed and he turned to leave. He walked out into the courtyard. In the other buildings, life looked normal. Even through the closed windows, he could just hear the chatter of little ones in their high-pitched voices. He saw single parents cleaning up after their dinner meals. Other windows showed the light from televisions flashing off walls.

Just outside the second building, all the windows were blacked out. He couldn't see any TV reflections or parents. No baby babble. Just a stark building with no signs of life. Demetrious knew there was a lot going on. Devious things happened in the night. His plan was simple: walk a half block away and call for a ride home. Before he took a step, he heard a voice calling out to him. The voice was soft, yet very familiar. He turned in the direction of the speaker.

"I knew I could find you here."

Demetrious looked surprised. "Booker, what are you doing here?"

49

They both said little on the way to the apartment. A fast in and out for a meal to go and they were walking into the front door of the apartment complex in less than thirty minutes.

Booker wanted to get some answers now before Demetrious withdrew into his bedroom. "Okay, what were you doing at the Brick?"

Demetrious popped open his food bag. "The bigger question is what were you doing there?"

"I wasn't worried. Not even with that stupid drone over my head. They knew I was there. I was looking for you. Again, what were you doing there?'

"You don't want to know."

Booker plopped his bag of food on the arm of the chair in front of the television. "I'm trying to look out for you. I called the café and they said you had something to do. Gave you the evening off. And you weren't here. The Brick is bad for anyone who goes there."

"I guess that includes you, Booker. You shouldn't be there. You might get dirty."

Booker asked, "Did it have to do with the guy who turned himself in? He goes by the street name Brim. My guess is you know him."

"You're right. I know him. I know just about everybody in Caston's crew. Brim isn't all that bad. If what they are saying is true, then he got greedy."

Booker had a stern look on his face. "These are all direct ties to you. A million reasons why you should never step into that building again. What did Brim do?"

Demetrious stared at Booker. Glaring eyes boring into his half brother. "Is this Booker Johnson the reporter asking me? Or is it my brother who supposedly is protecting me? 'Cause if I tell you something, I don't want to see or hear about it on television."

"Fair enough. I guess I have my own ties. Forget I asked anything about Brim. The main thing is you're okay."

"Look, Booker. Here's the deal. I provided them with some information. That's it. I don't sell drugs and I don't approve of anything they are doing. That's all I'm gonna say."

For the next forty minutes, the two men ate separately. Demetrious in his room, Booker in front of the TV. He was there when the eleven p.m. news came on. He flipped around, catching the coverage of the Olson murder. The other two stations now had the home surveillance video Booker had hours earlier. He started to list what he needed to do in the morning. An email came through and yes, Clipper scheduled a news conference for ten a.m. He kept rolling over in his mind how the Tally and Olson murders were so different. Tally was a horrendous death and Olson was shot twice. One victim was killed in the park, the other was killed in front of his sometimes home. The work could be two killers. Or one man who wanted the police and everyone else to think the murders were done by multiple suspects. Definitely something to ask Clipper.

And he wanted to know where was Whispis Dulan? Was he hiding somewhere? Or did he leave? Booker also wondered about the mysterious female voice who first called him.

Still, what was tearing at Booker was Yang. He felt helpless to change the situation and find a way to keep her as a two-person unit. If the station was headed down that road and others would be doing the same as Yang, there was nothing to do about it except work even harder.

Claire Stanley sent him an email saying she wanted to keep Booker working with Coffee since she was familiar with most of what was photographed. The photography staff was a good mix of very talented people. Working with Coffee was a plus. Working with anyone was a plus. For Yang to work alone would be hard.

He was about ready to shut down everything for the night, then he looked over and saw Demetrious standing near him.

"There are some questions lingering out there about the both of us, Booker. Some things that need to be cleared up. To be honest with you, some things you should know."

"Like what?"

"Not tonight. I've been talking it over and it's time to clear up everything. There is one person who can tell you and it's not me."

"Then who is it?"

Demetrious stepped back as if to end the conversation. "Our mother will be here in two days."

50

When Booker walked in the door Friday morning, Grandhouse was already there working on things. She was up at the assignment desk making phone calls and helping gather information from the morning crews. Information Stanley passed on to everyone else in the newsroom. Booker walked past the hallway separating the newsroom from the edit booths and he smelled the strong fresh aroma of Cuban coffee. He made his way to his cubicle and sat down to check everything he could on his computer.

Again, Booker was not planning to attend the morning pitch meeting. He was already penciled in to go to the news conference. Coffee walked past and kept going, sipping from a large water bottle. She just looked at him for a second. The quick look meant she was loaded up in the van and waiting for Booker.

He was ready.

Clipper made arrangements for the crews and newspaper reporters to be outside. She had a podium all set and ready. One by one, each station put up their microphones. Each mic had a square clip attached to it, with the number of the station on the clip. They looked like tiny billboards on each one, or mic flags. Soon the podium was stacked with mic flags from South Florida and Palm Beach County sent down a crew.

Clipper approached the lineup of microphones and introduced herself.

Coffee already called the station and would be sending a live feed of the news conference to the Channel 27 website. Clipper started, "If anyone does not have the surveillance video from a homeowner, we will be providing that to you in a matter of minutes. An email is going out to news outlets showing the victim just prior to the incident at or around one a.m. We want you to pay special attention to the car. We get a side look at the vehicle and it is in a darkened situation. We don't have a make and model just yet."

Booker looked around to see if anyone from the detective unit was there. So far, no one, just Clipper. "We have finished the autopsy. Our victim, Mr. Ben Olson, was shot twice. We are still awaiting toxicology results. The main reason we called you here today is to make another plea to the public. If anyone saw or heard anything, we are urging you to call the tip line."

She paused. Booker jumped on the moment and asked the first question. "Is there any connection between the two deaths, Greg Tally and now Ben Olson?"

Clipper answered, "We have not made a connection between the two murders. As you know, there's a very different set of circumstances for each of these cases. We're not ready to make that connection just yet, if there is one."

A question from another reporter, "Is there an indication on what is the motive regarding Ben Olson or Greg Tally? Was this a robbery? Revenge of some sort?"

"All of these questions are still under investigation and right now, we are not releasing a motive in either case."

Booker raised his hand and spoke at the same time, "Can you give us any more information about Olson's trip to the Orlando area? We know detectives from here were sent north."

Clipper pushed a lock of hair back into place. "What we can release at this time is very limited but Mr. Olson did travel to a motel in the Orlando area. What he did there and how he ended up back in South Florida is part of the investigation. One more question."

"From what you know so far, in Ben Olson's case, was this the work of one person? Or can you say right now if others were involved?"

"Initially, we saw one perpetrator was involved, however, at the moment, we will go where the investigation takes us. Thank you for coming." With that, Clipper turned and left the room. Three photographers, at almost the same time, snapped cameras out of the tripod head.

Booker knew what was coming next. Decisions were being made. Producers were watching the feed come in with the news conference. If the producers and managers did not think there was enough new information, they would knock down the coverage from a full live-shot to just a twenty-second mention over video and possibly a sound bite from Clipper.

Coffee was already packed and ready. "What's the plan, Book?"

"I've got to call Claire Stanley. We'll find out."

Booker didn't have to wait long. His cell phone rang. "Yeah, it's Booker." The voice was Claire.

"We're gonna knock this down to a VO for noon. We have all the video that came in the feed. Right now, you're not in the noon. That leaves you free to get a new angle. See ya Book."

She was gone.

Booker filled in Coffee. If he didn't come up with a new angle in the afternoon, he, along with Coffee, would be subject to covering anything breaking, like a major accident or a house fire. He wanted to stop by the station and get in front of a computer.

When they pulled into the parking lot, they drove past Booker's car. There was something placed on the windshield. "Stop," he instructed Coffee.

"I'll tell you what. I'll let you out and I'll park the van. See you inside."

Booker got out and walked to his car. Someone had placed a manila envelope under the driver's side windshield wiper. He looked around and saw no one. His car was too far away for the security cameras to pick up anyone. There was something inside the envelope. He picked up the package and inspected the outside. There was no message, no name, nothing. He opened it up. Inside, there were two things. A note and a burner phone.

51

Booker took the envelope and sat in his car. The note was short and simple: Wait for a call at three p.m. Be alone at the time.

That was the whole message. Now, he had a decision to make. Should he let the station know or just make an excuse and get away. Booker made a call to Claire Stanley. He explained that he had to do something away from the station. She gave him the afternoon off.

After telling Coffee he was going to be away, Booker drove to his apartment. He brought a meatball sub sandwich with him. He read four newspapers online, he scanned the Rich the Revealer blog, he checked all emails going to Channel 27. When he walked past his wall of photographs, he stopped yet again at the picture of Misha. He wondered what she was doing now, if she found someone new. Booker snapped out of it when the burner phone rang.

It was 3:03 p.m.

Booker spoke, then listened. "I'm here."

"We need to talk. Not on the phone but in person."

"Whispis?"

"I want to be very careful here. There is something we need to do and we need your help."

"We?"

There was a long pause until Whispis continued. "There are just two of us now. There is a lot to tell you and not on the phone. We have to meet."

"First, tell me if you knew Ben Olson."

"Yes. But you have to stop asking questions. We have to sit down and meet. To do that, I need you to follow some directions, okay? Our lives are very much in danger. Greg and Ben are gone. There were four of us who broke away. Two are dead. We're trying to stay alive."

"Broke away from what?"

"Dammit Booker, stop asking questions. I told you we have to meet. Are you listening?"

"Yes. Go ahead."

"They might be watching your apartment. When we get off the phone, leave your place. I have a car waiting for you in the overload parking lot near the airport. You'll find a green beat-up Jeep Wrangler with the key on the front passenger side tire. Leave your car. You got that so far?"

"Why can't I just drive my car and meet you."

"There's a chance they put a tracker on your car. Please Booker, just do what I'm saying. Go to this location. Leave the burner phone under the front seat of your car. Get into the Jeep. You'll find another burner there. You'll get directions on where to meet us. Now, when you leave your place, make sure you are not followed. That is very important. Can you do that?"

"I can. No more questions. I'm doing what you asked. Just be careful."

"The same to you, Booker. They already came at you once when they smashed into your van. They will come again. Be careful."

Conversation over, Booker wasn't sure what he was getting into or where he might be at the end of the night. He decided to pack a very small bag with a few essentials. The one thought that kept hitting him was there was finally a connection between Greg Tally and Ben Olson. Booker also reasoned the killings could be the work of one or more persons working to eliminate the men. Before he left, he had to leave some kind of message for Demetrious, if not a warning. Booker wrote a short note to him saying he was working on a project and might not be home that night. Not to worry. He pinned the note to the extra bedroom door.

He cleaned up his sandwich mess, grabbed his bag, and left. When Booker reached the front door of the apartment building, he carefully checked the street. Everything looked like a normal day. He hustled to his car, got it started, and circled the block three times before leaving the area. There was a direct route to the overload parking lot but he didn't want to take a straight drive. Booker went through neighborhoods, back roads, backtracked, and when he got close to the lot, he waited.

Six minutes later, Booker saw the old Jeep. Before he drove next to the car, he again sat and waited. Booker wanted to make sure he was operating without anyone watching him. He drove up and parked next to the Jeep. He checked to make sure no one was inside the car. He walked around and found the keys on the top of the tire. Booker went back to his car, left the burner phone as instructed, and grabbed his overnight bag.

For another fifteen minutes he sat in the driver's seat and waited. The entire time he kept looking for someone who might have followed him.

A whirlwind of thoughts swept through Booker. He was about to contact one, maybe two people who may have committed crimes. Every move he was making took him farther away from his familiar grounds. Booker suddenly felt uncomfortable about the situation. There was also the question of whether to contact Channel 27. Right now, he was doing things without their knowledge. Booker also knew he could very well be talking with the actual killer. Maybe this was a trap. He didn't know how much time he had before the phone would ring. The time to do something was now.

Booker called the one person he could trust the most at Channel 27. "Hello, it's Booker. Is Claire there?" A minute passed. "Hey Booker, I thought I gave you the afternoon off."

"I don't have a lot of time but I want you to hear something."

"Sure, Booker. What's wrong?"

"Well, nothing is wrong yet. Here's the deal. I'm in contact with one or two people who are running from the killers of Greg Tally and Ben Olson."

"What! You need the police!"

"No police. I have to hear what this man says. His name is Whispis Dulan. I had someone on the desk do a background check on him. He claims he is running for his life, that he's been hiding out. Claire, I think he wants to talk."

"Where are you now?"

"I'm in transition. I'm working my way to meet him. If this goes through I'll need a photographer. Please, can you keep this quiet?"

"You sure about that, Booker? I have to tell the boss something." There was a long pause. "I can keep this in a tight loop. I'll tell just the boss. If this goes off, I'll send Coffee. She has to agree to go to this."

"Knowing Coffee she'll jump at the chance."

"What about the police?"

"Not yet. I'm going to text you the phone number to Brielle Jensen. She's the detective—"

"Yep. I know who she is and the fact she came to the station."

"Gotcha. Claire, I'll speak with this person. If Coffee comes, she has to take a private car. She has to put her gear in the car and meet me at some point. Also, she has to make sure she is not followed. Got that so far?"

"Do we know, in Dulan's past, has he been violent?"

"So far, no. Look for my call. I'll be calling your cell phone number. I'm not sure when this will take place. This is Friday. This might go into Saturday or Sunday."

"I'll approve the overtime. The main thing is that you and Coffee are safe. What about if you call me and leave the line open?"

"He might see or hear something and run off. No, I've got to at least give the appearance I am doing this his way. Just wait on my call."

"Okay, Booker. Be safe."

Booker sat in the car and continued to survey the area. He was looking for any car, any person that might look suspicious. He also felt better after talking with Stanley. Now the question was, what would happen next.

Three minutes later, the phone rang and Booker answered. "Yes, I'm here."

52

"Booker, there will be two of us. There is a motel off A1A and Gufston Street. The surveillance cameras don't work there. We can meet you there."

"You already know since I work in television, everywhere I go, I also go with a camera. I have to let just a few people know so I can arrange for a camera crew, one person, to meet me."

"Can they be careful?"

"Yes. I need an hour to make the call and get someone there. They will be traveling in a private car. No news van."

"Okay. Go to room 157. When you get there, knock four times."

"I can do that. Again, I need time to get my photographer there. So, you're ready to talk on camera?"

Dulan's heavy sigh came through on the phone. "We're going to lay out exactly what we did. Then, we're going to turn ourselves in to the police. But here's the thing, Booker. When we meet with the police, we want you to go with us. We want you to accompany us all the way."

"You've been thinking about this."

"For a long time. It was Greg who tried to get us to get out. Get away. We didn't listen at first. There is no place on this planet we would be safe. That's why we decided to just tell all to you and tell it again to the police."

"How do you want to do this? Your number is not coming up on this phone. You want to give me a number or you want to call me back?"

"I'll call you back. Go ahead. Make your arrangements. But if we see anything funny, it's off. Is that clear?"

"Clear."

Booker called Coffee. "Junice?"

"Booker, no matter what, just call me Coffee."

"No problem. Did Claire fill you in?"

"Yes. What kind of cloak and dagger deal are you getting me into?"

"I need your help. There is an element of danger in this. The people we'll be interviewing say they are running from the people who killed Greg Tally and Ben Olson. So, don't mention this to anyone, for now."

"Understood. How are we doing this, Booker?"

"This will be a two-person interview. You'll need your light kit. You can't take your news van, just your personal car."

"Claire mentioned that. And she said I had to make sure I was not followed."

"You okay with that?"

"Dude, if you think I'm afraid, you got the wrong person. I'm up for it. Just tell me where to meet you."

"It's that old motel just off A1A and Gufston?"

"Yep. It's three blocks from the ocean. What room?"

"157. Here's the thing. Once we do this, they also want to turn themselves in to the police. I'm not sure if that is going to be tonight, tomorrow, or what."

"Got it. I always keep a getaway bag. The station requires we have one so they can send us out of town in a heartbeat. Anything else?"

"No. Meet me out front of the place. I'm driving an old Jeep. And Coffee, please be careful."

"I got it. See you in a bit."

Booker ended the conversation and waited again for a phone call. The burner phone rang. "Booker."

"You ready?"

"I'm set. There will be just one person coming. A photographer. Again, she will be in her own car. I have to ask. Will you be going to the police today?"

"Maybe. Maybe not. Is that a problem?"

Booker was working everything out in his head. "No problem. It's just that once we speak with you, I would suggest you get to the police as soon as possible. And contact Detective Brielle Jensen."

"Jensen. Got it. We'll see you there."

Booker put the phone away and decided to drive around a bit, rather than just driving directly to the motel. He kept looking at his mirrors, down the streets to see if anyone might be following him. So far, nothing.

Friday afternoon meant the state road, A1A, would be packed with people. People from all over the world were always attracted to the beaches. The water was warm and the horizon on the ocean was the perfect background for a photograph. Rather than some isolated place where Booker and Coffee might stick out, the beachside motel might be just the perfect place for a secret meeting.

In less than twenty minutes, Booker reached the motel. He did not see Coffee. Rather than park right away, Booker circled the block. Convinced he was alone, Booker parked several spaces from the entrance of the place. Dulan was right. Booker could not find any surveillance cameras. People were walking by seemingly only concerned about the intensity of the sun. Booker got out and looked around, then decided to wait in the car for Coffee.

A Honda pulled up behind him. It was Coffee.

Booker got out and met her as she was getting out of her car. He stood by the trunk and waited. "I can help carry something."

Coffee opened the trunk and lifted a large suitcase. "I'll take this. You can get the other case. Booker pulled out another suitcase. Coffee pulled a large bag with a long strap and looped the strap over her head. "I think we got everything."

Booker walked like he was a tourist on vacation. No tie and his shirt was open at the collar. They walked to room 157. Booker knocked the required four times. He could hear movement coming from inside the room.

The door whipped open and Whispis Dulan waved them inside. They walked past him and into the room. Dulan looked out at the street as if looking to see if anyone was there. He closed the door.

"Do what you need to set up. We are ready."

Coffee looked around the room. She pulled two chairs together, separating them by one foot. There was a small area to be used for a meeting. Coffee was all business. "I'm glad we have this space. I'm trying to keep the beds out of the shot." Once she lined up the chairs, Coffee stood up her tripod.

Booker had a question for Dulan. "You say there's two of you?"

"He'll be here in a few minutes." He looked down at the faded carpet, then back at Booker. "I gave Ben your card. The last time I saw him I thought he was going to call you. When he was," he paused. "When he was killed, that's when we decided to call you and do the interview."

Booker could see Coffee wasn't sure about something. "What's wrong, Coffee?"

"Even with the door closed, there's some noise from outside. When your friend gets here, I've got to do a few things."

"Ok." Booker had a lot of questions for Dulan. The nervous man sat down in one of the chairs. He kept looking at the walls, at anything rather than Booker.

Coffee was at the curtains, pulling them to block out the sun. Then she started working on the lights. She opened the suitcase and pulled out three of them, each with a light stand. Two of the lights were in front of the chairs, slightly at an angle. The third light was turned toward the wall. Dulan watched her with fascination. He kept his eyes on her as she moved about setting things up as she had hundreds of times before.

Booker didn't want to ask a question that might cause some anxiety for Dulan, yet he had to question. "Is your friend coming soon?"

"He'll be here. He's doing some last-minute packing. When we talk to you, we'll be prepared to go to the police. Where we end up after that is anyone's guess." Dulan got up from his chair and went over to the curtain. He tried to keep his face and body away from the window, while peering out at the street and the people walking to and from the beach. He whispered, "He'll be here. I know he will."

Dulan sat back down in the chair. There were just two chairs in the room and Booker planned to sit on a standing suitcase when the questioning started. For now, he was trying to keep Dulan calm.

Booker asked, "What does your friend look like?"

"Can't miss him. He wears glasses, almost bald, dark-skinned, and always with a worried look on his face."

"Okay."

Coffee had her tripod in position. Her camera was still in the suitcase. She was looking at the arrangement of lights, probably to see if they were in the exact needed position. She asked Booker, "Sit in the second chair. I want to get the lights right."

Booker sat down next to Dulan. Both of them were looking at the motel door like someone with bad intentions might come crashing through at any second. Dulan rubbed a spot on his arm. "I'm getting a bit nervous waiting for him. He should be here."

Booker reasoned with him. "Like you said, he's got packing to do. We're fine. He'll be here."

The door swung open and blazing Florida sun temporarily blinded them. They held their hands up to block the light from their eyes. Dulan was reaching like he was searching for something to use to protect himself. A figure filled up most of the doorway and the light subsided just a bit.

A man's voice spoke. "I'm here. We can get started."

53

The man closed the door and made sure it was locked. He looked around the room, finally sitting down next to Dulan. He leaned over and asked a question. "How much did you tell them?"

"I was waiting until you got here." Dulan looked a bit more relaxed.

Booker reached out for a handshake. "I'm Booker Johnson. We're just about set up. Can I get your name?"

The man hesitated. Booker knew even basic facts can be difficult if a person was operating on the bad side of things. And for Booker, giving up a name meant moving from the obscure and hidden to the very public. "Clarence," the man said. "Clarence Coleman. My friends call me C.C."

Booker studied Coleman. He was average build, and wore glasses that he would adjust every few minutes. Coleman looked and sounded college educated. More than anything, Booker wanted to explore how all of them were convinced to do something heinous and devious with no guilty feelings, until now.

Coleman and Dulan watched Coffee. She snapped the heavy camera into position on the tripod head. Her fingers were working fast now, checking the camera. She pulled out a piece of paper and gave it to Booker, who held it up. Coffee aimed the camera at the paper.

"What's she doing?" Dulan asked.

Coffee's voice came over the top of the camera. "I'm getting a white balance. You have to use white so the camera will get the colors right. Got it. Thanks." She took the paper from Booker. Then she went to each man and made sure they had the lavalier microphone in the right position. Back behind the camera, Coffee nodded to Booker, meaning she was recording.

"Thank you both for sitting down. What is it you want to say?"

Both men looked at each other as if waiting for the other to speak first. Dulan spoke up. "I have been part of a criminal enterprise. I'm ashamed of it. I want to speak about it and then tell the police what I've done."

Booker pressed him. "What have you done, Whispis?"

"I was part of schemes and scams to convince people to remove themselves from consideration for important positions, CEO positions, anyone in the command position of a company, we would convince them through blackmail, lies, deception, and antagonizing victims so they would remove their names as candidates for that position."

Booker again. "Can you give me a specific example?"

Coleman spoke. "Recently, you interviewed a woman. Her name is Mikala Williams." He stopped for a moment, as if weighing what he was about to say. "We convinced her to not go for a CEO position."

Booker was writing notes. "How did you do that?"

"We spiked her drink at a club. Got her woozy. We knew the route she would drive and we waited. When she went down the side street, we were there. Another person pulled out in front of her and she crashed into him. We had that person all made up with fake blood and made it look like she was the cause of perhaps a fatal car crash."

"Was the fake driver Greg Tally?"

Coleman answered. "Yes. Greg was part of our group. We got her into position to answer the phone call. The call told her that she was at fault, that another DUI would mean jail for her, and convinced her to drive off and we would clean it up and protect her. For a price."

Booker looked up from his notes, "Why would you do that?"

"Greed," Dulan said. "Absolute pure greed. We were making so much money at the time, we didn't think about it. We just wanted the money."

"How much money?"

Coleman looked at Dulan then back to Booker. "We each got ten thousand dollars for that job."

"Ten thousand!" Booker exclaimed.

"Yes. I know. We finally got to the point that we were ruining people's lives and we wanted to quit. Stop all this. It was Greg Tally who convinced us we should leave the group. And then we heard about his death. We knew if word got back that we wanted out, we would be next."

"Was Ben Olson a part of the group?"

Dulan's left leg slightly bounced up and down. "Yes. Ben Olson was in on, let me think, fifteen jobs."

Coleman echoed him. "At least fifteen jobs. Probably a lot more."

"And who was directing this? Who is the top man?"

"We don't exactly know." Dulan's words were slow and plodding, like the question had bothered him for a long time. "We were recruited by word of mouth from someone on the phone. The voice, sometimes, sounded mechanical. The very first job, the first time, we got the money before we did anything. Eight thousand dollars. We just felt obligated to do what they asked."

Booker searched their faces. On his personal BS meter, to Booker, they were sounding believable. A couple of times, he would look over at Coffee, who was panning the camera from left to right and back, depending on just who was talking. "Did you ever see this person who was on the phone? Or get a name?"

Coleman was shaking his head. "No. We tried a couple of times. Toward the end, we did encounter someone. We used to have an apartment where we could meet and discuss things out of view of the public. One day we saw a shadow of a man standing outside. After that, we decided not to meet there anymore, that it wasn't safe. We just know the guy from his hands."

"His hands?"

"He was wearing black gloves."

54

Booker focused on his next question and didn't want to stray back into memories of a man with black gloves. At least, not yet. "This man with black gloves, did you see his face? Would you recognize him?"

"Not a chance," Coleman said. "He kept his hands out in front of him but he kept leaning back, then we think he went to a car."

Dulan said, "We don't have any proof but we think he's the enforcer. He might be the person responsible for the deaths of Greg and Ben."

Coleman again, "That's why we're here. To speak up for them. To let people know what we did. What we did was wrong. Very wrong. We hurt a lot of people with our lies."

Over the next thirty minutes, Booker had them detail all kinds of scams and surveillance missions to use as blackmail to convince people to give up on their dreams and take a different job. They were all high-level positions.

"Let's take a ten-minute break." Booker looked back at Coffee. She gave him a thumbs-up and shut down the camera. Coffee pulled a bottle of water from the suitcase, sat on the edge of a bed, and took a swig from the bottle. "Don't forget Booker, I need some two-shots and some three-shots."

"No problem." Booker was making a mental note of things he had to do. Coffee needed more video of them sitting there. A two-shot was two people, a three-shot was all three of them. He also needed to check out the mass amount of information he was getting. There was no way he was going to just throw on all the interviews on the air until he checked out some of the admissions. Doing that might take a couple of days. If they turned themselves in, that would speed things up as police would also be checking their claims. In his notes, Booker wrote one sentence and underlined it three times.

Man with black gloves.

Water break over, Coffee was back, standing next to the camera.

Booker was ready with the next question, directed at Dulan. "Who are you running from, and why?"

"We both firmly believe that our lives are still very much in danger. I don't think they were counting on us talking to you. And we weren't just going to let them catch up to us and become the next victim. As to who? We don't fully know ourselves."

"Again, you never met with anyone to plan these deals?"

"No. Just the crude voices on the phone and the money. The money made it real. But we think we know why Greg was killed in such a horrific manner."

"Yes," said Coleman. "We think they were trying to scare us out of our hiding places. See what happened to Greg and start moving about instead of laying low. When we made moves to leave, they found us."

Booker scratched his head, "How exactly did they contact you to do these, as you called them, jobs?"

Dulan jumped in to speak, "Through the dark web. How can I explain it, these were recall messages."

"Recall?" Booker asked.

"Yes. We saw the information on the target person. We memorized it or wrote it down. The recall message disappeared. I don't know how they did that, but we have no real email to show anyone. But once we got the message, we acted on it."

"Then," Coleman said, "Money was wired to our accounts, which were set up out of the country."

"So, in your own personal bank accounts?"

"There were no payments going to our personal accounts." Coleman was almost done. "Just the wired offshore accounts. The more jobs we did, each payment increased. We were addicted to the money."

Whispis held up a finger, "Mind you, we didn't hurt anyone. But we caught a glimpse of a name or two, people who were targets. And later we found out something happened to them. They moved away, false arrest. So others were hired to do what we were doing."

"Anyone confront you?"

"No. I last spoke with Ben Olson the day before he was murdered. And again, I gave him one of your business cards."

"Detectives told me. Reported that my card was found in his pocket. Now, even though you didn't meet with the arrangers of this, you four did meet?"

Dulan spoke first. "We were working together to pull these things off. Again, I'm certainly not proud of what we did."

Booker stared at both of them. "Did anyone threaten anyone? Either by message or by physical threat?"

"As far as I know, we did not." Coleman was animated, using his arms and hands when he was speaking. "I'm almost certain someone used our information to do what you describe. But again, I did not see that directly. I only know what I did."

"I want to mention this at this point," Booker said, "You are both saying you did things that could become felonies. Possible jail time. I want to make sure, on the record, that you're telling me these things of free will. You can walk out of here anytime you wish. You're telling me these incidents are true?"

Both answered yes. "We knew what we were doing." Dulan looked for a moment at the carpet. "We knew and we kept going until we had enough. We tried to tell them we were done. The answer we got back was we were supposed to keep going or there would be deadly consequences."

"That's when we knew," Coleman sounded angry. "We were trapped. We had no choice. We either had to keep conning people or risk being killed. I mean, someone could come through that door right now and blow us away."

Booker let the answer hang for a few seconds before another question. "Were any of your victims politicians?"

"No." Dulan was adamant. "We stayed away from them. Too much scrutiny."

Again, Coleman raised his hand and started talking. "I remember one time we put illegal drugs under the passenger seat of a guy looking to be the next southern regional director of a big company. All I know is police were called, a tip. They pulled him over and he got arrested. The guy got off because they didn't find his DNA on the drugs. But there was enough stink to move out of the running for the position. We got eight thousand each for that job."

Dulan listened, then it was his turn. "We did surveillance to get dirt on people. And when that didn't work, we invented the dirt. We did anything we could to remove that person from a position."

Booker kept the disgust for their deeds within himself. He kept firing away questions. "What was the end game here? If all those people were moved out and new people got the positions, why was it done? Who profited?"

Dulan shook his head. "We wondered that. A lot. Any time we tried to broach that subject, we were shot down."

"Gentlemen, if you wanted to reach your contacts now, could you do it? Any way to call, email, or find them?"

"We tried once or twice. Got nowhere." Coleman was getting into the habit of staring at Dulan when he spoke. "When Greg Tally made his run and tried to run off, we were all shut off. I felt they knew how to reach us. We didn't know how to reach them. We were just open targets. And again, when Ben was murdered we just wanted to speak to you and the police."

Thirty seconds of silence told Coffee the interview was over. Booker got up and stretched. He sat back down as Coffee got the camera off the tripod and moved about the room, getting video of them sitting and talking. Once that was done, she started to pack up. "Booker, I'm assuming there won't be any walking shots outside?"

"No. We can go."

Once Coffee packed up her gear, it was decided they would let her go first. Dulan looked through the curtains. "I don't see anyone."

Coffee walked out the door and went immediately to her car. She came back and got the second suitcase and left. Booker gave Dulan the key to the

Jeep. "I'll get a ride back with my photographer. At some point, I'll get my car checked for a tracker. What do you two plan to do next?"

Dulan stayed by the window, looking. "We're going to a quiet place. We're not going to tell you where. On Monday morning, we will contact you. We want you to go with us to the police station. Just be ready."

"You sure you don't want to stay in touch over the weekend?"

"Look Booker, we trust you and everything but we just want to prepare for Monday. Do you know when you'll put this on television?"

"I have to check a few things but it will be soon. I'll probably release a lot on Monday. Thanks for contacting me."

Coleman let out a deep sigh. "I just wish I could go back and change a few things. We really messed up a lot of lives."

Booker opened the door and walked to Coffee's car. He didn't want to look back. Just go, he thought. They'll be safe another seventy-two hours.

55

"So, how did it go?" Claire Stanley was waiting for Booker.

"Great so far. We've got a lot of stuff to check out."

Stanley motioned to him to follow to her office. Booker sat down, however his mind was on other things. "I'll be here this weekend," he said. "A ton of video to go through. I'll send you a detailed account of what we can put on television."

Stanley was listening so intently, she didn't even blink. "That was my first question. I want everything verified for anything we air on TV. If anything is doubtful or needs to be checked out, we don't air it."

"I'm way ahead of you on that. The one thing I know we can air is what happened to Mikala Williams. We have her interview, now we have two more. We're almost there. I do have a favor. Can I work with Coffee tomorrow morning?"

"A Saturday. That's overtime for her. Is she okay with that?"

Booker stared through the glass office wall looking for Coffee. "Yeah, she's fine with that. I have to track down Williams. If I can get her to verify something, I think we can have a piece ready for Monday."

"Fine. I'll okay the overtime. What else do you have?"

Booker detailed the many scams and cons done by Dulan and Coleman. He told her about the surveillance trips and the ploys used to steer people from certain top-level positions."

"Wow. And they're turning themselves in on Monday as well?"

"Yes. They're going to call me. We'll meet them outside the police station and we'll get video of them going in."

Stanley nodded approval. "Very good. Are you sure they won't run?"

"We have them on video confessing to misdemeanors and felonies. I don't think running will help them at this point. These guys are scared. Scared of the people they worked for. Their plan is to turn themselves in and plead for immunity from prosecution. If they can confess and testify against whomever, they are hoping they will get a light sentence or probation."

"Are you sure they're not tied to any of the murders?"

"They considered the victims, Greg Tally and Ben Olson, friends of theirs. They were part of the cons. All four of them had an agreement to get away from all this. Two of them didn't make it. Now, these two want to cooperate with the police."

"Okay. Go home Booker. Get a good meal. Be careful tomorrow."

"For sure." Booker left her office. Stanley packed up, turned out the lights, and headed for the big hallway and the exit doors.

Booker sat at his desk, making one last check to look at a few emails. A person tapped him on the shoulder. It was Yang.

"Hi Booker."

"Merilee, how are you doing? Again, if you need any help with the transition, I'm here to help you."

"I just wanted to say thank you. Thank you for everything." The smallest tear in the world formed in her left eye. "I heard what you did. You tried to get the one-man band gig back so I could stay where I am. That was very kind of you."

Embarrassed a bit, Booker was caught in the emotion of her tearing up. "What's up?"

"Today is my last day here. They agreed to let me out of my contract. I told them I just couldn't work in the setup they were planning. You probably read about the reporter in West Virginia. She was working by herself and she was hit by a car. She survived just fine. But I don't want to work these streets alone. I just can't do that."

"What do you plan to do?"

"I always have my eye on something else, just in case. I have a job lined up in Philadelphia. They are expanding their investigative unit. I'll have a producer, photographer of course, and time to work on a story."

"I'm happy for you."

Yang reached out and hugged Booker, stepped back, and was ready to leave. "Keep doing what you're doing, Booker." With that, Yang turned and walked away. Booker saw Coffee leaving an edit booth. She had transferred all of her video into the system. For Booker, it was time to go. Saturday morning would come fast.

56

Booker leaned back in his lounge chair and sat in silence. No TV or radio. No sports streaming on his cell phone. Nothing. Just quiet. He saw the note was gone and assumed Demetrious read the paper and moved on. He went through a drive-through for something to bring home, ate and sipped soda from a cup. He didn't even want any wine. Just a big sampling of quiet.

There was one thing bothering him. More than anything, he should have called his mother about Demetrious, yet he didn't. He could have called her just to say hello and he held back. The real truth was searing right into his thoughts. The truth was the last phone call to his mother was months ago. Far too long of a time for a family talk with one's mother. That last call was about the pending arrival of Demetrious. Maybe, Booker thought, he wanted to know more about what happened many years before. And now it seemed, Demetrious knew more than Booker.

The door opened and Demetrious walked In. "What is this, a morgue? You got it so dark in here, can I turn on some lights?"

"Go right ahead." Booker took another sip.

Demetrious rested a pizza box on the kitchen table. "Look Booker, we never talked about this but is it okay if I bring a lady over here?"

"Sure. I don't mind."

"Thanks. Not tonight. Maybe tomorrow."

Booker studied his half brother. "I thought you were working midnights?"

"Not anymore. Things are happening. Good things. There are two more Internet Cafes in this zip code. I brought in a few ideas and got more people to come in the place. Now, they want me to help manage the other two cafes. I got a raise. This weekend, I plan to look for a car. Nothing special. Just something to get around."

"Something the ladies will like?"

Demetrious was smiling. "Not that special, but I'll get something nice. I thought you were working late or something."

"Got it done. But I will be going in to work tomorrow."

Now it was Demetrious's turn to check out Booker. "Dude, you look a bit down. Everything alright?"

"A friend of mine resigned today. She's a good reporter. Hate to see her go." He took a sip and came up empty, just a bit of air in the straw. "But the turnover at every TV station in the country has always been high. People come, people go."

Demetrious flipped open the pizza box and lifted a gooey slice of double cheese toward his mouth. "Ya want some?"

Booker could barely understand what he was saying between the chews. "Naw, I'm good. Hey, did you call our mother? Or did she call you?"

"She called me. We talked. She'll be staying at a hotel. I can give you the information. Will text it to you. Say, you want to take her to dinner? Or have dinner here?"

"If it's okay, I'd like to have dinner here. Give us more time to go over things."

"No problem." Demetrious stacked three more slices on a plate, grabbed a bottled water, and headed for his bedroom. Booker leaned back again and closed his eyes. He was going through all the questions he could have asked Dulan and Coleman and didn't. The list was too long. Maybe he could make up for it on Monday. He got up, took one long look at Misha's photograph, and went to bed.

57

Mikala Williams agreed to meet Booker at a park. Four times in just over a minute, she kept looking over her shoulder. Not too far away, a man was sitting at a park bench watching them. Coffee was set up with the camera and stood next to her tripod, waiting.

"I hired that man. He's a private investigator. For now, when I have to meet people, he goes with me." Williams looked upset. "I got a death threat after the interview."

"Sorry to hear that. Police involved?"

"Oh yeah. Unknown caller left some stuff on my voice mail. After today, I have a new number. I'll send it to you."

Booker pulled up a folder and rested it on his lap. "Thanks for meeting with me. Any regrets about talking with me?"

"Not one. Zero. I had to say something. Can't let these fools get away with that. Had me thinking I hurt or killed someone. After I stopped feeling foolish, I knew I had to talk with you."

Booker pulled out two photographs from the folder. "I'm going to show you a couple of pictures. See if any of these men look familiar to you."

He held them up. Williams studied them like she was studying paperwork to buy a house. "This was some time ago, but yes, I recognize this face." She was pointing to a picture of Coleman. "He's the guy who told me

I could go to jail and later handed me a cell phone. Told me to talk to someone who could help me. Worst advice ever."

"And the other man?" Booker held up a picture of Dulan.

"He really looks like the second guy that night but he stayed back. Plus I was so drunk and high, it's a wonder I can remember anything."

"So, you're sure this man was there that night?"

"Him, yes. The other guy, not so sure."

"Thanks, Mikala. I can tell you I interviewed both these men."

"Interviewed them? Like in front of a camera interview?"

"Yes. Both admit to setting you up. It was a con, all meant to deprive you of a chance to move up and become CEO of that company."

"Wow. And where are these guys now?"

"More on that next week. I wanted to show you the photographs first off camera before I interviewed you. But is it okay if I ask you these same questions again, but on camera?"

"Sure."

Coffee moved her whole setup, tripod, camera, everything. She moved a few feet from the two of them. Booker had a handheld microphone. Coffee got a white balance for the camera, focused the shot, and nodded to Booker she was recording.

"Mikala, I've shown you two photographs. Do either of these men look familiar to you?"

"Yes. This one. He is the one who convinced me, and he was rather good at it. He was the one who said I was going to jail unless I did something. Then he handed me a cell phone. Had me speak to someone. It was all arranged. They convinced me to abandon my application and remain in my old job, which I did."

"If you had a chance to say something to him, what would you say?"

"I would say you need to experience the justice system. You need to pay for what you did. I really wanted that position. I was more than qualified and you robbed me of the chance to show what I could do to advance the company. And you should be sorry."

Booker thanked her for taking the time on a Saturday morning. Coffee got a bit of video of Williams walking down the path. She put the camera away and they were back at the station.

"Okay, honey, what are you doing the rest of the day?" Coffee was about to put away her camera.

"I've got a few things to do. I got a warning to check my car for a tracker. I found nothing."

"Book, just make sure you take some time to enjoy the weekend. You work hard."

"Take care, Coffee."

Booker was in the station with the weekend staff of a handful of producers. Two Saturday reporters were already on the street, covering stories. He turned toward the hallway exit and saw a young face.

Grandhouse.

"What are you doing here? I have to be here, you don't."

"Booker, I knew you'd be in. I want to learn. And the best way I can learn is to watch you up close. Anything you want me to do?"

"Yes. I'm going into the edit booth and I'm going to look at the video of all the interviews. Then, I'll be done. But there is something you could do." Booker brought up something on his computer screen. "I'm going to send you a list. This is a list of companies that Dulan and Coleman say they had people removed as potential CEO candidates. I want you to find out just who did get those positions? Who benefited? What are their names? Are they still there? If you can find it, what kind of salaries did they get, what kind of compensation packages for being hired. People reaped the reward when others were scared off. I want to know the names."

"Sure. I'm on it."

58

Sunday morning, Booker spent part of his time staring at the burner phone. Demetrious left a note saying he was with his potential new girl-friend and don't expect him back until Monday, sometime. Booker had a free day.

He read all he could on just about every topic. The apartment complex had a small gym, so Booker availed himself of the treadmill. He walked off the equivalent of seven miles and lifted light weights. Booker thought about the sit-up bench and passed. Maybe another time. He grabbed his towel and headed back upstairs. After thirty minutes in the shower, he was ready for lunch.

When he checked his phone, Booker saw he had four emails. All from Grandhouse. In the first email, she listed information on the people who moved into top positions. The resumes were impressive. His stomach was growling, he could easily go to the beach, take a walk by the beach, or pay for an airboat ride in the Florida Everglades. Instead, Booker was at his computer, studying his cell phone emails and doing work. No wonder Misha left him, he reasoned. He pushed all of it away from him, grabbed his keys, and left the apartment.

More than anything, if he had another chance with Misha, he would show her a different Booker. A Booker who would wake up on a weekend morning, head to the Florida Keys, and only stop for a fantastic restaurant with a view of the ocean. There was a reason the speed limit in the Keys was so low. Yes, driving down A1A too fast was a hazard. Yet at the same time, a trip with Misha brought back a ton of memories. The lower speed in the Keys forced you to slow down and admire the surroundings. Sunlight glistening on the water, boaters and fishing lines, a horizon all full of shades of blue. There was no rush in the Keys.

Booker snapped out of the daydream and started compiling a new list. He went online and looked up addresses and the lifestyle that came with success. Or, thought Booker, was it something else? Some of the people on the list lived in a much fancier and pricier home than their public salary indicated. Social media afforded him a trove of information. A theory was developing in his mind. For now, he would only keep it to himself. There was no proof for any of it, yet he could see a possible pattern developing. If he got the chance, he would ask Dulan and Coleman about what he was thinking.

His kitchen table was now a working station for all of the facts he was gathering. He placed a stack of photographs on one side. If he could just convince Demetrious not to mess with the paperwork, he would leave everything in place.

Booker headed to a restaurant. He tried to keep his mind on just a fish sandwich and he knew just where to go get one.

~

HIS HANDS GRIPPED the steering wheel and he lightly stepped on the gas, staying at least four cars behind Booker Johnson. He didn't like taking off the black gloves, not even to drive a car. He was tired after spending the night watching Johnson's window. The gun was kept next to him, pushed down in the narrow space between the seat and the console. A suppressor was attached. The man with the black gloves was upset with himself. He was supposed to kill the last two fuck-ups who left the group. All he had to do was follow and kill. Simple.

A right turn off the main street. Black gloves could easily pull up to Johnson's car, lower the window, and squeeze off a few rounds. He had to make new arrangements since he lost track of Johnson. His best guess was that Williams met with them somewhere, but the man got blocked in by traffic and lost him. The man at the wheel guessed Johnson was meeting with the two who left. He missed his chance. All the work to track them was lost. He lost them again. When Johnson stopped and parked, he stayed back and watched. No matter what, he would not lose Booker Johnson again.

59

Booker got into the station before six a.m. The staff knew he was working a special detail so no one questioned him on what he was doing. Coffee was not far behind. She had the van geared up and ready. No suitcases today. They would be out in the open and not hiding anything.

Still nothing from the burner phone.

Twenty-two minutes later, the phone rang. "Booker here."

"We're ready," Dulan said.

"How do you want to do this?"

Dulan's instructions were straightforward. "We're going to park as close to the police station as possible. We'll get out and leave the thing. Our walk-in will be quick. We planned it that way so we're not in someone's crosshairs too long. Once we're inside, they'll probably take us to two separate rooms, do the questioning, and then we'll go from there."

"Give us a few minutes to get there and set up." All Booker had to do was look at Coffee. Both of them started walking to the van. "You'll see me out there. Watch yourself."

"You too." Dulan was done.

Booker took out his car keys and placed them on the counter near the assignment desk. A hand reached out and took the keys.

THE MAN WATCHING the Channel 27 news building was parked far enough away to not be noticed. He watched a man walk to Booker's car. The figure couldn't see Booker's face but he had the same blue sport coat he was seen wearing outside the apartment. He watched as Booker opened the door, took out something from the car, closed it up, and went back inside the TV station. Fourteen minutes later, a Channel 27 van rolled out from the back parking lot. The van stopped, Booker climbed to the passenger side, and the van left. The sun was still twenty minutes from rising and things were still a bit dark. The man behind the wheel followed the van, staying at least four to six cars behind. The van got on the I-95 Expressway and headed north. The figure with the black gloves grew excited. The van would take him directly to the two hiding targets. Once he found out where the van ended up, he would take out all of them. They kept traveling. Black gloves slowed down just a bit to make sure he was not detected.

THE RIDE to the main police station was around fourteen minutes away. Coffee kept moving her eyes from the road to the rearview mirror. After several eye movements, Booker had to ask, "You see anything?"

"Naw. I'm just a bit jumpy."

They found a parking space and got out. Coffee was a whirl of movement, unlocking the camera, getting everything ready. Booker took the wireless microphone with the Channel 27 logo. He knew once they set up outside the station, inside, people would be wondering why they were there. Tongues might start wagging. A passerby might even pick up the phone and call a rival TV station and ask what was happening. Booker didn't want any more reporters showing up. They stood outside, waited, and watched for any sign of the arriving two men.

They were also looking for anyone who should not be there. Presumably, thought Booker, a police station should be the safest place around. Without an idea of which way Dulan and Coleman would be coming from, all eyes were on the sidewalk, going in all directions leading up to the front door. Inside the building, more and more office lights were coming on.

Twice they spotted a car parking and it was not the men in question. Another time, Booker was certain someone was watching him. On a second and third look, he found no one.

Coffee noticed Booker pacing up and back on the sidewalk. "You a bit nervous?"

"Trying not to show it," Booker told her.

She regripped the heavy camera. "You think this will work?"

"If it doesn't, the station will be here covering our deaths. You still up for this?"

"You bet. I'm not afraid."

Four minutes later, a car parked. Whispis Dulan got out, easing himself from the driver's side seat. Coleman came next. Both men looked like they didn't sleep at all. Coffee was already moving in their direction. It was Booker who had to catch up to her.

Booker got prepared for what reporters called the walk-back. Coffee was recording in the camera. She was moving backward the entire time. She had to keep the camera focused, make sure both men were in the frame and at the right exposure setting. It was on Booker to watch her back. If she was headed for a curb and a possible fall, Booker had to make sure that didn't happen. If she moved toward a fire hydrant, Booker had to gently grab her top and pull her away. After several yards, Booker felt comfortable the sidewalk ahead was clear enough for a couple of questions. He extended the microphone to Dulan. "Any thoughts about changing your mind?"

"Not at all. We have to make things right. We're going to do this."

Booker paused to make sure Coffee was moving without anything in the way. "Your victims, was this just centered in South Florida or were there victims in other states?"

Both men kept walking. They looked elsewhere but not at Booker. The question made both of them shut down. He asked again, "If we check, were there victims in, say, Georgia or nearby states? What about across the country? How big and how far did this go?"

Dulan's lips smashed into a flat line. Coleman looked down at the pavement. Finally, it was Dulan who uttered just a few words. "We were called into that late. This is the last thing I'll say. Apex."

And with that, they sped up their walk to the front door of the police department. In Booker's peripheral vision, he was seeing two, maybe three bodies. He did not and could not pay attention to the incoming objects because he had to watch out for Coffee and be ready for anything else coming from the duo about to walk inside.

Booker heard a clash of noise and saw a microphone hit the ground. Next to the microphone was a prone reporter. Clendon Davis, his rival from another station. Davis and his photographer were now next to Coffee and recording the men. Davis got up and joined the moving pile of bodies. Dulan and Coleman entered the building and walked up to the officers inside. They were directed to the metal detectors. Luckily the front doors were glass. Coffee kept recording. On the far side of the lobby, Booker saw Brielle Jensen. She greeted both men and they were quickly ushered out of view.

Coffee, for a moment, turned off the camera.

Davis approached Booker. He was out of breath. There were sidewalk scratches on his right hand. "Whatcha working, Booker?"

Booker Johnson stayed quiet. Coffee was now getting video of the outside of the police department. The building, the doors, the sign just above. She was almost done.

Booker turned to Davis. "You okay? That was a bad fall."

Davis ignored the question. "The PIO didn't know anything about this. Clipper said she would get back to me. What are you working Booker?"

"In due time, Davis. In due time." Booker wasn't trying to be coy or smart, just silent.

Something else caught Booker's attention. A man moving on the other side of the street. The man looked like he was late for something. Booker tried to get identification on the figure. The man stopped, appeared to see Booker, and turned around. He was leaving.

"Coffee," Booker shouted. "The man across the street."

Coffee wheeled around, tilted up her camera, and was recording in under two seconds. She was trying to get a focus on anyone moving or running on the other side of the street. "He's gone," Coffee said. "I'll have to check later to see if I got anything."

Davis looked utterly lost. "Well, I'm not moving until I learn more."

Booker whispered to Coffee. "If it was someone who wanted to hurt us, shooting at a police station might not be the best idea in the world. I have to call Claire."

Coffee looked like she needed a big sip from her water bottle. "Working with you, Book, is never dull."

Booker took out his cell phone and called a number. When the voice came on, Booker posed his question. "Did it work?"

"Hello. For a good four miles or so. It was great being the fake Booker Johnson. I went to your car like you told me, rummaged around, and got into the news van. Some guy followed us almost to the Palm Beach county line. Then all of a sudden he sped up and got off the Expressway."

Booker said, "It worked. He thought he was following me. Did you need to call the police?"

"No. We used Coffee's van and everything like you set up. He must have bought it. He thought I was you. Once he figured out he was following the wrong van, he took off. And did you get what you needed?"

"Yes. It was good. Thanks for coming in early and posing as me."

"No problem, Booker. Anything to help out. Take care."

Booker went over to Coffee. "There was someone following the other van. Guy thought it was us." Before he called Claire Stanley to give her an update, Booker went to the van and brought Coffee some water. They would be planted in front of the police building for the next few hours, just in case Dulan and Coleman came back out.

Booker called on his phone. "Morning, Claire."

"How did it go?"

"Good so far. We got a bit more information and a short interview. I have all the video I need with us. We can put together a package for the noon."

"Okay, good. I'll let them know. Unless something happens, you'll probably be the lead. Are we exclusive on the walk-in?"

"No, Davis got here at the last minute. But the interview is exclusive. I'll talk to you later."

Conversation ended. Coffee gave the van keys to Booker. When a parking space closer to the building became available, he would move the van. By 9:20, the third station arrived with a camera crew. Now everyone was there. Booker sat in the van and started writing. Coffee found a piece of shade under a tree and kept watching the front door of the station, just in case they came out. Claire Stanley indicated another crew would be on the way to help watch the door.

Booker kept thinking about the man across the street. He would worry about that later. For now, he and Coffee had work to do getting everything ready for the noon newscast.

And, he had a new word to fixate on.

Apex.

60

An hour after Dulan and Coleman went into the building, Clipper came outside. She had that look on her face, like she was suppressing anger. And all of it aimed at Booker. She kept a stern appearance as she approached a semicircle of reporters. "Morning all. I don't have a lot to say for the moment."

"You planning a news conference?" The question came from Davis.

"Not at this time."

Davis followed up. "Then what can you tell us?"

Three cameras and two newspaper photographers all aimed at the face of Clipper. "I can tell you that two men have turned themselves in to the police. At this hour, they are being questioned. What happens next depends on what they tell us."

From a newsprint reporter, "Are they confessing? And what are they confessing to?"

"As you can imagine, this is a fluid situation. And anything they say will be part of an investigation. Until such time that I have some direction, I can't say anymore. Thank you." And with that, Clipper turned around and walked back inside. A few minutes later, his cell rang. "Booker here."

"It's not often I call a reporter. Let me change that to never call a reporter." Clipper's voice made Booker walk away from the throng.

"Hello."

"Okay, Booker, I know you have some things working but I don't like to be caught blindsided. I got filled in but I still can't say anything. Your story runs at noon?"

"Yes. Just know the two men in there are scared. They told me a lot on camera. Now, they're in your hands."

Booker could just about hear Clipper patting her foot. "I can't comment on anything but we'll see how the day goes. I'm getting hounded by the other reporters."

"When you're ready to tell us something, we'll be out there."

"I'll be watching your story."

Booker went back to the van to write his story. Most of the package was already written and he just needed to top the story with the new video of the two men going into the station. A second photographer from Channel 27 showed up. Drewhill pulled out his camera and he stood next to the other photogs waiting outside the front door. No second reporter, just Drewhill. Booker got a text saying a third crew was headed to the jail. If they are booked and if the bond wasn't too high, they could get out. Someone was by the jail door just in case.

Booker could sense the other reporters were doing whatever they could to find out details about the story. And that Booker had something no one else did.

A two-minute, fifteen-second video package was sent by microwave back to the Channel 27 feedroom. Booker stood in front of Coffee's hot lights and the brilliant sunny day and got ready for the intro from the noon anchors.

He heard, "Here's Booker Johnson with the story."

"There is another major break in the murder of Greg Tally. Channel 27 interviewed two men who say they worked with Greg Tally in a for-hire deal that had the men scamming, blackmailing, and tricking people into not applying for major positions. We're talking about CEO positions in several companies. We'll let you hear what they did in their own words. These men told me their story, then they turned themselves in to the police early this morning."

On television, viewers saw the lengthy story put together by Booker. He did have to read his script to an executive producer just to double-check and make sure everything Booker was about to say and show was backed by facts. The package included the information and sound clips about Mikala Williams. There was also an interview with her reacting to what Booker found out.

Booker tagged out live. "Once the men are interviewed by the police, we'll know if they are being charged. As far as we know, both Dulan and Coleman had clean records before all this and were never arrested in the past. For Channel 27, I'm Booker Johnson."

When Booker heard the word clear in his earpiece, he headed to the van for a bottle of water. Now, everyone in South Florida knew what he was working on. The other reporters were on their cell phones, presumably talking to Clipper to confirm any of what Booker reported. She would be swarmed by calls all afternoon.

"You think they'll let us get lunch?" Coffee was putting her camera away.

"I'll tell you what. I'll work with Drewhill. You go get some lunch."

"Fine, but what about you, Booker?"

"If I can get a bathroom break, I'll be fine. I have to stick it out."

"Okay. You sure?"

"I had the edge at noon. Over the next few hours, all these reporters will be working to figure out an edge that I don't have. Something new. Just because I have the edge now, I could lose it later today."

Coffee was just about done putting away the stand lights. "You want me to bring you something?"

"Anything from a drive-through will be fine."

"See you in an hour or so." Coffee got into the van and drove off. Booker took up a position next to Drewhill. "Okay, Booker, you think these guys are coming out that door?"

"I really doubt it. One, if they charge them, they'll come out the jail door. If they get immunity, who knows where they'll be. I just know they'll be in the court system."

"So, we stay here?"

"For now, yes."

61

Booker and the other reporters got word late in the afternoon, the men would be charged with seven counts of fraud, based on the facts presented to the police. Two of the charges were misdemeanors, the rest were felonies. Clipper said she was not doing a news conference but she would answer individual reporters if they called her. The information also meant the men would not be coming out the front of the police station, but instead, they would be leaving from the jail.

When Booker got to the jail, Dominguez was already in position. Drewhill was sent to another assignment. Coffee and Booker would stay with Dominguez at the jail door. Booker called the jail reception number and was told their bond was set at twenty thousand dollars. Under Florida law, they had to post ten percent of that amount. The group of reporters had moved from in front of the police department to the jail. They knew Booker already had a sizable amount of information and interviews from watching his story at noon. For other reporters, this was their one chance to try and catch up to Booker. They camped out and waited for the two to come outside and maybe, if they could, get an interview and recoup some of the story.

Coffee stayed in the van and prepared stories for the five and six p.m. newscasts. Dominguez would stay by the jail. If needed, Coffee could always back him up. Booker still never worked out in his mind just what Apex meant. There was nothing in the interviews that suggested what type of crime was being planned or already happened.

Dominguez called Booker. "Hey Booker, I'm hearing one or both of them might be coming out in ten minutes."

"I'll be right there."

Booker had time to quickly eat a burger and do some writing before he went back out into the sun. The estimate was off by thirty minutes. Whispis Dulan came out first. He did not drop his head or run, like most who leave the jail and try to avoid the cameras. Dulan held his head up and almost marched out, saying nothing. Booker did not toss any questions his way. The reporters would be able to get copies of the arrest affidavit and facts about the charges. Still, they really wanted a comment. They got nothing. A car pulled up and the door opened. The car was driven by the wife of Ben Olson. She must have received a phone call. Dulan jumped in, the door closed, and the car left the parking lot. One gone. One to go.

Next, word came Coleman would be released in the next five minutes. He came out and, much like Dulan, he kept his head up and didn't say anything to reporters. Ben Olson's wife was back. Dulan was no longer in the car. She probably dropped him off somewhere. When Coleman got into the car, the cameras swarmed around it like bees on a new flower.

Booker was surprised by something.

Coleman motioned for Booker to get inside the car. The other reporters were a bit shocked as Booker, without a photographer, climbed into the back seat. Coleman was in the front next to Olson's wife.

He turned to Booker. "I just want to thank you for letting us tell our story."

"Are you getting immunity?"

"Not yet. They say they had to charge us first. Check out what we're saying. They don't want to be too quick to hand out something as important as immunity. We'll be in touch. But we have to get an attorney."

Booker started to get out. Photographers were still camped outside shooting video of Coleman. Booker turned back to him to ask one more question. "You said you guys set people up by stashing drugs on them."

"Man, Booker that was a long time ago."

"I know, but one thing. Back then, where did you get the drugs?"

Booker had his hand on the door and was about to get out. Coleman didn't answer the question until Booker moved away from the door and waited for a response.

"Where we always got drugs back then. From what I remember, there was a strong connection to the people who hired us and the dealers. The drugs came to us and we put them where they directed. But I know where they got their drugs. I know because a few times I had to go pick it up. It's a place you've probably never been to and won't want to go back. It's a real dump."

Booker asked, "You recall the name or location or the people that sold the drugs?"

"Yeah, we got our stuff from some apartment dump called the Brick."

62

Booker had new information for the newscasts. In the five p.m. and the six, he reported the men needed an attorney, that a request was made for immunity from prosecution in exchange for testimony. The men spilled everything they knew, all the scams they ran. For any state attorney's office, Whispis and Coleman represented a gift-wrapped investigation. The problem was going after the people above them. And where were they now?

When Coffee drove into the station parking lot, most of the dayside staff were gone for the day. Booker walked into the newsroom and found Claire Stanley still there, working. "So, Booker, the decoy worked?"

"I think so. We found somebody lurking in front of the police department, but that's about it." Booker found his sport coat hanging on the chair by his desk.

Stanley handed him a note. "A woman called for you. She insisted on speaking with you. Now, check this out. She claims some guy broke into her house, and by force and the threat of death, he made her pull away from a plumb CEO position. The thing scared her so much, she and her daughter moved two states away."

"And now?"

"Your story got picked up by the network. It's online. A lot of people saw it. She says she saw your report and she is no longer afraid to talk. She saw

Williams come forward, Whispis and Coleman do the same. She's ready to speak."

"Thanks. I'll call her tonight."

"Great. Woman says she will fly tomorrow. That's how serious she is about moving on this."

"Got it."

Booker dialed the number and waited. A woman answered. "Hello."

"This is Booker Johnson with Channel 27. You called?"

"Yes, I did. My name is Janet Kemper. I came home to find a man in my daughter's bedroom, holding a knife to her throat. He was going to kill her and both of us unless I withdrew my name from the CEO spot. I complied. I was so scared, Mr. Johnson, I left town. I never told anyone about this until I spoke with someone on your assignment desk this afternoon."

"Are you willing to speak about this on camera?"

"Yes, Mr. Johnson."

"You can call me Booker."

"Okay, Booker. Yes, I want to speak. I'll talk to you, to the prosecutor, whatever. When I saw that brave Mikala Williams come forward and it was the very same situation, I knew I had to step forward and say something."

"I'll be in the office early again tomorrow. Let me give you my cell phone number." Booker gave her cell phone information and email address. She already booked a flight and was arriving late in the morning. Booker planned to speak with her in the afternoon. He thanked her and ended the conversation.

The night assignment editor yelled out to Booker. "Book! C'mere. Need to speak with you." The voice of Kamden Starling boomed across the large room. When Booker approached, Starling stood up. His massive size and six-five height made him look like a defensive end for the Dolphins.

"What's up, Kam?"

"I don't know, Book. We got three more calls from people who said they were set up and ripped off by these guys. One described a scam but it sounded like some others in the group were involved. You opened the floodgates."

Booker took the paperwork with the names. "Thanks. I've got a lot of work tomorrow. Listen, did anyone mention anything called Apex?"

"Apex? No. I'll tuck it away though. If I hear anything in connection to your cases, I'll let you know."

"Thanks." Booker had more than enough material and leads for a follow-up. What bothered him was the obvious. A clear connection to the Brick. For now, he kept the information to himself. Booker reasoned it wouldn't be long before the police made the same connection.

As a precaution, he circled the block a few times, looking for a car in the shadows. Finding no one there, Booker made his way to the apartment.

When he opened the door, a voice said, "Hello, Booker."

"Hello, Mom."

63

Her voice brought up all kinds of memories for Booker. Mostly good. He thought about the day she bought him skates and he absolutely hated them. For twenty minutes he protested the gift. Then the eight-year-old Booker tried them on. He was still skating when the street lights came on and it was time to come inside.

She speed-walked to him and kissed his left cheek, then immediately started rubbing the lipstick smudges from his face. Then came a hard hug. She stepped back and studied him. "Love you, Booker."

"Can I get you anything?" Booker wasn't sure whether to order something or look in the kitchen.

"No. Demetrious got me something earlier. You had a busy day."

"Just another day in the office. Thanks for flying out here."

Her brown eyes almost seemed golden in the light of the living room. Demetrious had pulled a chair away from the kitchen and set it up for her in the living room. Booker was pleased to see her. "How was your flight?"

"Fine. California won't miss me for a few days. I came out here, back to Florida, because I wanted to thank you."

"Me? I didn't do anything."

"Sure you did. You gave Demetrious a place to stay, made sure he was okay. That means a lot to me."

Demetrious sipped on a soda and for some reason stayed in the kitchen with the lights turned off. Booker motioned to his big chair. "You want to sit here? Take my chair."

"No, I'm fine. I'd rather sit upright than sink back in a chair." She had a few more wrinkles lining her face than the last time he saw her in person. The streaks of gray hair far outnumbered the black strands. A lot more gray now. She pointed to the chair. "Sit there, if you want."

Booker instead went to the kitchen and pulled out another chair. He sat it close to her.

Pia Monroe Johnson sat in the small kitchen chair and looked around the room as if checking for all the things a mom checked. She wore a blue dress with a white collar. Her left arm was ringed with bracelets. Whenever she spoke or moved her hands, the gold bands clanged together. Her eyes bounced back and forth like she couldn't believe they were both in the same room.

"I hope you don't mind if I just get right down to why I came."

"Sure, that's fine." Booker leaned her way.

"I sent Demetrious here to live with you on purpose. I wanted you two to get to know each other. As far as I know, you've never seen him before he arrived."

Booker nodded.

"You're both grown and time has a way of marching too fast unless you slow it down." She turned and stared at Demetrious. "The other reason I'm here, Booker, is to explain about what happened. Things you don't know."

"You don't have to, Mom. You don't have to explain anything."

"I do, Booker. There is a narrative out there, I think from Demetrious, that I was cheating on my husband, your father. Demetrious likes to tell that story. Well, to be honest, it's just not true. The truth is I was divorcing your father, Booker. It was broken, whatever you want to call it. There was no cheating because there was no marriage anymore. In fact, he even signed the paperwork. He moved on and I was a single mom."

She stood up for a moment. Stretched her legs. Booker was about to ask her if she wanted anything and got the look from her that she was fine. "I met Roland in a weak moment in my life. I thought he was dashing, the very thing I needed. But as it turned out, he was a nightmare. The only thing that I cherish from our time together is sitting in the kitchen. I am here with the two most important things in my life. You two. Back then, I found out the hard truth about Roland."

She sat back down again. Her right hand smoothed down a crumpled part of her dress. There was a silence. Again, Booker fought off the urge to take over the moment. He stayed quiet.

"I love both you boys. I mean men. You're both grown. Booker stayed with me and when I got pregnant with Demetrious, I found out I had cancer. I knew I couldn't take care of both of you. Roland stepped in and proposed something. He wanted to raise Demetrious. I let him. I didn't want to do that but I did. And then the bills came. The cancer in my throat required time and money. But I got treatment, had two operations, got better, and fought off cancer. Been cancer-free for years now."

Demetrious picked up the soda can and started tapping it on the kitchen table. "Tell the whole story, Mom. I was sent to boarding schools. Roland didn't have time for me. But he said he would help out."

Booker was confused. "Help out?"

She cleared her throat and she roared. "Roland Caston paid my bills with drug money! That's how he was helping out."

Booker blinked a few times. "Sorry, Mom."

"You're sorry? I was helpless. I had to get the collectors off my back. He knew that. I also learned what he did for a living. I found out later. I couldn't stand the man, but it was too late. I owed him."

Demetrious tapped the can again. "I paid her debt."

"You paid him back?" Booker aimed his question directly at Demetrious.

"I can't explain what I did, but I did some favors. The debt is cleared. Trust me, you don't want to know."

"Booker, I'm hearing stories you're trying to talk to Roland. And Demetrious is doing things. I'm here to tell you both to leave that man alone. He is danger. Pure danger. And I don't want either of you getting hurt." She was pounding her right fist into the palm of her left hand. The clang of her bracelets echoed in the two-bedroom apartment.

Booker gave in. "I promise. I'll try to stay away from him."

"Please do. Nothing good will be there. Anything that comes close to him dies or gets hurt. If anything happens to one of you, I'll go after Roland myself."

Booker could see she was getting tired from telling the story. Her face was drawn and the anger deepened the wrinkles in her face. He knew she had a hotel room, yet he wanted to make an offer. "Mom, you can stay here tonight. I cleaned up everything, new sheets. My bedroom is yours, if you want it."

Pia Monroe Johnson smiled a mother's smile. "I'd like that, Booker, if you don't mind putting up with me for a couple of days."

"No problem. Just let me know what you want for breakfast. We'll make sure you get it."

She disappeared into the bedroom. Demetrious chuckled.

"What?" Booker asked.

"She already put her suitcase in your bedroom when she got here."

"Ah, gotcha."

Demetrious placed the metal soda can into the garbage bin rather than the usual loud toss. Booker brought his voice down to a whisper. "Are you still in contact with Roland?"

"Why?"

"I need to talk to him about something."

"You're kidding, right? You just told Mom you'd stay away from him. Now, you want to go see him. You better listen to what she said."

"This is important. You have to get me in to see him. I have to know something before the police come knocking on his door."

64

Tuesday, Booker was up at five a.m. He slept on the couch, showered in the guest bathroom, quietly gathered clothes from his bedroom, and went out to get breakfast. Demetrious left a note on the coffee table that he was taking the day off and would show Pia around, take her where she wanted to go. Booker had breakfast with her and took off for the office.

He got to his cubicle by 8:20 a.m. For the next twenty minutes he read all local newspapers, national news online, read the blog of Rich the Revealer, and had time to fill in Claire Stanley. The blog detailed the arrests of Dulan and Coleman. And the blogger mentioned cases the men were involved in. Booker took note of the blogger's comments and wrote down some information.

Booker already knew Janet Kemper was flying in and would be an afternoon interview. He went through the things he needed to do. First, he called the police PIO to make sure there were no new developments in any of his cases. Once Clipper confirmed everything was the same, he moved on to the list of people who called the night before.

He was taking notes on paper and worked with his computer. One person had a man walk out in front of him while driving a side street. The move was an old fake injury trick of getting hit by a car on purpose and then making a ton of medical bills and a possible lawsuit. In this man's case, he got a call to withdraw from being president of a middle-level company. He withdrew and swore the men he saw on television were involved. The man on the phone wanted to talk. Booker took down the information.

Booker spoke with three people, all of them were in denial before, obeyed the demand to stay quiet. He lined up one more interview to do after his meeting with Kemper. If nothing else happened, he would have two new interviews to keep the story going.

Grandhouse walked in and pulled up a chair next to Booker. "I just emailed you the list of people who took the positions of people who were made to move off. It was very interesting. Can I?"

Booker nodded yes and Grandhouse took over, moving to his computer and bringing up websites. "Something's not right," she started. "See, look at this." She pointed to a photograph of a home. "This is the old home of the man who took the position that Mikala Williams was going to take. I tracked it." She tapped the keyboard. New website. "Now, look at this home." On the screen was a much larger home, pool, gigantic backyard. "This is the new place. Worth about 2.6 million dollars. I got a fix on his income but this is a major step up."

Booker studied the website. "Maybe his new salary paid for this."

"Okay. Check this out." Grandhouse was at it again, bringing up more social media. "This is him. He's very open about his two new cars. A Lambo and a convertible Audi. The cars are beautiful and expensive."

"Thanks. Maybe he got a big raise."

She shook her head. "The company had to lay off one-third of its staff. I guess sales were off."

Booker took over the computer. "Let me check something." He noted the company was not privately held and stock was available. He did a stock check and found the company stock was down. Way down. Booker also did a stock history to find out just when the stock took a nosedive. "Interesting." He was busy writing down notes. "You have time to check any other companies?"

"No. Just that one."

"Thanks, intern. I won't be going out till later. You might want to hook up with a crew leaving this morning."

"No problem. See ya later."

Grandhouse took off. For the next two hours, Booker checked the names she found. He had to recheck them anyway. Grandhouse always did a good job, however, he had to check all of her information himself to make sure it was accurate. Booker looked up three people and the companies they were working for now. All three were hired after the other candidates were scared off. In all of the cases, the new hires did well. So well, they were able to move up and into jumbo homes and expensive lifestyles, all of which was found in social media.

Then Booker checked the stock prices of those same companies. Stock prices were stable for years, then the stock history line looked like a roller coaster ride. A general look at the stock prices gave Booker some direction on a theory but he needed more proof. What he had now was too speculative. The noon newscast was a few minutes off. He was told he would have Coffee for the afternoon interviews. There was one hour free.

Rather than taking a lunch, Booker called Demetrious. "How is she doing?"

"Mom? She's doing fine. She's not here right now. She rented a car and took off to get her nails done."

"Gotcha. What if I come by and we head to the Brick?"

"Booker, I'm trying to get you to stay away from that place. It's no good."

"I'll be there in ten minutes."

BOOKER WAITED for Demetrious to come downstairs. When he got into the car, Demetrious had a small confession. "The last time I was there, they wouldn't let me see him. I don't know how this is going to go."

"If I can ask, why did you need to see him?" Booker hit the gas pedal and picked up speed.

"I couldn't tell you before. Those people who overdosed? They all were using drugs that could be linked to Roland."

Booker pulled hard on the steering wheel. "What? Was he involved?"

"Technically, no. Someone was siphoning off some of his stash. Just street weed. But the stuff was stepped on with fentanyl. Too much of it. The result was four people dead. Directly, Roland had nothing to do with it. A guy in his crew stole the drugs and sold it to three people who made it deadly. I wanted to make sure none of that blew back on Roland."

"And?"

"He's okay. And then that guy turned himself in."

"You don't think that man won't turn and still blame Roland."

"He won't talk."

"I have to ask Demetrious. I don't know anything about Roland Caston except what I read online. Are you close to him? You're blood."

"I hardly knew him growing up. I think he wanted to keep me from the drugs. He's very private. I have never seen him use a cell phone. Not ever. He doesn't speak and only talks to Strap. He keeps himself so isolated. That's why he's never been to prison."

Booker made a turn, headed for the Brick. "You sure about the guy who took the blame on the fentanyl?"

"I'm pretty sure. All I can tell you is mom's debt has been paid. Booker, we really don't need to speak to him. Let's just turn around."

"I can't. He might have some vital information."

Demetrious looked concerned. "I know he does bad things, but I felt I had to protect him. It's not easy. Roland keeps all drugs away from the Brick. No drugs in or out. From what I gather, it's all collected and processed at locations around the county. So the police can come all they want. They won't find anything in the Brick."

"I'm not talking about drugs. This is something else."

"If it's not drugs, I'll wait to see what you have to say."

Booker pulled up on the street, avoiding the main parking lot. In Booker's reasoning, he didn't want a car blocking a quick exit from the place. He felt that could happen if he put his car in the lot. Before them was the middle building. A few people were outside, all of them giving hard looks to Booker and Demetrious. They walked to the entry area and waited. It didn't take long before Strap arrived. "What y'all want?"

Demetrious took a step forward. "We want to see him."

"Him? See who?" Everything made it seem like approaching any closer would be a bad idea.

Demetrious spoke a bit louder. "You know what I mean. This time I'm not leaving until I see Roland. Are you going to take me to him or am I going through you?"

Strap gave a half laugh. "So you're the tough man today. Wait here."

They waited. Strap disappeared down the dirty hallway. There were no lights and anyone could pull a person into one of the open doors and do whatever. Five minutes later, Strap returned. "Follow me."

They walked down the unlit hallway. They passed empty apartments. There was a slight odor coming from one place on their right. Finally, they walked inside one apartment and through the large hole in the wall and stepped into the so-called meeting room.

Roland was in his big chair. Standing next to him was Abrafo. Booker and Demetrious kept walking until a stern look from Strap made them stop.

Strap moved next to the big chair. "He's very busy today. Why are you here?"

Booker spoke up. "I have something to ask him. I would say in private but I don't think that's going to happen."

"He doesn't talk to anyone. Everything goes through me." Strap rested his hands on his hips. Something was protruding under his shirt. Booker figured he was armed, as always.

"Okay. If you want, we'll say this in front of everyone." Booker made sure his voice was heard. Nothing weak.

There was a long wait. Then, Roland Caston himself broke the silence. "Does Pia know you're both here? I don't think she'd like that."

"I just have something to ask and we'll be gone." Booker searched Roland's face. Would he tell him the truth? "Back some time ago. Maybe years. You, I am told, supplied drugs to someone who planted them on unsuspecting people. Got them arrested. All part of a scheme to manipulate them. You remember that?"

"I don't sell drugs. Who told you that?" Caston crossed his legs.

Booker's bullshit meter was striking red alert. "I'm not the police. I just want the truth. If what I'm told is correct, and I believe it is, you might be pulled into a very public police investigation. Did you supply drugs to people who planted them on others? 'Cause if you did, then you very well might know who is killing people to keep all that secret."

Caston stood up. He was wearing a full suit today. The white shirt looked to be heavily starched. The suit was double-breasted with a blue tie. His shoes were shined and he had a pinkie ring. He kept walking until he was just two feet from them.

"They can check me for a wire, I don't care." Booker patted his shirt. "I told you I am looking for the people who might be on a killing spree."

He looked at them like he was inspecting a newfound fossil. "My, my. Booker and Demetrious all grown up and making demands. A killing spree, you say? What makes you think I'm not part of that spree? You could both be dead in a snap of the finger."

Booker waited the longest one minute in his life. "I don't believe you're killing anyone. At least not today. But I also believe you know who is doing this. We're going to leave now, but I want you to think about something. I'm looking for connections. Any kind of connections from what's going on to a killer. You have the answers." Booker looked at Strap. "You have the guns. The only thing I'm armed with is this." Booker took out one of his business cards and tried to give it to Roland Caston. He let the card float to the ground and didn't touch it. He walked back to his chair and sat down. "Okay, sons of Pia. We're done. I hope you enjoyed your time here. And I hope nothing happens to you on the way back to your car." He had the confident walk of someone who was about to play a royal flush. Caston was almost back to his chair when he turned around and made his way back to Booker and Demetrious. He looked at them hard.

"Please tell Pia I said hello."

Before they could respond, Roland Caston's face turned wicked. "You know what, maybe I'll tell her myself. Just drop in."

It took all of Booker's strength to hold back Demetrious. Strap was there before a second passed and stood in between all of them.

Demetrious was held back but not his mouth. "You go anywhere near her and I'll put you under this shithole. You got that?"

The man who commanded an armed following, the drug dealer who never had to touch anything and made thousands of dollars a day backed off. With the wave of Caston's hand, Strap took two steps back and held on to the grip of his gun. Booker managed to get Demetrious turned around and moving in the opposite direction.

Booker and Demetrious left the large room. They walked through the hole in the wall that divided the two apartments, down the stinky hallway, across the entryway, and back out the door to the car. Above, they could hear the whirring noise of the drones.

Booker looked at Demetrious. "Thanks for coming."

"Let's not do this again."

BOOKER DROPPED off Demetrious and made his way back to the newsroom. Claire Stanley met him inside and she did not look happy. "Where have you been? Your interview has been waiting for twenty minutes. For a minute, I thought she was going to leave. Coffee is all set up in the conference room. C'mon Booker, move."

65

Coffee focused his camera on the face of Janet Kemper. During the preinterview and throughout, she showed signs of the trauma she suffered a year earlier. Booker asked the questions and Kemper detailed going upstairs and finding a masked man holding a knife to her daughter's neck.

Every moment of terror was still lined in her face. Recalling it all now for Booker only extended what she experienced. When she spoke about the threat to one day kill her daughter, her lower lip trembled. During the entire interview, she kept rubbing her hands. Kemper explained her daughter was still going through therapy and she constantly wakes up sweating with dreams of running from someone. Once the attacker was gone, she found he had opened the breaker box and turned off power to all sections of her house. She was not sure how he got inside. In the past twelve months, she moved away and thought about that day every day.

Kemper's one single wish and goal was to find the man and somehow punish him.

"Before the threat to abandon the corporate position, were there other, softer messages or hints aimed at you?" Booker followed her instructions to have her sit facing the door. Even in the security of the newsroom, she wanted to be able to see everyone entering and leaving.

"There were notes left on my desk, saying I'd be better suited where I was working. All of these notes had no signature."

"You go to anyone about it?"

She tried to stop scratching the top of her right hand. "Oh, sure. I told the board, the interim CEO, everyone. They listened politely, took note, and nothing happened. I kept pursuing the position and then the attack happened."

When Booker started with his next question, she cut him off. "The reason I am here is because I want to cooperate. With you, the police, anyone who can find this guy."

"And you didn't report it at the time?"

"No. No way. I took what he said as a very real threat. And I wasn't going to do anything that could jeopardize the life of my daughter. But I still want him caught."

"Do you want to stop for a moment?" Booker asked. "I can get you some water. We're almost finished."

"No. I'm fine. The absolute main thing is I want to see if my case is connected to the two men who spoke to you. The two people who admitted doing cons on people and convincing them to step aside. That's what I did. I stepped aside. I did nothing. Well, my days of stepping aside are over. I'm doing something."

"What do you plan to do next?"

"I have a meeting set up with the police. I sold my house so there may not be any evidence left but I can tell my story. Let the police build a case and we'll see where it goes."

"Did you ever wonder why you were targeted? And who moved into the position you wanted?"

"I have always thought about that. Why me? I do know the person who did get the CEO spot is still there. The company had some rough patches and the stock was bouncing, but now everything is okay."

"Thank you," Booker tried to comfort as best as possible. "As we agreed, I'll keep your daughter's name out of this."

"Thank you."

Booker got her a bottled water and a very short tour of the newsroom.

She thanked him again and after she left, he had a meeting with Claire Stanley. "Well, Booker, how does it fit in?"

"Well, for now her story stands on its own. We have no proof of any connection to Dulan or Coleman. And there's no connection, at least for now, to the murders. However, her circumstances are very much like Mikala Williams and others. Somehow, through a con, a death threat, or blackmail, they are all being manipulated. We could still run a story just based on her facts and don't connect any dots just yet."

"Sounds good. I'll let the producers know what you have."

Booker retreated to his desk and his growing stack of papers on the murders. He was about to go over the names and companies provided by Grandhouse when he got a phone call.

"Mr. Johnson, there's a person here at the front desk. He insists on seeing you."

"The name?"

"What's your name, sir?" Short pause. "He says his name is Whispis Dulan."

"I'll be right there."

Booker used his swipe card to get into the front entryway of the Channel 27 building. Dulan looked tired. "Hey, Booker. Thanks for seeing me."

"What's up, Whispis? You okay?"

"Well, depends on how you look at things. First, I'm glad we spoke up. It had to be done. But now, I've got other worries and concerns."

"Let's go outside." Booker led him out the front door, and walked to a shady area with patio tables and chairs. The space was designated as the official smoking area, however, no one smokes. Dulan started talking as he sat down. "If my court-appointed attorney knew I was here, he'd kill me."

"I'm here to listen. Go ahead."

"The state is moving forward on our immunity from prosecution request. We're doing all we can to provide as much information as possible. The charges, we hope, will go away once they complete their investigation. That part is the easy part."

"And the hard part?"

"Well, what we didn't think about was other investigations. We never paid any taxes on any of the money we got. Now, the IRS is coming after us. Both Coleman and I got letters indicating we're on the hook for any cash that is identified by the state attorney's office. I'm prepared for that." He stopped and took a deep breath like something was weighing him down. "And I got a letter from our victim, Mikala Williams. She's suing us."

"Before the charges are ironed out?"

"Yes." His body slumped down and his right eye was starting to redden. "We're being sued for what we did to her. By the time this is all over, I'll be pretty poor."

"She went through a lot," Booker reminded him. "Not just her, but other victims are coming forward. Not directly to your cases but people got hurt by this. Traumatized by this. You understand that, right?"

"Yeah, I understand. We were just thinking of the money. There is no excuse for what we did."

"If I can ask you. Is there more you can share on what Apex is all about?"

"I won't say this on camera but we heard a few things. One of them was this Apex thing. It's big. Way bigger than me, Colman, the four of us. Tally heard something about it. To me, I think that's what got him killed. Not just trying to get away from the group, but I think he knew about Apex. They couldn't let him get too far with that kind of knowledge."

"You staying safe?" Booker watched Dulan rub at the red eye.

"I changed where I stay twice already. I'm in contact with the police and they do check on me. No one knows I'm here unless you tell them."

"I'm good. I was just asking." Booker got up to leave. "I've got to get back inside."

"I've got a meeting with the state in two weeks. I should know a lot more by then. See ya, Booker."

66

Booker put together a package for one newscast, the six p.m. He was not the lead story. And he couldn't tie in the other cases since he did not have the good information to pull them together. He did a stand-alone story on what happened to Janet Kemper. Just her. The decision was made to stay away from even publicly trying to connect her case to the murders or the Williams matter. Booker just didn't have the needed facts.

Before he left for the day, he called the two other people who first called in to the news station. Both of them were told by their attorney to not say anything yet on camera. Booker agreed to let things settle. They could always talk at a later date.

Demetrious was working and Booker had arranged to take his mother to dinner. When he opened the door, she wasn't answering. Booker called out to her, "Pia?!"

His apartment was not that big and he soon found her sitting up against the far wall in his bedroom. "Mom, what are you doing there?"

"Is he gone?"

"Gone? Who?"

"I'm not gonna get up unless I know he's gone."

Booker took her hands and helped her get to her feet. Once he could see she was alright, he asked again. "Who? Who was here?"

"Roland."

Every impulse in his body tensed and his fists balled up tighter than a boa's grip. "What did he want?"

"Well, Demetrious was gone and when I heard the knock on the door, I thought it was you, Booker. I opened it and there he was. Big as a nightmare. I just tried to get away from him."

"Did he hurt you?"

"No. He tried to settle me down but the sight of him just shocked me. I wasn't ready for that."

"I'm here now. You're okay." He put his arm around her. "I'm sorry I wasn't here."

"I've got to be stronger. It's time for me to stand up to him. I've never been able to do that."

"What did he say?"

"Other than trying some of that sweet-talk crap on me, he said he wanted to see you."

"Me?"

"Yes. Said you two have been talking. I told you to stay away from that man, didn't I?"

Booker tried to explain. "There is something he knows about. A piece of information that I think can really help with a story I am working on."

"That man hasn't helped anyone in his life."

"But he did give you the money for your operations." Booker felt her break free of his hug.

"Like making an agreement with the boogeyman. You've got to promise me you'll stay away from Roland. Stay! Away!"

"I will. I will stay away." In Booker's thoughts, he was trying to figure out how Roland Caston knew where he lived. But then, if Caston wanted some information, Booker was sure he could find a way to get what he wanted.

After several minutes, Booker had her ready to go out to eat. He drove her to a place that was once a go-to restaurant for Misha. The place had semi-dark corners for couples to talk in hushed flirtations. On one side of the restaurant, a man played soft piano. The tables were spaced far apart from each other with a lit candle. It used to be Misha's favorite spot.

Booker ordered fish and Pia did the same. Dinner conversation was about his future at the station, what he wanted to do, and what happened to his girlfriend. "We had a conversation about where to live. I like South Florida. She wanted to follow a job in Texas. She took the job, I stayed. When she left, I really missed her."

Pia was digesting his words as much as the fish dinner. "I thought you two were getting serious."

"Well, we were kind of headed in that direction, then this job offer came up and she had to go."

"You two talk on the phone?"

Booker kept chewing. He was trying to think of a way to answer. "No. I haven't talked to her in months."

"There's nothing wrong with long-distance love." Pia smiled the way Booker always remembered her in happier times. They talked about Demetrious and she thanked him again for taking him in on short notice. Booker enjoyed the time with Pia. There were no conversations about the news, or death, or Roland Caston.

They returned to the apartment and after saying goodnight, Booker was caught up in thoughts on what Caston wanted. And despite the warnings from Pia, he knew more than anything he had to make contact with him. Somehow.

THE NEXT MORNING Booker entered the newsroom. Walking down the hallway, he saw a few postings for a goodbye party for Yang. Booker made a note to check for the mass mail and get the information. He would miss her.

He made the walk to his desk with a list of priorities. He had to figure out what Apex meant. And there was the question of Roland Caston. The man had no phone contacts and he hated the experience of going back to the Brick. Booker got on the computer, read articles, and waited to see if the producers wanted to keep him on the murders or a follow-up to the black-mail and smear campaigns. What he did notice was people giving him a side glance as they walked by.

When that happened, Booker knew he must have been the subject of some newsroom talk.

The usual slip-slide of early morning conversation was missing. Not one person was milling about the assignment desk. For some reason Booker had the strong impression everyone knew the details and he was about to be the very last one to know.

He realized something was off when he saw the face of Claire Stanley. She would not look directly at him at first, opting to look down or at some notes. When he did try and connect with her, she looked like she had just suffered the loss of a friend. Booker realized she was waiting for something. Five minutes later, the news director walked into his office. Booker looked over at Stanley and she was gathering up some notes. Her face was worn, the edges of her eye bent down.

She headed straight for him.

"Booker, what have you done?"

"Me? I haven't done anything."

She stood next to his desk, looking straight into the office of the news director. Stanley turned to him. "I thought I could trust you. Now I'm not sure."

"Claire, what are you talking about?"

Inside his glass-encased office, the news director gave a nod to Stanley. A signal. "Okay, Booker, come with me. I just have to be blunt. I think you're about to be fired."

67

Ken Diven never smiled much. When the ratings were excellent and Channel 27 was winning in every time slot, Diven still looked like a truck had just crashed into his house. He kept the same disaster look when he hired someone or when he had to let a person go. The thing about a newsroom was everyone in the place saw the people enter and leave his office. A floor-to-ceiling glass box gave everyone a view to the action. People walked by and looked away, rather than peer into the dreaded box.

"Sit down, Booker." Diven's voice was cordial and for sure, was not a typical on-air voice. Past problems with nasal issues sometimes gave him a voice that needed to sneeze. Diven's worth was not in front of a camera. He had a national reputation for spotting talent. Good, hardworking TV reporters who were not what he called 'surface reporters,' meaning they were eager to dig and go deeper than what was printed in a news release. When he hired Booker, part of the welcome speech was about that very topic.

Today would be different.

"Booker, have you heard of a man called Roland Caston?"

"I have. Is this what all this is about?"

Diven pulled a folder from his briefcase. "What this is about Booker is Roland Caston. I want to be clear about something. What you say or don't say will impact your future here at Channel 27. No matter what happens, there is a discipline policy in place and normally you would have fifteen days to change course or explain. But in this matter." His voice drifted off and he reached for a Kleenex to wipe his nose. "Again, what do you know about Roland Caston?"

"He's a known drug dealer. The possible head of a criminal enterprise. So far, Caston has evaded the police and any attempt at his arrest has not been fulfilled."

He took out a few sheets of paper from the folder and placed them on his desk. He also spread out several black-and-white photographs. "Take a look at these photographs, Booker. Do you recognize Roland Caston?"

Booker saw immediately Caston entering his own apartment complex. Another photograph showed Caston leaving Booker's building and getting into a black SUV with Strap at the wheel. A gun was clearly showing when Strap opened the door for Caston.

"We're very concerned, Booker. We have received a sizeable amount of information and photographs about you."

"Me? I can tell you flat out I have nothing to do with this man."

"That's not what the information is saying." The calm, even-faced Diven spoke with absolutely no emotion.

"What information? Who is saying this?"

"We're being told that you are part of this criminal enterprise. That you have benefited directly from drug proceeds of a man who might very well be connected to murder and the drug-related deaths of many in this community. The very community we're supposed to offer the truth."

"That's a lie, Ken. Flat-out lie. I've never benefited from this man. I'm investigating him but I am not in league with Roland Caston."

"On the face of it, I can believe you, Booker, but this is not looking very good for you."

Claire Stanley could offer nothing. She was not sitting in to defend Booker. She was there as a witness. A person who could swear, if needed, to everything being discussed in the glass box.

Booker's voice took on a stronger tone. "I need a name. Who is saying this? There is absolutely no truth to any of this. My career is at stake here. I've got a right to confront the person or people accusing me of working with a drug dealer. So far, I don't see anything but guilt by association."

"I see your point, Booker. I do. In fact I agree with you. What I have here is flimsy. Just some photographs and some words from an unnamed person who presented all this to us. When we got this, the claim was this was going to the newspapers. We were being given the chance to get out in front of this. To ask you about it. The claim is, Booker, that you are a part of the Brick."

There was a moment of heated silence as if Diven waited for Booker to say something. Then, he pulled out more photographs. "We have dozens of pictures of you walking into the Brick. Of you with members of Caston's crew. Pictures of you with another man, who I'm told is your brother. In all of this time and these visits, did you mention any of this to Claire Stanley?"

"No." Booker's voice was now so low, he was barely audible.

"Did you do any stories on Caston?"

"No."

"I have to ask, Booker. Did you accept anything from him in violation of station policy on not accepting gifts?"

"I have not once, repeat, not once did I accept anything from Roland Caston. Nothing. Not one cent. I know he is a very dangerous man, surrounded by dangerous people. He had and still has valuable information pertaining to the stories I've been working on."

"I hear your words. But I got to tell you, Booker, all of this is pushing me toward a very hard decision. A decision I never once thought I'd have to make regarding you. Why would you want to get so close to this man?"

Booker lined up his thoughts. "You can see what's happening. I'm getting close to something. I first started reporting on the death of Greg Tally and kept pushing. And what happened? Someone tried to run me off the road and push me down an embankment. I'm getting somewhere." Booker took a photograph and tossed it toward his boss. "All this garbage is meant to slow me down or eliminate me from getting to the real truth." He pinched his fingers. "I'm this close to exposing what this is all about and what I'm asking now is don't fall for this mess. Let me keep going. I'm resting on my past, my stories, and my reputation for digging. I rest everything on the truth. Don't let this stop what I'm pursuing."

Claire Stanley was no longer silent. "Booker has led the way on this series of stories. No one else in this market has uncovered anything like Booker has. Look at the interviews, people are coming to him. To Channel 27. Nowhere else. I say let him look into who is taking these photographs. Clearly he's being followed."

Diven looked divided. "I know your work, Booker. But I can't ignore this. I spoke with the general manager of Channel 27 and he agrees with me. So, as of this moment, you're being suspended for fifteen days with pay. You have to turn in your swipe card. After the fifteen days, if we still feel this is a matter for the police and you're implicated in anything, you will be terminated."

Booker looked out into the newsroom. From across the space of desks, he saw Grandhouse. She was wiping something from her eye.

Diven wasn't finished. "Do you understand, Booker? I have to hear you respond to what I just told you."

"I heard it all. I'm suspended. All I can tell you is the truth will come out."

68

Booker got out of the office wear and put on jeans and a polo shirt. He kept reading over the spread of company names, COO names, CEO position holders. Aside from their own businesses, Booker had also linked them to shell companies. He pressed himself to work out all the connections to motives.

Booker made phone calls to stock experts and contacts he had developed over the years. He pored over business records online, searched social media sites, and drew up conclusions. The next time he was called into the office he would be better prepared. He took information given to him off camera by Janet Kemper. He made four more phone calls to Mikala Williams and got new information about the person who got the position she wanted.

Pia was in the bedroom taking a nap. He decided he would not burden her with more worry by talking about his job status. Booker just wanted to keep his head down and investigate on his own. He still had no idea what Apex meant.

There was a knock at the door.

Booker checked the peephole and opened the door to a smiling Merilee Yang. She had her hair down and falling all around her shoulders. Her white running shoes were marked up in street scuff and her faded jeans had four slits on the left leg.

"Hope you don't mind me dropping in." Yang stood at the door looking at Booker and the inside of his place.

"Step right on in." Booker showed her his collection of papers and stacks of photographs.

"Wow, looks like you've been working hard at this." She walked down the kitchen table, examining the papers.

Booker spoke over his shoulder as he headed to the fridge. "I don't have much. Got cold bottled water."

"That's fine."

Booker handed her a bottle. "So you're leaving and I'm about to be fired."

"No, you're not!" She took a hard swig of the water. "Any other station would just snap you up. You know that." Second swig. "I heard about what happened."

"Welcome to my palace of conspiracy connections."

She pointed to the list of names. "How is it going with this? I pulled some info out of Grandhouse. You making any headway?"

"A bit."

She waved her hands over the table. "So, what am I looking at here?"

"What you're looking at is a group of opportunists who blackmail, run con games, threaten, and even murder. They move their victims out of key positions by intimidation or violence, put in their own people, and manipulate what they can. Very dangerous."

Yang leaned down to look at the photos. "Still active?"

"Very much so. I just can't prove it all yet, but I think I know what's going on." She waited for him to explain more. Booker grabbed his bottle of water and chugged.

"I'm gonna miss you, Booker. I came by 'cause I thought you were down. You picked me up more than once. I'm here to repay the favor. But now that I'm here, you don't look like you need a pick-me-up."

"I am so absorbed in this right now. I'm not alone. The victims in this are convinced they were picked for a reason."

There was a sparkle in her eye that caught Booker. Yang always had that way of talking with a smile.

He placed the bottle down. "My clock is ticking. I'm on a tight timeline. I have just days to clear my name."

"So they think you're a drug dealer? That's ridiculous."

Booker looked to his room to see if Pia was awake. Apparently not. Attention back on Yang. "I admit I've been to the Brick. But mostly for personal reasons. I never saw any drugs there. They're too smart for that."

"I'll leave you to your charts and stuff. Listen, Booker, if you need anything, please let me know. I'm here for you, okay?"

"I know."

Her smile stayed with her, out the door and down the hallway. Booker moved back in front of the table.

His cell phone rang.

"Booker . . ."

"My, you have been busy." The smooth voice of the woman who first called him was back. "How are you, Booker Johnson?"

"You probably already know how I'm doing. You called me about Greg Tally. How do you fit into all this?"

"I have an offer for you, Booker, and I want you to take it."

69

Booker pressed the phone to his ear, trying as hard as possible to listen for any sounds to give him a clue to where the call was being made. For a moment, Booker thought he heard a train in the background, then dismissed that idea.

"What kind of offer?"

The woman on the other end had a golden voice. "Ah, I like the fact you're just not dismissing the idea. What we need to do is meet."

The call came up UKNOWN. Booker had no way of tracing the call and was now trying to stay on as long as possible to hear any location give-aways. "Explain to me why I should take up any offer from you?"

"You're about to lose your job, for one."

"You heard about that?"

The woman's voice laughed. "I hear about everything. You don't have much of a choice. Just hear what I have to say."

"You mean in person?"

"Why sure, Mr. Johnson. In person. Face to face."

"Where?"

"I don't like many public places. I'll tell you what, I'll text you a location later today. We'll meet tonight. Say nine p.m. or so?"

"A text? Okay. Why did you first call me?"

"Why, Mr. Johnson. I thought you'd figure that out by now."

Booker could tell there were certain noises. Sounds he couldn't make out. "You wanted me to help you bring the missing members from your group out in the public."

"Very good. Excellent, Mr. Johnson. They were like roaches in the exposed light. I had to step on them."

"And, is that what you have planned for me. Step on me?"

"Oh no. I have some very special plans for you. No stepping. And I want you to hear them directly from me. No place else. Are we on for tonight?"

"Yes."

"I know you have plenty of time available. Now that you're no longer a reporter."

"We'll see about that. Why can't you just tell me where you want to meet now?"

"I like games, Mr. Johnson. Games. And we're playing one right now. In fact, we've been playing games for a long time, you and I. It's time to meet."

"And why did you . . . ?"

She was gone.

Booker sized up exactly what he heard on the phone. Maybe it didn't matter. Where she called from and where they will meet could be two very different places. He was clear on one thing. The woman on the phone was behind the murders. The best thing before him was he had time to think about his next move and make plans.

Booker took his cell phone and started taking pictures of the layout on the table. More than anything, he wished he could use the software programs at Channel 27 to do some research. That was not an option.

His thoughts also centered on what she might look like, just judging from the voice. Did she sound like she was thin? Was it even possible to determine just by a voice?

"Booker?" A voice called from the bedroom.

"Yes, Mom?"

"Shouldn't you be at work? I've been here alone. Demetrious took off to see his girlfriend." She was shouting from the back bedroom.

Booker called back. "You want something to eat?"

She walked into the kitchen. "I didn't want to yell anymore. Yes, Booker,

I'd love something. It's almost what, three pm? For us older folks, that's prime eating time."

He did not want to tell her about his situation at the station. Being placed on suspension and facing a firing was not something he wanted to share with her just yet. And he felt like his time to do something was rushing past him.

"I'll tell you what. I'll go out and get us something."

"You want me to come with you, Booker?"

"No. Just stay here and I'll be back in a few."

"What is all this?" She walked around the table, admiring the paperwork and the lists.

"Just stuff for work." Booker gathered up all of the paper and stuffed it all in a briefcase. "Back in a few minutes."

70

Just past eight p.m. Booker was waiting for the text message on where to go. He made arrangements with Demetrious to take Pia with him to the café. She wanted to stay up anyway and volunteered to help him run the place.

Booker put on a gray polo shirt and black slacks. Over the polo, he planned to wear a blue sport coat. The same one he wore on many news stories. In his wandering thoughts on what he was about to do, Booker checked and rechecked what was going to happen, even if he didn't have a location.

For his tiny moment of inspiration he looked again at the picture of Misha. He studied her face and thought of the hundreds of times he kissed her cheek, held her hand, and insisted that she walk on the inside of the sidewalk while he stayed closer to the curb. Somehow he let her down by letting her go. While they were together, he knew each day there were just three words to keep her by his side. Just three words that could and should keep any couple on a loving journey.

Just three words.

Make her smile.

He did that every day.

Booker saw a text message pop up on his cell phone. The message said, GET IN THE CAR. DRIVE TO SAND DOLLAR PARK AND WAIT.

Booker knew what he had to do. He gathered his phone and tapped out a text message. Then he gathered up the briefcase and his coat and went out the door. Twenty minutes later, he was just a couple of blocks from Sand Dollar Park. Even though the place was named after a sea urchin, the park itself was in the middle of the county and not by the beach. He pulled into the parking lot and started looking. All he could think about was keeping himself in a spot where he could escape if needed.

Sand Dollar was one location where the park was accessible after six p.m. There were no gates. Booker parked under a street light. He was sure, if needed, he could drive straight across the grass if he was blocked in. The directions made him think about Whispis Dulan and the directions he needed to meet. If Dulan had any dealings with the woman on the phone, if she was directing him, he understood where Dulan got the idea.

9:07 p.m. Booker waited. Just to make sure he was seen, he turned on the engine and let his car lights show his location.

Nothing.

9:14 p.m. A text came in. Go to the miniature airport. Now.

Like a few other parks in Florida, Sand Dollar had a place to fly model planes. However, Booker remembered the place was closed down by the park district and now there was just a large abandoned field. There were a lot of complaints by motorists after seeing a plane loop around and drop suddenly to the ground. Many thought the plane was real and 911 was flooded with calls about falling planes. All false alarms.

When he drove up, Booker was surprised to see the place had the outside lights on. The field was lit up. There was no one there except Booker. He decided to get out of the car. Booker put on his sport coat and walked to the spot where once pilots would command their tiny planes. He stood there waiting. He looked out over the open field and didn't like his location. If he wanted to run, he might be an easy target for anyone with a weapon. There were no buildings or walls to hide behind. There was one small storage place with doors that looked locked.

Off to Booker's right, a black SUV moved slow down the park driveway. The super dark tinting on the glass made it impossible to see inside the vehicle. The SUV parked directly in back of Booker's car, blocking his path to back up. Booker adjusted the breast pocket of his sport coat.

The passenger window rolled down.

"Hello, Booker Johnson."

The female voice was coming at him through a bullhorn. Booker started walking toward the sounds.

"Stop right there, Mr. Johnson."

"I want to make sure I hear you. I don't want to miss something you say." Booker took a chance and kept walking toward the SUV. When he got to within fifteen feet of the car, the driver's side door opened.

Booker stopped.

The man who got out was perhaps six-foot-five. He was wearing a black balaclava. Booker's gaze was stuck on the man emerging from the car. Maybe, Booker thought, he was taller than six-five. While the lighting was dim, one thing was clear. He had a gun on his right hip. The figure did not stop there. He pulled an AR-15 from the SUV and placed the weapon on the hood of the car. What struck Booker more than the guns was what the large man had covering his hands.

Black gloves.

Booker imagined the big man with gloves holding a knife to a teenager's throat, shooting twice into the body of Ben Olson, throwing Greg Tally into the razors of a makeshift tree chopper. And ramming a truck into Booker's news van. He was facing the enforcer.

The imposing figure stood near the car yet within easy reach of the AR-15. The light from the parking lot lit up the top of his frame and made him look like a robot. He stood there waiting for instructions.

The female voice was back, coming from the passenger window. "You don't like listening to directions, do you Mr. Johnson?"

"I'm here. If you wanted to make me an offer did you have to bring all the heat with you?"

"You mean the guns?" The voice said. "One has to be careful."

"Okay. What is your offer?"

"You have the chance to really make an impact on your life. You have this one great chance to make it to a level that will bring you all the money you would ever want in life."

"And why would I want to do that?"

She answered, "You mean make all that money? That answers itself. I mean, look at yourself. Booker Johnson. Washed-up reporter with no future and zero chance of another job in television. There's nothing for you there. Nothing!"

"I haven't been fired yet."

"Oh, you don't understand, do you. What your office got was just part of what information I have on you. You won't stand a chance of keeping that job. I could send them the rest and you will be done. Just plain done."

"There's something I don't understand."

"What is that?"

Booker wanted to push things a bit. "Why would you want to hide?"

"Hide? Why, Mr. Johnson, I'm right here."

"I mean why would you want to hide behind the voice of a woman? You're using a voice disguiser. Show yourself."

There was a long pause. The man with the black gloves pulled the weapon from his hip and pointed it at Booker. The long pause became a full twenty seconds.

"Okay, Mr. Johnson." The bullhorn was gone. The contraption connected to the bullhorn was thrown into the back seat. A man stepped out from the SUV. He was almost as tall as the figure with black gloves. No longer holding a bullhorn, the man on Booker's left stood out from the car. "How did you know?"

"I wasn't quite sure. Just playing a hunch. Something I've been accused of doing for years. But on the phone your voice did sound a bit mechanical."

"Your hunch was right." The man was not wearing a mask. In the park light Booker could see he resembled the size and shape of the man with the weapons.

Booker decided to go all the way. "Good evening. Or should I call you by your name? Rich the Revealer? The blogger."

"My, Mr. Johnson. You are right on target tonight." The man who called himself Rich looked to his left. "Meet my brother. I won't give you his name tonight. Maybe at another time. Right now, I still have an offer I want to make you."

Booker took three more steps toward The Revealer. He shouted to

Booker. "Stop right there. One more step and unfortunately he will be forced to shoot you."

"What is this offer?"

"It's simple, Mr. Johnson. I want you to join my organization. More than anyone I have encountered you have the ability to find out things about people. All kinds of things. In my line, I would want you to find dirt. Things I can use."

"Things you would use on people, like you did with Mikala Williams?"

"Yes, like Mikala Williams. Like Janet Kemper, like a lot of people. People who would not move out of the way. People who had to be shown they needed to go."

"And if I refuse? What then? I'll end up like Greg Tally or Ben Olson? You'd kill me?"

"In a heartbeat, Mr. Johnson. Just like we had to kill both of them. You would die right here. Right now. If I give the signal you would be reduced to just a pile of flesh and blood."

"Maybe I want to know more. Maybe you convinced me. Maybe I want to know all about Apex."

"Ah, you know or heard something but you don't know what it is or what it's about, do you, Mr. Johnson?"

"You know what? You can just call me Booker. Just plain ole Booker. You see I figured out what all this was about, as you say?" Now he had their attention. Booker wanted to move even closer yet stayed back.

"So, here it is," Booker said. "You moved people out of the way and put in people you could manage and manipulate. Then you had these people feed you information. Valuable information. Insider trading information. You and your group made millions. Not in big bundles all at once, that would get the attention of the federal exchange. No, your money came in small victories with cash going to shell companies. And those companies stashed money out of the country. You weren't just happy threatening people in South Florida. No, you were planning on taking this nationwide. That was going to be Apex."

"How do you know so much?"

"I just figure things out. You see, I figure Greg Tally found out this, didn't he? And all of this scared him. He didn't want to be a part of a national con. He tried to get away and you killed him."

"All that being said, Booker, you still have not answered my question. What you say next will determine the scope and depth of your very next breath. I could use your talents. Come join me. Be a part of Apex. Or die right here."

"You tried to kill me once. Your brother here tried to run me off the road."

Booker looked at what was in front of him. One man fully armed and the one in control. Running now would probably be foolish. Booker leaned his head toward the chest pocket of his sport coat and started talking.

"I'm Booker Johnson, Channel 27, and you are looking live at the men who have murdered, conned people, and carried out physical threats. All of which you have just witnessed them admitting."

A shocked Rich the Revealer started shouting at Booker. "What is this? Who are you talking to?"

"As you said, it's simple. Everything you have just said to me tonight is part of a live television special seen right now by probably a million viewers. This is going out on our station, and out on the web. You are being seen everywhere. By hundreds of thousands."

The Revealer turned to his brother. "Shoot him!"

"I wouldn't do that!" Detective Brielle Jensen stepped out of the storage building. The doors were not locked. The Revealer moved to go toward the SUV door. "I said stop right there!" Jensen shouted. He stopped.

The man with the black gloves did not.

He dropped down low and tried to hide behind the car. When he rose up to take a shot at Booker, there was a loud exchange of gunfire. The gloved man went down, a bullet hit him in his shooting hand. Three more officers moved out from the shadows of the trees and closed in. They had both men in handcuffs and on the ground.

Jensen yelled back to Booker. "You okay?"

"I'm fine."

71

Booker walked up closer and used the cell phone camera that was strategically put into the body of his sport coat. Booker had spent an hour fitting and adjusting the phone just right. He had cut out a tiny bit of the fabric for the camera lens to catch the action. A microphone was connected to the cell phone and the wire stretched through the sleeve of the sport coat with the mic just sticking out enough to gather audio. The camera in the phone sent back a live picture and audio feed of what was happening. Others in TV markets, including South Florida, have used a cell phone to do live TV. Booker was still on the air.

"The men will be processed by the police. Tonight, you witnessed a well-orchestrated takedown. I don't want to call it a confession but you heard the comments and the admissions of a man who talked about the murders of two men and the campaigns to smear the careers of so many. There will be a lot more on this starting tomorrow morning. For now, this is Booker Johnson reporting live in Sand Dollar Park for Channel 27 news."

Booker was mentally and physically exhausted. He leaned up against the wall of the storage building. Booker knew his personal car, the SUV, and everything in the close surroundings would be part of a crime scene. He would have to be interviewed by the police. He knew all that going into the setup. A Channel 27 live truck pulled up, followed by a gray car. In the

Channel 27 truck was Coffee. And in the gray car was the news director, Ken Devin. They both got out and had to wait for clearance on how close they could get to Booker.

A paramedic was treating the man with the gunshot wound. Mask off, he looked a lot like his brother. The Revealer sat in the back of a police car. He glared at Booker.

Jensen made her way to the storage facility. "So, again, Booker, you're not hit?"

"No, I'm fine." Booker looked at the officers who were also there to back up Jensen. "Bri, how did you know I was here?"

"With two men dead and others possibly a target, including you, we expanded police surveillance. We've been watching you. That brought us here."

"Thank you."

Booker was about to ask another question, then Jensen held up her hand as if to say she could not say anything else. All conversation between them had to end. Booker understood and he knew why. Jensen's actions would be investigated by the Florida Department of Law Enforcement, or FDLE. In Florida, all police-involved shootings were handled this way. Routine. Any continued talk between them might end up in the FDLE file or a courtroom. The less said, the better.

Still, Booker thought he needed to explain to Jensen. "Yes. When I called the station to set this up, they clearly did not want to do this live. I had to convince them. How would it be to have me killed live on television? They really did not want that. Back at the station, in the control room, they had their fingers ready to stop the live feed. But yep, the safe phrase was Green Turtle and if I said that, they would also stop the live feed."

Another car showed up. PIO Carol Clipper. She walked to where Booker was standing. Jensen made her way back to the other officers. Clipper had his attention. "This time, Booker, they informed me before anything happened. This will come out in the news conference but we've been working on this group for some time now."

Booker said, "Jensen was amazing. She shot that gun right out of his hand."

Clipper whispered to Booker. "I'm sure she will tell you this one day but she wasn't trying to shoot his gun hand. We're trained to shoot center mass. That guy probably moved."

"Thank you."

Jensen was yards away watching Booker talk to Clipper. Then, Jensen turned and walked off, her dark uniform blending with the night.

72

Twenty minutes later, Booker was free from being inside the yellow tape and able to talk to Coffee and Devin. She had her camera on her shoulder ready to shoot video. "You're gonna be asked this a million times, but are you okay?"

"I'm fine. There was a shot fired in the air and I should have just dropped to the ground but I wanted to keep the framing right and stayed upright. But I'm okay."

Coffee looked around at the scene, then back to Booker. "And you even had a safe phrase for the station to stop video?"

"Green turtle."

"Why that?" She asked.

"I didn't want to use a word that might anger or scare that guy with a gun. If I said green turtle, I know he would just be confused."

Ken Devin approached and wiped away a mosquito. "For the record, Booker, you're no longer on suspension. But for awhile, you were off the books. Welcome back. I see you're okay. I had my concerns but this turned out okay." Devin headed back to his car.

Coffee was moving all over the park, busy shooting video of the scene, the two men, and a few more seconds of Booker. She got video of the men being whisked away and she finally set the camera down. "Okay, Booker, how did you pull this off?"

"When I got a phone call from this woman who would not identify herself, I knew she had to be involved. I contacted Claire Stanley and we did a short conference call with Ken. I convinced them to do this as a live broadcast. Very risky, I know. Without me knowing it, Stanley contacted Detective Jensen that I could be in danger. Jensen kept track of my phone, knew where I was, and followed me. When I got to the park I texted Claire it was going down."

Coffee's face contorted into a look of concern. "So you were expecting no help from the police?"

"Correct. Probably stupid on my part. Claire, I guess wanted to involve them anyway. I never spoke to them. Ken Devin gave the okay to put all of this on television, which was a very bold move. This could have ended badly."

It was well past eleven p.m. when Booker was free to get his car and drive home. Pia was home asleep. Booker texted Demetrious to find out he got her a ride to the apartment. He just couldn't sleep. Too much adrenalin.

BOOKER WALKED into the office in the morning and found several messages on his desk, all of them giving thanks he was safe. One person was waiting for him to arrive.

Grandhouse.

"Why didn't you call me? I wanted to be a part of this." She had a notepad in her hand like she was ready for the next assignment.

"You couldn't be a part of this. Too dangerous. Your parents would have my hide."

Grandhouse looked at her notes. "The man arrested. The one calling himself Rich the Revealer. His real name is Solen Bender. His brother is Cleo Bender. They are both on the bond court list, I checked."

"Good work. Thanks."

She wasn't done. "For now, they are not being granted bond. We have a crew at the courthouse covering that angle."

"Thanks. If I go out today, we'll make arrangements for you to be there."

"Thanks. I'd like that. Oh, and you have a guest in the lobby."

When Booker went to the lobby area, he did not expect Detective Jensen to be there. "Hello, Booker. I don't have much time. I'm going home to shower and eat."

"Been up all night?"

"That's right. All night. What I'm about to tell you will be released by the PIO at a news conference at eleven a.m. Both men have been talking. And when they keep talking, we keep listening. That took all night. We just finished not too long ago. They admitted to the killings, the threats, and intimidation. We're just not sure we'll be able to track the money they stole. I'll let other units in the department and the feds to worry about that. I just stopped by to see if you're okay."

"Thank you, Brielle. I mean, Detective. It was a bit touch and go but thank you for being there. You saved my life."

"No problem, Booker." She didn't look tired. Booker shook her hand and she was out the door.

He wasn't sure what or how Channel 27 wanted to do the coverage. All of that was soon cleared up. Stanley met him as soon as he walked back into the newsroom. "Booker, you will be on set. For the noon newscast, you will introduce a package and then coming out of it, the anchors will ask you some questions. All of the other angles will be covered by other reporters. Any questions?"

"No."

Before Booker walked to his desk, he got another message from the front lobby. There was a person to see him.

"Who is it?" Booker asked.

The lobby security guard shrugged his shoulders. "He asked for you. He claims he is a judge. A Judge David Napston."

73

"Booker, I have always found your reporting fair. I respect that. I just wanted to tell you this before I go public." He looked every bit like a judge you would see on television. His silver hair and expression like he was about to make a ruling.

"Yes, your Honor."

"I explained all this to the chief judge. I was about to file my papers and not run for my judge position. You see, I know Solen Bender. Back when I was in the civil division, I conducted a civil trial regarding a bad accident. He managed to fight off any severe criminal charges but the jury awarded the plaintiff four million dollars. I know he was upset with me. I went against his lawyer's motion to dismiss the case. And then . . ."

"Judge, you don't have to get into this if you don't want."

"No. It's important. This is something I have to do. You see, Booker, I'm an alcoholic. I had a really bad drinking problem and I don't think it impaired my cases but someone was watching and got video of me just before I went to the courthouse. Video of me drinking in my car."

"The Bender brothers."

"Yes. They did not identify themselves in the email I got, but the police just told me they admitted to sending me the videos. A smear campaign, they promised, if I ran again. I was the only politician they blackmailed. For them it was personal. And also for me. I have been forty days sober. I'm proud of that."

"Congratulations, Judge."

"I plan to run again. Let the voters decide if I should stay or not. Some lawyers are filing motions to dismiss cases because of my drinking. I'll let another judge decide what is right." He got up to leave.

"What's most important is you're taking steps to make things right in your life."

"Thanks, Booker. I know you're busy today. But you come to my office and I'll explain it all on camera. I want to apologize to the people of South Florida. I'm only going to tell my story to you."

74

Three weeks later, Booker Johnson was among the last to enter the restaurant. An outside space was set up just for guests of Merilee Yang. Booker saw her in the middle of a throng. Reporters, producers, photographers, assignment desk, they were all there. She was getting congratulations and every soul there had a drink in their hand.

Booker ordered a sparkling water. He waited until there was an opening in the crowd of people. The music was just loud enough. There were trays of shrimp, tiny barbequed steak bits on long toothpicks and chicken wings. Booker picked up a plate and walked down the tables of food.

"So you just show up late and don't say hello?" Yang moved in and hugged Booker. "Thanks for coming. There's plenty of food."

"Don't worry. I'll eat my share."

"Booker, that was a great interview you did with Judge Napston. I had no idea he was under pressure like that." Yang dipped a shrimp in some sauce.

"He was very grateful to have the opportunity to tell me his story. It's been weeks since the arrests and I'm still finding stories peeling off from the Bender brothers. And it looks like Detective Jensen will be okay. The report is weeks away but the word is the shooting will be justified."

"Great news. I also heard about the Brick."

Booker tried to fit one more food item on his plate. "A shocker. I haven't been there but they tell me the Brick is closed. Everybody is gone. The Narcotics Unit raided three locations. Arrested fourteen people and seized, they say, around four hundred thousand dollars and drugs. Roland Caston is nowhere to be seen. Vanished. His people, Strap, Abrafo, all gone."

"Yeah, the station did a story on it. The building owners were happy. They're in the process of renovating that second building. Painting, patching up holes. I heard the place was a mess. Any idea where they went?"

"Nothing. He'll turn up somewhere. I promise." Booker sipped at his sparkling water. "I don't want to hog all your time. Don't you have to mingle at these things?"

Yang put her paper plate down and waved her hand at the large group. "You've been in this business long enough. In one year, at least one-fifth of this crowd will be moving on to another job. This biz is just a long series of hellos and goodbyes with some news in the middle."

"You're right. People come and go. My mom went back to California. My brother Demetrious is thinking about joining her. Not sure what he's gonna do."

"Just know, we, I mean I will miss you."

She stared hard, looking into his eyes. "Booker, you haven't heard the news."

"What news?"

"I'm not going anywhere. I'm staying at Channel 27. I plan to work my way off a one-man gig just like you did." She snapped off a hard bite of a shrimp and smiled.

"If you're not going, why is everyone here?"

Yang picked up another tasty morsel. "We had the place booked, the food catered, and we just decided to have a party anyway. Even though I'm not going anywhere."

"Yang, you're amazing. Congratulations on staying here."

Yang plucked a shrimp off Booker's paper plate. "And what are you going to do? You were on what? Three networks, about ten radio stations, and I don't know how many articles. They all wanted a piece of Booker Johnson."

"I'm not sure what I want to do. Right now, I'm perfectly happy working for old Channel 27. I am thinking about getting another place to stay but we'll see." Booker pointed to her guests. "Go on, Merilee. Enjoy yourself. This is your stay home party. I'll see you in a bit."

She gave a soft laugh and peeled back into the crowd. Booker took his plate and wandered to the far corner of the space. The building was off the Intracoastal and the Atlantic was not too far away. He smelled the ocean and let the breeze swarm over him. Somewhere out there, he could see the water kiss the sky and extend the blue horizon like one giant carpet.

He thought about what Yang said about his next move. All he wanted to do now was go back to his stomping grounds covering the courts, and doing what he could to expose the wrong dealings. What he could not tell people was that it was Booker himself who leaked information to certain outlets and bloggers that he was in trouble with Channel 27. That part was real. He was suspended. Booker also had information possibly from an unlikely place. A note was left for Booker and slipped under his door. No name. Booker suspected the note came from Roland Caston, yet he had no proof. If it was Caston there was just enough information for Booker to figure out who was behind the group. Booker took the information and ran with it.

A day after the arrest of the Bender brothers, Caston broke from his norm and called Booker. He never admitted leaving the note but Caston apologized for showing up at the apartment unannounced and scaring Pia. When the conversation and call were over, Booker did not think Caston would disappear.

A cruise ship was inching across like some giant caterpillar on the ocean. They were probably headed for any number of stops and exotic locations not too far from the Florida coast. Booker thought about the next few days. Channel 27 gave him some time off. He could do whatever he pleased. He just had to figure out what was a priority.

His cell phone rang and Booker picked up before the second ring. He pressed the phone to his ear.

"Hello, Booker. How are you doing? This is Misha."

THE ARRANGEMENT
Book #2 of the Booker Johnson Thrillers

The truth might be more than reporter Booker Johnson bargained for.

TV reporter Booker Johnson just doesn't know when to back down. Fresh off his fourth Emmy win and back in the classroom, he teaches the primacy of truth in journalism. But there is danger in pursuing the truth at all costs. And despite being told by his superiors to move on from the scene of a suspicious accident, Booker just can't leave well enough alone.

Booker's investigation soon plunges him into the gritty world of crime boss Parson Manor, where corruption reigns supreme, and where Gibby Manor is being trained to follow in his father's criminal footsteps. Meanwhile, on the other side of the law, rising star prosecutor Cain Stocker prepares to unveil a 37-count indictment against Parson Manor.

Unbeknownst to Booker, his relentless investigation is hurtling them all toward an explosive collision. The battle between criminal and prosecutor takes an unprecedented turn. And in a race against time, Booker's determination to report the facts leaves him caught in the crossfire, teetering on the edge in a dangerous game where the stakes are high...and the consequences deadly.

Emmy Award-winning reporter Mel Taylor and Wall Street Journal bestselling author Brian Shea deliver a gripping thriller, perfect for fans of Michael Connelly and Harlan Coben.

**Get your copy today at
severnriverbooks.com**

ABOUT MEL TAYLOR

For many years, Mel Taylor watched history unfold as he covered news stories in the streets of Miami and Fort Lauderdale. A graduate of Southern Illinois University, Mel writes the Frank Tower Private Investigator series. He lives in a community close to one of his favorite places – The Florida Everglades. South Florida is the backdrop for his series.

Sign up for Mel's reader list at
severnriverbooks.com

ABOUT BRIAN SHEA

Brian Shea has spent most of his adult life in service to his country and local community. He honorably served as an officer in the U.S. Navy. In his civilian life, he reached the rank of Detective and accrued over eleven years of law enforcement experience between Texas and Connecticut. Somewhere in the mix he spent five years as a fifth-grade school teacher. Brian's myriad of life experience is woven into the tapestry of each character's design. He resides in New England and is blessed with an amazing wife and three beautiful daughters.

Sign up for the reader list at
severnriverbooks.com

Printed in the United States
by Baker & Taylor Publisher Services